ALWAYS THE RIVER

The river gives and the river takes
away - a genealogical mystery
spanning the centuries

Leona J Thomas

Dedicated to Steve and his Yorkshire family
- past, present and future

SUE'S FAMILY TREE FOR KATE LAURA INNES

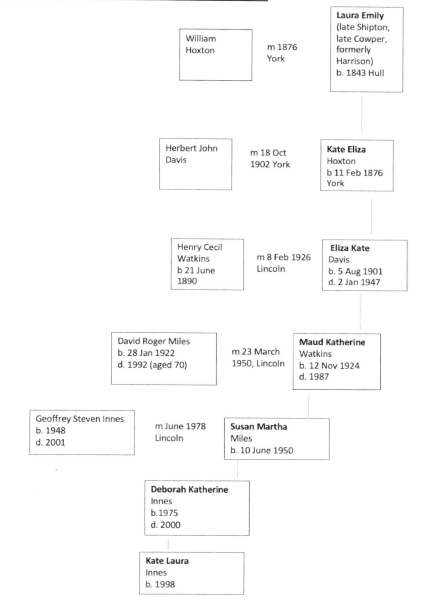

William
Hoxton

m 1876
York

Laura Emily
(late Shipton,
late Cowper,
formerly
Harrison)
b. 1843 Hull

Herbert John
Davis

m 18 Oct
1902 York

Kate Eliza
Hoxton
b 11 Feb 1876
York

Henry Cecil
Watkins
b 21 June
1890

m 8 Feb 1926
Lincoln

Eliza Kate
Davis
b. 5 Aug 1901
d. 2 Jan 1947

David Roger Miles
b. 28 Jan 1922
d. 1992 (aged 70)

m 23 March
1950, Lincoln

Maud Katherine
Watkins
b. 12 Nov 1924
d. 1987

Geoffrey Steven Innes
b. 1948
d. 2001

m June 1978
Lincoln

Susan Martha
Miles
b. 10 June 1950

Deborah Katherine
Innes
b.1975
d. 2000

Kate Laura
Innes
b. 1998

1

It was the stench. The stench of a thousand river journeys. The swirling brown silted waters beneath my feet, perched too close to the edge of the dock. Hands on me, roughly pulling me back. Stern voices. Tears.

My first childhood memory.

Over the years I heard many instances of people lost to the grasping current of the river as it swept past the wooden quaysides. Drunks. Small children. Careless workers. Hopeless souls. They were swallowed up and spat out miles into the estuary. Some were never recovered. Some are still asleep at the bottom of the muddy sprawling inlet.

A slap from an older sibling – it might have been Hannah – drummed that lesson into me. Never go down there, never stand near the edge. NEVER!

But it was a place where people could go to disappear. It both fascinated and terrified me. I was never to be far from it.

S amuel slung his canvas bag over his shoulder and set off from the quayside towards the buildings that led from the docks up into the oldest streets of the city. Narrow, dingy and where many of the poorest were to be found, trying to make enough to pay for a night at the doss house or a drink to obliterate the reality of crouching in a corner of a doorway or under an overhanging stairwell. Samuel strode past them in the fading light, making his way to his shelter for the next few days. As a mariner he would pick up jobs here or there, and often brushed shoulders with familiar faces on board vessels, on the dockside or in the many ale-houses that plied their trade to slake the thirst of sea-men, porters, loaders and scavengers. One of these was Davy, who was a couple of years older than himself. He was married to Caroline – a girl from Lincolnshire like Samuel himself, and he often found a bed for the night with them when he was in port.

He'd left home when he was seventeen, leaving behind his parents and siblings to come to the port of Hull to seek work on the docks and quays, bustling with ships coming and going, cargoes loading and unloading and all the other ephemera of a crowded noisy centre of commerce. His father was a carpenter and boatwright in a small village in Lincolnshire and Samuel had learned the use of tools and boat construction by osmosis at his side. But there were older brothers to carry on the family trade and Samuel had more of a hankering to be sailing on the water rather than to build craft to sail upon it.

But it wasn't the romantic image that he'd had of sail-ing the seven seas – instead it was hard backbreaking graft, long hours, sweat, toil and for little pay. Some-times he travelled to nearby Goole and picked up work on the many barges and wherries that plied the river Ouse, coming to and from York or else on barges on the Aire and Calder canal, having come from Leeds or Knot-tingley. Other times he picked up work on sea-going boats sailing out of Hull supplying goods to the coastal ports of Lincolnshire, Kent and the East Riding, becom-ing familiar with ports such as Grimsby, Felixstowe and Gravesend. In the end, they were all the same. With the minimum of schooling he was passably able to read and write and sign his name, which at least put him ahead of many of his peers with whom he brushed shoulders and shared bunks and lodgings.

When he and Davy struck up a friendship, he was always glad of a place to lay his head when in Hull. Davy had married Caroline six years earlier but they had lost two daughters, born and died within a year of their birth. Getting a couple of rooms on Catherine Street was a step up and Caroline was now expecting another child. They were glad of the few shillings Samuel paid for his bed and board, and he was glad of a friendly face on return from a day's work and a fellow to share some ale with in the nearest public house. Caroline's brother Frank also stayed with them so with two men's wages and lodging money from Samuel, they were able to keep themselves above the poverty line and pay the rent on time.

But there had been times when they had been forced to live hand to mouth, especially when the two babies had arrived. Squalid accommodation with vermin rife in ramshackle tenement housing had brought about the inevitable result. Caroline was but a shell of a woman, gaunt and pale. Her days were spent doing all the jobs that being a woman entailed – washing, cleaning, cooking the meagre items of food they could afford, and taking in a bit of mending when she was able. When her brother came down to Hull from Lincoln, the extra money he earned gave them the ticket out of the lowest of the slums and one step up into two rooms and a kitchen with a shared lavatory for the four families who lived in the block. Samuel dossed down in one room with Caroline's brother Frank, who also worked as a mariner, while the couple had the other room, which would shortly hold another baby if it was spared.

Samuel wasn't in a hurry to take a wife – although the thought of someone to share his bed at night was inviting. He spent his money on his lodgings, food and drink and what little he had left after that seemed to disappear. But he was now in his mid-twenties and he was expected to start to shoulder some responsibilities and maintain a wife, home and children. He hadn't got his eye on a likely spouse yet, but there was time. What was the hurry?

◆ ◆ ◆

My eyes are sore and I cannot sew another stitch in this dim light. My fingers ache and my belly rumbles with hunger. Soon I will go to the kitchen and join her at the table for what constitutes our evening meal. I'll try to avoid that unnerving son of hers with his wandering hands and lecherous looks. Doesn't take a genius to work out what he thinks he can get if he backs me into a corner. Well, he can think again.

I am going to get out of here at the first chance. Just because someone working for a local charity that looks out for destitute girls seeking some employment found me this place, doesn't mean that I have to be here all my days. I want more from my life than this drudgery for a pittance that she lets me keep after she extracts her board and lodging from me.

I know how to read and write and I can tot figures with the best of them. I have a future to plan for.

But first I have to get out of this place …

Samuel sauntered down the road to the docks, the light was fading and a cold wind was whipping up. Soon he would be loading goods to take to Grimsby on the evening tide. He'd spent the last hour in the tavern with Davy and Frank, and there they had parted company as Davy set off down Hedon Road in the direction of the Alexandra Dock while he headed to the end of Great Union Street towards the Victoria Dock. At the far end of the dock he could see the railway tracks that threaded in and out like so many ropes. The tops of the cranes stood out in silhouette in the dusk and the shouts and noise from the loading and unloading which never stopped, day or night, came in waves on the gusty wind. A few other figures flitted in the shadows – women who were looking for a few coins in return for some company and their own offerings. Not for Samuel. He knew what you got from that kind of trade. Shouldering past a couple who were obviously striking a bargain in that department, he headed for the looming gates of the dock and the work that lay ahead of him.

The vessel he was working on tonight was at the far end of the basin, where they would be loading coal and timber. As he skirted the side of St Peter's Church he saw a figure hovering by the Drypool Swing Bridge. Cutting back towards it for a few steps, he could make out that it was a woman and she was walking under the bridge and standing on the grit and mud near the gentle curve of the river as it headed out into the estuary. She stood with a shawl pulled around her slight shoulders. What was she doing? Uncertain whether to advance or retreat, he stood hesitating for a few moments and in that time she took another step forward, her eyes staring intently ahead of her. She remained like that for another few moments and then seemed to take a deep breath, her shoulders rising and falling, before she slowly turned and made her way back to the pathway that led to the road. Samuel stood mesmerised, watching her as she came nearer, and only when she turned to head back towards the town, did he move. This caught her eye and she turned, peering into the gloom.

He didn't know what to say or whether to say anything, but in the end he raised his voice just enough so that she could hear him. "Are thee aw' reet?"

She looked at him for a moment or two, seemingly not registering his presence, and then a slight smile spread over her face. "Of course," came her reply, almost lilting.

With that she turned to continue on her way, but Samuel advanced a few more steps so that she could not ignore him. As she turned to look at him, he was mesmerised by her eyes. They were the palest grey, almost clear, with an outer ring of darker grey around the iris. They seemed to look through him, and he felt that they were so transparent that he should be able to see into her soul. She still had that faraway look and seemed almost in a trance.

"Tha should be careful. 'T'sn't safe walkin' there."

At this she let out a small breathy laugh and looked at him as if he was a half-wit. "I was visiting – a friend," was all she said as she took a few more steps away from him.

He felt himself drawn towards her and in a few strides was by her side.

"I am perfectly well. Thank you for your concern. I must go now."

"Let us help 'ee," he offered taking her elbow.

This time she paused and turned to look at him directly, studying his face for a few seconds, and then indicating with a small nod of her head that he might do as he had offered.

When they drew level with the roadway that led back into the town, she made to draw away and carry on her journey without another word. But Samuel held her a little more firmly and was about to ask her what she had been doing when she fixed him again with her direct stare, such that it made him feel both uncomfortable and intrigued at the same time.

"Wher're ye goin'? Will tha be aw' reet?" he asked.

"Quite alright. But you may walk with me if you feel the necessity and it would please you."

He was not sure if this was an invitation of the kind he should, and would usually, refuse but nothing in her dress or manner indicated that she was a street girl. Her clothes were dark coloured – he could not tell their exact hue in the gloomy light, but they seemed well kempt and not the ragged vestments of those who were forced to spend their lives upon the streets. Brushing against her skirts he could feel the woollen cloth and the bulk of petticoats beneath. She had a knitted shawl pulled tightly about her thin shoulders, covering a bodice of dark fabric, velvet or similar. Her head was covered in a small bonnet loosely tied under her chin, the ends of the ribbons dangling down, occasionally caught by the light gusts that swept off the river.

Pushing aside thoughts of being late to work, Samuel turned and fell in step with her and they made their way up Great Union Street together. Neither spoke. She slowed down as they approached a side opening leading into a court of typical dwellings that shared a common courtyard.

"Thank you," she said, looking at him but almost through him, or so he felt. Those eyes again.

"Ah'm Samuel ..." he stumbled over his words, "Samuel Cowper."

"I am Laura ..." and with that she turned and headed into the gloomy courtyard without a backward glance.

Samuel stood shaking his head to clear the fog that seemed to be enveloping it. Turning to head back the way they had come, his feet began to pick up speed as he realised he had but minutes until he was due to report for work. Grateful that the road sloped down towards the dock area, he made the quayside just in time, as the hefty boat master roared at him and cursed him for his tardiness.

It was rich and deep, the occasional ripples belying the filthy depths. Curls around the wooden piers. Gaps between them choked with the floating rubbish that washes up here. But sometimes the force pulls things out into the stream and then they are dragged away on the grasping tide. On their journey.

I feel the pull of the water drawing me in. But I am not for it. It is not for me. It is not my time to join it. But I visit it and it tells me tales. Tales that would turn your stomach. It has a cruel sense of humour. It is a grasping clutching thing.

I have nothing to give it – this time.

'So he is a thing called Samuel?' it asks me. I don't tell it too much – for now. Some things you share with a friend, some things you don't.

Increasingly Samuel found himself outside the court-yard of buildings on Great Union Street as he made his way home from trips, as he walked to work on misty mornings and drizzly afternoons. He always stood and loitered for a while, drawn there, hoping that he didn't look too shifty. But which house? For weeks he never saw her come or go. Then one evening as he was passing on his way from the docks he caught sight of her coming out of a rough wooden doorway and crossing to the water pump that stood in one corner. Unsure of whether to speak or not, he hesitated just long enough for her to see him as she turned to set down the bucket and work the handle. She kept her pale eyes locked on his as she continued filling the bucket, her look hard to read. Annoyance? Bemusement? Interest?

Samuel found his feet moving him forward into the yard and stopping by the well as she stood and straightened, her hand reaching for the small of her back as she arched and pulled up straight.

She looked him in the eye and half-cocked her head, with a questioning look.

"Ah … Ah" – Samuel stumbled over his words. " 'ow are 'ee?" What a stupid thing to say, he thought the moment the words spilled from his mouth.

"Well, hello," she said. "Samuel." It was a statement rather than a question.

"Ah … ah was jus' passin' an' …" he babbled.

"And you thought you'd come and say hello to that girl that you thought you had rescued."

Again a statement, not a question.

"Aye, naw. Ah mean …" Good grief man, pull yourself together. " Aye. Ah 'oped all was reet wi' ye."

"Yes, yes I am fine. And I have not succumbed to any ill fortune, as you can see." A small smile hovered over her lips. "And you?"

"Oh, jus' comin' back from me work. At t'docks."

"Are you a docker? A porter? A ship's master?"

"A mariner 'ee could call me. Any goods t' deliver by river or sea, ah'll tak job t' deliver 'em."

"And where do you live? Where is home?"

"Ah'm a Lincolnshire lad but lodgin' with me friend Davy an' his wife whiles in Hull. 'T'other places ah find a lodgin' house."

"And where do they live in Hull?"

"St Catherine Street. Naw far from 'ere. But ah pass this way most times when ah'm headed t' docks."

"And are you finished for the day now?"

"Ah am. What about 'ee?" he asked, surreptitiously look-ing at her hand for a tell-tale ring.

"I have some laundry to deliver and then I should be done for the day."

"Ah could walk wi' ye – if tha'd let me – an' then would 'ee let me buy ye supper?"

She fixed him with that look that seemed to pull him in and drown him. "Wait there."

She disappeared into the door from whence she had come, water slopping over the rim of the bucket. A few scrawny kids went running past him, dodging his legs and racing out into the main street. An old man staggered from the communal privy, coughing and spitting the phlegmy residue onto the midden in the corner. Samuel scuffed the dirt at his feet, shifting his weight from foot to foot as he contemplated why this woman had such a hold on him. She was not a beauty. She was passably fair, but it was that look that fixed him with those eyes that were both defiant and drawing him in.

He turned as he heard the scrape of a door and she was coming down the few steps towards him, her woollen shawl around her shoulders, her dark hair tucked under her bonnet, her skirt held up and her boots dodging the muddy ground by the water pump. She linked her arm through his and together they walked from the courtyard out into the busy thoroughfare, their footsteps mingling with the clatter of horses' hooves and the rattle of cart wheels.

He's one of mine. You toy with him.

You seek to possess him but you shall not.

I shall … in time.

You want some recompense for losing him? You will have to wait.

The time will come. Be patient.

Have I ever let you down?

He is my way forward. He will be my future.

He thinks me fair – fair enough for a mariner's wife.

I can curb his thirst for time spent in the alehouses and taverns.

I will command his time and his body. I will have him and keep him close.

And I will get out of this foul pit I have found myself in.

You ask how I got to this? Indeed. How?

Disowned by those who should have looked out for me. Brothers and sisters with ideas above their station. Oh, so Martha married a doctor and took a house on the Holderness Road. Six children under her skirts and her nose in the air.

What does she know? Dripping tales into Ma's ear.

He was very small.

And very light.

And very frail.

It was so easy.

Wait. Wait! I told you!

You – must – wait …

2

The old car coughed and spluttered and finally juddered to a halt as the driver pulled into the designated parking space and cut the engine. There was a split second of silence before the sound of mildly hysterical laughter erupted from the interior and shattered the calm of the late summer afternoon, causing a passing elderly couple to look up and cast frowns in their direction. Doors were flung open and from either side the passengers spilled onto the tarmac, stretching cramped limbs and taking in deep breaths of the warm fresh air, glad to be released from the overfilled vehicle that had imprisoned them for the journey north from Lincoln to York.

"Well, we made it!" announced the older of the three occupants, her voice betraying a hint of surprise and also relief.

"Well done Gran! And well done Cynthia," one of the girls responded, patting the bonnet over the now overheated engine of the lime green old Citroen 2 CV.

"Which one is it Jen?" enquired the taller of the girls, squinting up at the building in front of them, shading her pale grey eyes against the sun.

"The top one on the far right – see the yellow blinds?" replied Jen, already leaning into the overstuffed car to retrieve the first of many bags and bundles.

"It would be the top one! Typical!" snorted Gran, shaking

out her long full print skirt where it had stuck to her legs throughout the journey in the packed stuffy little car. But she laughed and linked her arm through the taller girl's and announced, "Come on then – let's get this show on the road! Kate – grab a few of the bags and let's get climbing!"

Kate burst out laughing and gave her Gran a hug, before diving into the car and joining Jen with a few more bags draped over her arms and shoulders.

The next half hour or so consisted of repeated trips up and down to and from the flat, carrying all the paraphernalia they would need for the girls' coming term at York St John's, the university they both had been accepted for and where they would study for the coming three years.

By the time the girls had completed the last of the trips, Gran had the kettle on and coffee brewing alongside a plate with slices of carrot cake sitting alongside three mismatched mugs on the kitchen worktop.

The girls had quickly decided on who would have which bedroom, sharing the bathroom and open kitchen/living area in the small but adequately fitted out flat which belonged to Jen's parents and which they normally let out as an Airbnb but had kept as an option should any of their children need it if they came to York to study. Gran had been relieved, as it would have been a struggle to finance Kate's studies as well as accommodation but Jen's parents were more than happy that Jen would have such a sensible flatmate and were only asking that the girls stumped up the running costs of food and heating.

Flopping down on the sofa, the girls let out groans and

gasps as Gran finally shut the front door. Bringing over a tray with mugs and plates, cake and kitchen roll folded for napkins, she sat on the chair opposite, brushing her long purple hair back from her eyes and tucking a stray strand behind her ear, before retying the multicoloured scarf that held it behind her head.

"Well – here's a toast to you both," she announced lifting up one of the mugs. "Good luck girls! I'm sure you'll be happy here and I wish you both the best. Cheers!"

At that, all three mugs were raised and clinked together as the girls laughed and joined in, their voices echoing round the flat and out of the open windows, across the car parking area and carried on the wind towards the spires of the Minster beyond.

3

O ver the next few weeks the girls settled into university life. Freshers Week was the usual riot of hustle and bustle as new friendships were made, loners found themselves willingly (or unwillingly) swept up into the hurly burly of student life and the gregarious ones soon discovered the best places to socialise on and off campus. The city soon found itself home to an influx of young and sometimes rowdy students, but as usual it took it all in its stride, having been a place of meetings and congress for centuries. By now most of the tourists had vacated the city and the young ones had the run of its cafes and bars, or sat in groups in the parks on waterside benches. But soon their courses would begin, and Kate and Jen were eager to knuckle down to their studies after a few crazy evenings with new-found friends.

Kate phoned Gran every evening at first and told her all her news, but soon Gran said that she didn't need to, and just to be in touch every so often. Kate was embarking on a new life now and it was important that she grasped the opportunities with both hands and didn't feel tied to her old life. Gran assured her she was fine and in fact, she had decided to enrol at the local community centre and do one or two evening courses – she just hadn't decided which yet – it was a toss-up between pottery, life drawing and furniture upcycling. But Kate still texted most days and occasionally sent a picture of something or someone to make her laugh.

To be honest, Kate was feeling a little homesick – naturally. Her Gran had raised her after her mother had died when she was only tiny, and Grandpa had died just after that so there had only been the two of them. Granny Sue was far from being conventional – Kate loved that about her. She was very bohemian and her house was a mismash of styles and periods, housing an eclectic mix of collected and handmade items – some her Gran's handiwork and many from car boot sales and charity shops. Gran was in her late sixties but you would never have guessed. Growing up in the sixties and seventies, she was truly a child of that era and had never really left behind the flowing clothes and bright colours. She had dyed her hair purple a couple of years ago in defiance at turning sixty-five – only a number she assured Kate! Sometimes people would even take them for mother and daughter, both willowy with flowing dark hair and clear grey eyes.

Kate knew very little about her mother, Deborah – Debbie as she was always called. She had had Kate when she was twenty-two and there never seemed to have been a father on the scene. Kate's birth certificate was left blank where that piece of information would have been recorded. Kate occasionally used to daydream about what he might have been like. Did he sweep Debbie off her feet or was it a more sordid one night stand? Was he already married or did he run when he heard that Debbie was pregnant? She wasn't really sure how her mother died other than she had drowned; Gran said little and Kate never pursued it. But in the end, she closed that part of her mind, and decided that being brought up by Granny Sue was wonderful and being loved by her was all she had ever needed.

Before the real hard work began, Jen and Kate decided to explore the city and discover its hidden nooks and crannies and get a feel for the place. So far all they seemed to have seen were its cafes and bars where live music played and they flooded out late at night, wending their way home through dark streets. Above them the floodlit tower of the Minster kept watch and the gargoyles smirked at their unsteady gait, as they had for centuries.

"We need to keep ourselves in shape! All this sitting about's not doing us any good," announced Jen one afternoon. "Come on, let's go for a run – let's see if we can follow the walls!"

"Sounds like a great idea," agreed Kate so that evening before supper they set off in joggers and tee shirts to follow the outline of the city walls. Starting at Lord Mayor's Walk they headed round behind the York Minster then down Museum Street till they found themselves by the bridge crossing over the River Ouse. Taking a breather, they watched as two boats left the Rowing Club and set off downstream, their oars in perfect synchronicity. And of course, there were some lithe male bodies to admire too!

"Come on – can't stand here gawping all evening!" scoffed Jen and they crossed over and followed the river bank south. Soon another bridge came in to view and they were able to follow the path up and onto it. Catching their breath, they crossed over the road and stood and looked downstream. There were still a few late tourists looking for somewhere to eat, hovering in doorways perusing menus.

Kate leant her elbows on the rough stone of the bridge and looked down at the water slowly swirling beneath her. Suddenly she felt faint and her legs struggled to hold her as she slumped forward on the parapet. Closing her eyes she tried to focus on the present but something was pushing at the edges of her mind, something familiar but not welcome.

"Are you alright?" It was Jen's voice coming through from somewhere in the distance. She was aware of a hand on her elbow and the roughness of the stone under her bare arm. It was as if something slammed into her and she was hurtled forward and found herself standing next to Jen on the bridge, unaware of how she had got there.

"Kate! Kate, are you alright?" The urgency of Jen's voice snapped her concentration to the present and she fought to regain her balance and stand upright.

"Yes. Yes, I'm fine…"

"Maybe we did too much for our first run out in ages. Come on let's get back. We can just walk it from here," Jen said with some concern in her voice. "You sure you're okay? You were … somewhere else."

"Come on, I'm fine," Kate replied as she tried to convince herself that it was just a case of too much exercise and not enough practice.

By the time they had walked back through the streets and across Lord Mayor's Walk, the light was going, street lamps were glowing and windows were being illuminated as lights were switched on, exposing cosy rooms just before blinds and curtains were pulled to keep out the darkening evening.

By the time they reached the flat, Kate just wanted to jump in the shower while Jen scoured the freezer for a spag bol to shove in the microwave. As Kate came through in her pyjamas, Jen grabbed her dressing gown from the bedroom and shouted, "Put the plates to warm. I won't be long," as the bathroom door slammed behind her.

Kate lay back on the sofa and found herself trying to piece together the fleeting images that she had seen on the bridge …

4

S oon Samuel couldn't get back quick enough from the voyages he made inland or out to sea. To see his Laura – that was all that filled his mind, and body. She beguiled him. She was witty, smart, she could read and write and her language was better than that of many of the guttersnipes he had rolled with before. She was no slip of a girl. She said she was but two years younger than him, but she seemed wise beyond her years. She never said much about her family but he suspected they had parted on ill terms. Nevertheless she did seem to hold some affection for her mother on the very few occasions she had spoken of her.

After a few weeks of her company, he knew that she must be his completely. And she seemed to be more than willing. Davy's lodging was no place to go, so fumblings in the chilly alleyways and dark doorways seemed all he could hope for. His hands roved over her and his mind envisaged what lay beneath her woollen skirts and flannel petticoats. Her thighs were soft and warm and he sought what lay beyond until he ached with the pain of it. But she would step away and hold him at arms' length while her eyes still said 'come here'. She tortured him and enthralled him at the same time.

"We must be betrothed Samuel. We have to plan for our future. Between us we can make a life for ourselves and one day soon we will get another step further from the gutter. Wait and see."

With that he kissed her hard and fierce before he knew what had come over him. His answer.

Samuel would try to see her as often as he could on return from his trips while Laura would find excuses to collect or deliver the laundry for her landlady. It was mending and altering items from the laundry that Laura spent her time doing in exchange for board and lodging and a few spare shillings at the end of the month. With her bundle of dried sheets and pillowcases, linen shifts and shirts bundled up and slung on her back, she would meet Samuel at the entrance to the court and together they would walk up to the town where Laura would deliver her bundle to some merchant family's door. And on the way back there was a detour via an alehouse or tavern to enjoy the fruits of their labours.

And in a dark alleyway discretion was thrown aside and Laura found her skirts being thrust aside and her bodice pulled down as Samuel made demands on her that she was not totally averse to. His kisses rained upon her as the damp ran down the wall behind her. She tried to resist but there was inner voice that wanted what she had been denied for so long.

Samuel found a place to rent at the end of Great Union Street in a part of town called The Groves, an area of closely packed housing that had sprung up as the population of the town had exploded. It was two rooms and a kitchen, not unlike the house in which he lodged with Davy, but on a front street called Lime Street, rather than a courtyard. And it was far enough away from the tidal Sutton Drain which, at low tide, was lined with black, putrid matter that acted like suction if any unwary drunk were to fall in or urchin go mudlarking there.

And all the time the swishing of the river as its tidal flow swept up the banks and under the wharves, whispering its demands of promises made, debts to be paid.

Be patient, be patient.

It is not yet time …

The Banns were read for three consecutive Sundays at the local St Peter's Church. They were married at the end of that October by which time she knew she was not alone in her body. She signed her name as one – but there were two.

Her body was not her own. It belonged to Samuel. She was his property and his to command. But she entertained another and felt it move inside her as well. It demanded as much, if not more of her attention than her husband.

Their rooms were small and cramped. Their furnishings just the bare minimum but Laura had plans. This was not for ever. She made it clear that they must set aside whatever they could, although she did not share her aspirations with her husband. His needs were plain – food, a good drink, honest toil to sweat at and a warm bed to sweat and toil in some more.

And when he took her in his arms and she looked at him with those eyes that took him out of himself to a place he became lost in, then he was sated and content.

The months passed, her belly gently swelled, he worked and she planned.

And the river flowed.

Waiting …

Her life had changed – but only in small ways. She still toiled at sewing till the light had faded, taking in dressmaking and mending for a few shillings, using the contacts she had made while in the employ of the laundress. The rest of the time she scrubbed and cleaned, fetched water from the communal pump at the back of the street, walked up Lime Street and down Great Union Street, seeking out bargains to make the few coins stretch a bit further. Under her layers of clothing she wore to keep out the biting east wind, there were stretchings and turnings, hidden from view.

Samuel was usually away for a few days at a time, and there were always a few coins to put in the pot on his return. But she knew he was spending others in the alehouses along the canals or rivers of Yorkshire, or in the taverns of Kentish ports. On his return they would stretch the coins to a pie and a bottle of stout, with a few slices of rough bread and an apple if one could be found at this time of year on a stall in the market. But it was a basic existence, not that it bothered Samuel. He was a 'take it as you find it' kind of man, with few thoughts of tomorrow and none for the future beyond that. His mind focussed on simple needs – a full belly, a drink or two to take the edge off the hardship of sleeping on a wooden bunk board or in a vermin-infested lodging house, male company to exchange jokes and ribald conversations with and a woman to warm his bed on his return home.

When he was apart from her, he couldn't fathom how she seemed to possess him. It was like a mist came over him and blotted out images from his memory. In his mind she was the slim girl with the dark hair that welcomed him home and laid a hot meal on the rough wooden table before him. She was the one who extracted from him the few coins he brought back and put them, God knew where. She was the one who darned the holes worn through in his rough woollen socks and repaired the tear in the sleeve of his jacket, so it would last a few more months. She was the one that would find a pot or a blanket to pawn when there was no work on the day they needed to pay the rent. She was just – there.

But when she took his face in her rough hands and lifted her face to his, he was pulled into her looking-glass eyes and transported to another time and place. When her lips found his and her hands laid on his chest, he dissolved and became a malleable substance that she could hold and form and shape to her will. He moulded to the mirror image of her form and they fitted together and around each other and inside each other. The hours evaporated and time stood still. His own will had been sucked out of him and he moved to her tune, her will, her bidding. No words were needed – it was an unspoken script that he had learned unbidden. Then there was no hard pallet beneath, no cold icy draught seeping through the gaps in the windows and doors, no coarse woollen blankets. There was nothing. He was suspended and in-sensate. He was nothing. She had taken it all.

5

K ate was on her phone giving Gran the latest news about her course. She was doing the English Literature and History course and one reason she had chosen this was that it included using the social and cultural history of the city – 'history in situ' as Kate called it, and she couldn't wait to explore the history of the city with the tutor for that module.

"I've got some news too," announced Gran. "You remember I fancied doing some evening classes at the community centre? Well, Sally talked me into coming with her to enrol for the genealogy course. She got a DNA test for her birthday and she got the results last week. She uploaded her results and discovered cousins which apparently link with her tree so now she can't wait to learn how to dig further."

"What about you Gran? I've never really heard much about our family roots – do you know much about our ancestors?" To be honest, Kate had never felt she wanted to ask too much as she didn't want to dwell on the death of her mother as it might prove upsetting for Sue.

"Well, to be honest, I don't really know that much. My mother, Maud, never told me much when I was growing up and neither Mum nor Dad seemed to have many old photos or family things so I never really asked. How I wish I had now. Always the way isn't it?"

"Ooh – quite exciting then. Maybe you'll unearth some skeletons in the cupboard! Keep me up to date with your findings won't you? When does it start?"

"Next Thursday evening – 7 till 9. But I also enrolled in the Life Drawing class – hope there's a hunky chap to draw!"

"Gran!" squealed Kate, as they both dissolved into giggles.

"And I'm going to do an afternoon class on Mondays on furniture upcycling, so I'll be busy."

"Keep you out of mischief, more like!" Kate giggled again.

Later that evening, Kate found herself thinking more about her ancestors and what Sue would discover. And after all, they were her roots as well.

6

S tumbling and slipping down the icy streets to the docks, Samuel set off to pick up any work going on a cold, bitter, grey winter's morning. The yellow light filtered from the east through the smoggy atmosphere of a thousand chimneys but it was not yet daylight and few people were around. He felt he should have remembered something but as usual, his recall of the previous hours were patchy at the best. He felt exhausted, hardly rested and ready for a day's work. But work he must. She had made that clear. Fair exchange.

A few others joined him as he made his way to queue up at the gates, waiting for the hiring men to take their pick. Blowing on his numbed fingers and stamping his feet, he had his eye on the coal carrier berthed at the dock. He knew the master and had sailed with him on a few occasions. Before sailing he and the other hired labourers would join the dock workers to empty the heavy trucks of coal that had been brought by rail into the siding by the dock. It was hard heavy work but paid slightly better than purely loading and working on the craft, so there was always a scramble to get that opportunity. Samuel nodded at a few familiar faces as they huddled closer and slapped their arms around their bodies to engender some heat and dispel the creeping cold. Their breath rose in clouds, the vapour hovering and then dissipating before being replenished with more from the gathered mob.

An hour later Samuel was at the dockside with another docker, tipping the cart-loads of coal into the hold of the boat tied up, awaiting its cargo bound for Gravesend.

The weak light of the winter sun combined with the low angle caused him to squint, the shafts of pale light giving token illumination to the scene, as coal dust rose in clouds as the loads were tipped out, rumbling and crashing into the gaping maw of the hold. The sun brought no heat with it and the quaysides were still slippery from the freezing temperatures of the previous night.

Turning back to collect the next load, Samuel felt his foot slide away from him, his other leg twisted back and he clattered to the ground, cracking his ribs on the edge as he slipped over and wedged between the boat and the rough wooden piers of the dock. A sickening crack and a tearing wrench caused his stomach to heave and from the very depths of him came a screaming yell, drawing all eyes to the scene. It was as if the scene was frozen in the wintry air. For a second or two there was not a movement or a sound. It was as if the world held its breath. Then it seemed like every voice, tool and piece of machinery leapt into motion and a cacophony of sounds erupted. Shouts and yells, tools clattering to the ground, feet running, hands grasping, bodies jostling. Darkness closing in.

She was startled from her reverie, still huddled under the thin bedclothes that held no remainder of his warmth, nor comfort of his body. The only trace a hollow in the greasy pillow that lay by her head. More hammering and shouts – her name in urgent tones.

"Lass! Are ye there? Wake yer sen! 'Tis yer husband – 'e's had 'n accident! Are ye there?"

Reluctantly dragging herself from the tangled cocoon

of bedclothes, she crossed the room in a few steps and unlatched the door, still shaking sleep from her head. A burly man and a scrawny sidekick stood upon her doorstep, their breath wreathed around their heads.

"Missus Cowper? 'Tis Samuel – 'e's slipped an' fell. They've taken 'im t' Infirmary. Will 'ee cum?"

She stood, frozen. Not with the cold, but with something more primeval. A brief nod of her head in affirmation sufficed to give them an answer as she shut the door, leaving them to depart, but unsure if they should stay or go. A few moments later the clattering of their boots signalled their departure. She sat on the edge of the bed, reaching across to her shawl and pulling it round her. This was not how it was supposed to be.

Leaving the red brick building of the Workhouse Infirmary where he had been brought two weeks earlier, she walked alone and unaccompanied by neither friend nor family, along Anlaby Road in the direction of the docks. And the river.

Crossing the Drypool Bridge, where he had first seen her, she slowed and found herself on the tidal shore of the river. A steady drizzle of rain soaked her through and sat on the surface of her woollen shawl like a thousand tiny diamonds. It was just the two of them. What to do now? They had not had a chance to lay down roots or make plans. It seemed like they had had all the time in the world. Fool! Should have known better girl! Taking your pleasures without getting a solid foundation under you.

I nearly had him. But not quite.

I can wait.

A debt has to be paid …

He went to his rest in a pauper's grave with neither marker nor headstone to attest to him ever having lived. Money didn't stretch that far. The rent had to be paid. Pawning the few items of any worth bought some time but without his wage coming in, her pittance from mending and sewing was soon found wanting. The thought of going back to lodge with the laundress and her unnatural spawn of a son turned her stomach. A flip and a ripple of agreement from within her belly settled her mind. But all they had now was a day's grace until they would be out on the street to fend for themselves.

Without really thinking where she was headed, she walked through the main thoroughfares that headed further into the centre of town. The shops and offices were brightly lit although it was still early afternoon. Carts and carriages interwove their way through the accumulated slush and mud at the sides of the road and prim ladies picked up their skirts for fear of slipping or stepping in the accumulated filth.

Her feet took her without her mind taking charge and, as she realised where she had walked to, her spirits momentarily lifted. Memories of family meals, cosy bedtimes, playing games and sharing secrets with siblings. But they were shadows. Long gone. The house looked the same. Red brick with a stout door and the windows on the upper floors shedding beams of warm light into the cold misty afternoon, now almost evening. Her eyes were drawn by the noise of a cab arriving, the horses hooves approaching round the corner and in her direction. Pressing herself back into the shadows, she watched as it halted at the house and a man alighted, holding out his leather-gloved hand to a woman who followed him down whilst holding her skirts above the road surface. She had a fur muffler around her neck and a fine wool coat of a deep blue colour. Quickly they stepped towards the illumination from the front door which carved a beam of light to lead them into the bright interior. A servant holding the door bobbed a greeting and the strong tones of the man thanking Betsy carried through the eerie stillness. As soon as they had crossed the threshold, the door was shut and bolted against the approaching dark and cold of the night.

They were strangers. They were not the people she knew. They were obviously not visitors but residents of this place. There would be no flash of recognition or a welcome for her here. How long since she had enjoyed the comfort of the warmth and security this place held? Nine – ten years? But then memories of less happy times. Cruel words and bitter recriminations. Tears. Leaving the place without a backward glance, her head held high but her heart in shreds. She had been sure her pride and her strength would be her helpmate.

They had obviously moved on, who knows where. No communication found her to inform her. No sibling with an ounce of sympathy sought her out. That chapter of her life was well and truly closed. It was as she always knew – she was mistress of her own future. And that was the path she had chosen.

A final lingering look before turning away, and then she headed back towards the main part of the town. She could not rely on husband or family to support her, only herself. As darkness crowded in she heard the swishing of the flow of the water alongside the street she trod. A gap in the pathway drew her in and again she found herself on the mud encrusted shore, the ruts and ridges hard and frozen, causing her to stumble and stagger to gain a solid foothold.

You made your choice. I am waiting.

I am your friend, your family, your ... lover.

You can come to me anytime.

Not yet.

Not yet.

Remember your debt.

I have not forgotten ...

7

The next week or two was spent knocking on doors, visiting sweatshops and backstreet laundries in the hope of a some promise of paid work. If she was fortunate, she would get some 'slop work' – making cheap clothes, trousers or waistcoats, skirts or coats. This earned her a few shillings a day which enabled her to get a room in a cheap lodging house for a week. But then she had to get food on top of that. Scrounging the market stalls at the end of the day for left over items, a bruised apple, a couple of wizened potatoes, some stale bread, enabled her to make a scant meal to fill her belly, washed down with some watered beer.

Other times the sewing work was not forthcoming and she had to resort to a day working 'at the tub' where she would spend ten to twelve hours, up to her elbows in huge vats of hot water washing linens, by the end of which her hands and arms would be red raw as a result of the harsh caustic soap. Then a few hours' sleep before repeating the same routine the next day. By the time she fell onto her thin mattress, her back ached and she felt faint with the steam and the stench of the carbolic. She became listless and felt her energy being sucked out of her.

And then one morning she awoke, the bed soaking and her body drenched in sweat. Barely able to reach for the chamber pot in time, she voided the little that was in her stomach before doubling up with pain. Most of the day she lay in her own vomit before drifting into a restless sleep as dusk fell. Although the walls were thin and afforded no privacy, no-one came knocking at her door to enquire for her wellbeing. There was no-one left to care.

Barely aware of the change of light in the gloomy little room, she awoke to another type of aching that pulled at her core and dragged her down. Hauling herself up off the soiled mattress, she crawled towards the door in an attempt to reach the outside privy. But before she could reach the door, another pain stabbed through her and she felt the wetness seeping through her skirts and between her legs. Letting out a howl of pain, she realised it was blood she could feel, sticky and warm. Another cramp of pain and something slithered from her, warm and still.

◆ ◆ ◆

So you have come at last.

Have you brought me something?

Is it yours to give? You know the rules.

Yes, yes. Take it.

I have nothing left – nothing.

You have taken all I ever had.

The bundle was caught in a little eddy that circled around it, licked at it, tested its weight and curled around its form, before embracing it and carrying it off.

I watched it until I could see it no more as the darkness of the night swallowed it up and I was left – alone, truly alone.

I had paid my debt.

The best part of the following day resting on her mattress gave her time to think what she could do next. Having missed the best part of two days' wages, however meagre, she was now without enough to pay for her lodgings and no-one was going to give her credit. She would be out on the street with only the clothes she stood up in and the other few belongings that had not been pawned over the last few weeks, or were so worthless as not able to raise a penny or two. And she was never going to sell her body on the streets – of that she was quite sure, whatever depths she may have sunk to. The only other choice was the casual ward at the workhouse. She would be required to stay a minimum of two nights and do some work to justify her keep. Here she would at least get a roof over her head and some slops to fill her griping belly. But the ignominy of that chilled her to the core. How had it come to this? Even the thought that it was only a temporary measure crushed what little pride she had left.

She gathered together her few belongings – a piece of mirror, a comb, a length of green velvet ribbon, a scrap of lace edging, a small sliver of perfumed soap, a leather drawstring purse, a pencil stub, a reel of cotton and a small skein of darning wool, a small needle-case with a few needles and pins inserted into the flannel leaves, two buttons, a few menstrual rags, a neckerchief that had belonged to Samuel, a linen chemise and a pair of woollen stockings. All these she put into a blue striped ticking pillow cover and tied the bundle with a length of twine. Her other belongings were worn on or about her.

Two flannel petticoats, a cotton petticoat, a light set of stays, a flannel chest cloth, a pair of drawers, a pair of stockings held up with woollen knitted garters, a pocket on a tape tied around her waist under her woollen skirt, a chemise, a faded velvet bodice, a woollen jacket, a shawl and a bonnet with green ties. Her only embellishments were a faded fabric rose pinned to her jacket and the thin silver band Samuel had placed on her finger the day they were wed. Thrusting her feet into her only boots and lacing them up, she took a moment to glance around the gloomy room and then picking up her bundle, crossed to the rough wooden door that led into a corridor and the creaking worn wooden stairs that brought her to the main door.

She passed no-one.

She heard no-one.

No-one even knew she had gone.

All she knew was she had to head west along the Anlaby Road, the same way she had hurried to see Samuel when he had been taken to the infirmary. And here she was again, tramping the same road but in very different circumstances. If ever she needed to acknowledge the fact that money was a woman's only power in this world, it was now. Without the support of a man she had few choices without money behind her, and even then the choices left to her were few. Every step she took reinforced this knowledge within her.

As the twin square red-brick towers of the workhouse

came into view behind the high red-brick wall, she felt an involuntary shiver. To enter here would be to admit that everything she had tried to do in her life so far had come to nothing. If this was to be her lowest point, then she had only one way to go. Weak and exhausted with both lack of food and lack of child, it was only the thought that it would be a temporary measure that spurred her on. Time to take stock, fill her belly and make plans.

Entering the gates with one or two other unfortunate souls, she determined to keep her head up high and swallowed down the shame and bile that threatened to weaken her resolve. Upon entering, an official directed her to a counter where she had to give her name and age, her reason for admission and whether she had any illness or disease. She was asked whether she was for 'the casual ward' or if she intended to stay here longer. Indicating the former, this was noted in the register and she was herded through a doorway to the right with a handful of other women who had been separated from the few men who had entered at the same time. Tears and howls of anguish from women torn from their husbands and older male children threatened to reduce her to a similar state, but biting her lip hard she managed to grit her teeth and move forward. Girls and younger children were hugged close to the ragged skirts of their mothers as they snivelled and rubbed their noses with the backs of their sleeves. Each woman's few belongings were then taken from her and labelled with her name, while she was instructed to remove her clothing and head through the icy tiled corridor into a communal bath where they were instructed to scrub themselves clean. The odious brown of the water, filthy from the countless unwashed bodies that had passed through it that day, reminded Laura of the river .

The river ...

No, not again.

Never again.

Having dried themselves on the pitifully thin rags that masqueraded as towels, they were issued with identical grey and off-white clothing. A thin petticoat and chemise, a thin serge skirt, a blouse of indeterminate colour to be covered with an apron that reached to her ankles. No attempt was made to match sizes so while some were almost tripping up on their skirts, others were showing half a leg of mottled blue flesh. Grey stockings were handed out and gratefully pulled over cold feet, although they were pitifully thin and offered little warmth. Finally there was a scramble to find a pair of boots that roughly fitted from a pile in a crate in the corner. Eventually they were led through to their dormitories where those who had been here before scrambled for the beds furthest from the doors and windows. As it was almost time for the evening meal, they were soon joined by other inmates who had been working all day.

A bell was sounded and a warder led them into a dining room where serried rows of benches and tables stretched the full length of the hall. Each woman collected a bowl and a spoon and queued up to receive some watered down porridge which they called 'skilly', a chunk of rough brown bread, a small potato and a tiny slice of some grey coloured cheese. Returning to their seats no-one was permitted to start to eat until all were instructed to bow their heads and give thanks to the Lord for His munificence and their good fortune to be so well looked after in His care. Only after 'Amen' was echoed by nearly 200 voices, did the cacophony of spoons scraping bowls begin.

By the time the meal was over, Laura felt her belly at least had something in it at last. It wasn't much – but it was better than nothing. Laying on her pallet and pulling the thin blanket over her, she curled up to conserve what little warmth her body could engender and thankfully fell asleep as the cries of infants and scared children eventually abated.

The next morning followed the same dining regime – with the addition of a splash of cold water as a morning wash in the cold tiled washrooms. Only porridge and a hunk of bread to break their fast, then they were assigned their tasks for the day. As she was ' a casual' she was assigned picking oakum. Hunched on the floor over a pile of old ropes, the women picked the strands apart with a spike and their bare hands, then put the bundles of fibres into sacks. They would be sent be mixed with tar and used to caulk ships' timbers. Her hands were filthy, raw and sore from the rough fibres and what nails she had were torn and broken from trying to prise the fibres apart. As daylight started to fade, they were herded out into a yard for exercise, even though their backs and legs were aching from being hunched over the work on a cold floor. The men were kept totally separate and exercised in their own yard. A few children chased each other while the younger ones were balanced on the hips of mothers, or hastily put to their mothers' breasts to hush their cries. Some women congregated in small groups, exchanging a few words with those they knew, but no-one spoke to her. And she spoke to no-one.

Another evening and night of the same regime followed, and all that sustained her was the thought that she would leave the next morning and head out along the road in search of a fresh start.

8

S he headed west, facing into the weak sun that was fading fast as the day wore on. With her pack under her arm and her shawl pulled tightly around her she soon left the buildings of the city behind her and patches of green fields and hedgerows brightened her view and the air freshened as the smoky atmosphere was left behind. Passing through the small settlements of Anlaby and Kirk Ella, she found a barn to shelter in having just passed through South Cave. By now the light was fading fast and she had no more strength to keep going any further. From her pack she pulled a hunk of bread that she had managed to keep back from her last meal, and after gnawing at that and slaking her thirst from a small nearby stream, she pulled the straw about her and thankfully sleep overtook her.

The sound of a cock crowing and the calls of sheep awaking in a nearby field roused her from sleep. Hoping that she could make better time that day, she prepared to head along the road toward Eastrington. Luckily it was a fine morning and after a few miles with the sun at her back, she heard the approach of hooves as a cart pre- pared to join the road from a farm track nearby. Pulling the cart to a halt, the driver waited for her to draw level and then doffed his hat at her.

Considering her poor outfit and demeanour, this amused her somewhat but she gave him a pretty smile and wished him, "Good morning."

"Where be ye off t' lass?" he asked after he had returned the battered hat to his almost bald pate.

"Oh – anywhere along this road. Where does it go?"

"Well it'll go where 'ee want 't to, 'spose."

"Where are you going?" she asked, "Sir," she added hopefully.

"Well, I be off t' Goole wi' this load o' vegetables. Ye're welcome t' hop up if th'd be likin' a ride. Allus like a bit o' company," he added with a wink.

With a grateful smile, she hitched her skirts and climbed up, sitting alongside him on the board that served as a seat. He wasn't one for much conversation, which suited her, and with the old horse going at a slow but steady pace, she was soon able to see the smudge of buildings on the skyline ahead of her after a couple of hours, by which time the sun had risen high in the sky and its thin warmth began to seep through her woollen shawl.

As they turned south towards Goole, a glint of water caught her eye and as they came nearer, she realised they were approaching the wide sweep of a river.

A river!

"What river is this?" she gasped, clutching at the shawl at her neck.

" 'Tis th' Ouse, missus. Be'int a gurt big river indeed. Goes all t'way t' York an' out t' sea t'other way," he replied, looking at her strangely, surprised at her reaction.

She felt her pulse racing and tried to slow her breathing, as her chest heaved with the effort of getting air into her lungs. After closing her eyes for a few moments, she was able to calm herself enough to manage a slight smile to reassure him all was well.

"Ye all reet lass?" he asked, with a note of concern in his voice.

"Yes, yes. I'm alright. Thank you. A temporary moment of no matter. Thank you."

"We cross t' ferry here 't Booth. We'll have t' wait till there's space for Molly an' t' cart. Ye can go ahead if ye're in t' hurry?"

"No, no thank you. I'll go with you if that's alright?"

And so they tethered the old mare, Molly, and let her have some oats from the nosebag he attached to her bridle. Digging into his cavernous pocket he pulled out three apples, slightly wizened as it they had been stored all winter. Handing her one after rubbing a shine on it on his sleeve, he cut into the other with a penknife he drew from his corduroy waistcoat. The third apple he set aside – for Molly when they reached their journey's end, he told her.

They sat on a patch of grass on the bank and watched as the ferry crossed the slow moving current, expertly guided by the ferryman and what appeared to be his son wielding long poles. It was but a broad flat craft with a boards laid across it, which overhung the sides. A couple of smaller boards were placed in the stern, where passengers could sit. Along one side a rail had been attached. They were bringing a few passengers back on its return journey and two horses tied to the rail. They swung it round as it neared the bank and nosed its way to the mooring posts set into the muddy verge. A sloping track led down to the water's edge with some wooden planks on which to walk, and soon the passengers were making their way up it and onto the roadway beyond. When the ferry was ready for them the ferryman waved to them to get ready to come aboard and the farmer paid the fee – 6d for the cart and horse, and an extra 1d for Laura, which he didn't let on.

Once Molly and the cart had been balanced to the ferryman's content, and her reins lashed to the rail, Laura made her way to the stern and sat on one of the boards, her bundle clutched tightly to her chest as she tried to quell the rising panic she felt.

Surely she couldn't hear it. No. No!

She was free. Of course she was free.

Her debt had been paid – in full.

Hadn't it ... ?

This was a different one, a different place ...

Let me free!

By the time they had reached the other side, Laura found she had been clutching her bonnet round her ears to block out any sounds. To the others it looked as if she feared for its safety in the strong breeze that rose off the water. Her eyes were tightly shut, which only made the sway and rock of the craft feel all the more unsettling, causing her stomach to twist and her head to swim. A thud and a scrunching rasping noise made her open her eyes, and she was glad to see that they had reached the far bank in safety. With some amusement, the ferryman's son offered her his hand to steady her as she stepped forward over the edge and onto solid ground. With a wink he touched his greasy hat and wished her good day. The farmer busied himself with getting the horse and cart unloaded and reharnessed while Laura contemplated what to do next. They were still well out into the countryside and a couple of miles away from the main part of the town by the looks of it. Her first instinct was to start out straightaway to get herself away from the riverbank and all the memories that were crowding in on her. Turning to scramble up the embankment, she stood under an overhanging tree until cart and horse were finally unloaded and set upon the roadway in preparation of the next part of the journey.

"Are tha comin'?" called the farmer.

Glad of the company, she once more pulled herself onto the cart as the horse was urged forward with a slap of the reins and a promise of that apple and a rest in a couple of miles.

As the countryside and straggled cottages gave way to the outskirts of the town, shops and rows of larger buildings came into view with all the attendant hustle and bustle of people going about their business and traffic criss-crossing into side streets. In the far distance were the tops of cranes and masts which marked the dock area.

Eventually they turned into a market square where stalls were laid out and people were haggling over prices and children were chasing each other through the legs of stallholders who tried to clip their ears in annoyance as they dodged behind crates or sacks. Molly was tethered at the side of one stall where the farmer told her he regularly brought his produce. A buxom woman stood behind it, her pockmarked cheeks spoiling an other-wise fair face. She greeted the farmer and they had a short conversation, which included a glance in Laura's direction. She was just thinking that she would use the crowded throng to slip away, when she was beckoned over by the woman.

"Tom 'ere tells me tha've been 'is company t'day. Have 'ee a place t' go? Family 'ere?"

A slow shake of the head was all Laura could reply, as she clutched her bundle tighter.

"Well, that no good girl o' mine didn't turn up t'day so if ye'd gie a hand wi' t' stall ah'd pay tha summat for't."

Laura's options were certainly limited at this precise mo-ment in time so she hesitantly accepted the offer and came over to stand with the woman behind the stall, who introduced herself as Lizzie.

"No thieving mind! Ye'll get yer dues an' some o' the goods at t'end of day if tha stays an' do a day's work."

"Of course," she hurriedly replied with a nod of her head. Only then did she look the woman directly in the eye. Lizzie held it for a few moments longer than normal, then broke away, shaking her head as if to clear a fog.

The day passed quickly. It was a thriving market and the produce Tom had brought was fresh and of good quality. The money taken was stowed in a belt at Lizzie's waist and seemed to be filling up well as the day pro-gressed. Tom had long ago harnessed Molly to the empty cart and headed homeward, assuring Laura that he'd be home before nightfall, all being well, and bidding her farewell.

As the afternoon started to head towards evening and the crowds thinned as people headed home with their purchases, Lizzie tidied up the stall and together they put any tattered leaves and unsaleable items into a sack.

"Have 'ee a roof for t'night?" she asked her. "Thought not," she added when she saw Laura's hesitation.

"Ah'll pay tha summat for t'day's work but it'll not get 'ee a lodgin' for long. Nor a very good 'un. Ah can offer 'ee a bed and some warm food if ye come back wi' me."

Again Laura hesitated, which Lizzie took for a refusal. "Well, 'tis up to ye …"

"No, I mean, yes. I would be very grateful for your hospitality. Thank you. And thank you for today. You are very kind." That was the most words Laura had uttered to her all afternoon, and Lizzie's eyebrows raised a little as she realised that this was no girl from the Poor House or from the gutter. Nor did she sound like a farm wench newly come to town.

"Reet, tha' be sorted then," announced Lizzie, bundling up the last of the empty sacks and adding them to a barrow which she proceeded to manoeuvre around the empty stall, avoiding the leftover rubbish lying on the ground. "Cum 'head," and she set off at a brisk pace, down the incline towards the lower part of the town, with Laura following her, clutching all her worldly goods and possessions.

After about half a mile or so, Lizzie veered into a narrow street of terraced houses, matched by identical ones facing them. Stopping outside one at the end of the street, she turned down a ginnel and opened a high gate set into the red brick wall. She deposited the barrow and its contents in the yard which was small but packed with all manner of items. At one end was a large copper tub for laundry, sheltered by a lean-to roof and beside it a small brick privy. Washing hung from ropes strung across the yard, and dodging these, she led Laura towards the back entrance to the house. A door led into a kitchen with a small range to one side. In the centre was a well-worn table with a selection of mis-matched chairs around it. From the kitchen a narrow corridor connected with the front door of the dwelling. To one side a door opened onto a living room with a couple of worn armchairs and a small table set in the window on which sat, incongruously Laura thought, a large potted plant. Against the wall a settee-come-bed was covered with a throw and a couple of cushions.

"All me brood 'ave flown t'nest. Only one who drops by's me son John. 'E works on t' boats but 'e allus likes 'is mam's cookin' an' a comfy bed when 'e's in port." With this, she tossed her head upwards towards the top of the stairs. "T'other room is where me girls were but they've all got wed. Me man an' me slept down 'ere but 'e's gawn now. Just me'sen."

With that she led Laura up the narrow creaking stairs and into a small room with a small bed that might have slept two – she supposed her daughters had shared this.

"Thank you Lizzie. I am very grateful."

"Tha'll not get owt for free. If tha work wi' me at the stall an' do some laundry an' mending – can tha do that?" she paused as Laura nodded in affirmation, "– then ah'll give ye yer board an' lodgin' wi' a bit left over dependin' on yer 'andiwork. Trial period, mind."

"Of course. I am a dressmaker and I can do laundry and mending."

"Well, there ye'are! Aw reet? 'Ave we a deal?" At this Laura nodded and gave a hesitant smile.

While Laura untied her bundle and laid out her meagre possessions on the bed, she suddenly felt very weary and lost. Certainly luck had dealt her a good hand to find such kindly folk. But this was not the future she hoped for. But maybe she had to learn patience. Time would tell.

9

O ver the next week or two, Laura began to get back some of her strength and a hint of colour returned to her sunken pallid cheeks. Lizzie intended to fatten her up, stating that none of her girls would have been allowed to get into such a state. But Laura offered little in the way of explanation about her past life, and Lizzie realised she would get little in the way of information.

So I have exchanged one wash tub for another, one pile of sewing and mending for another.

Life seems to be following the same pattern – but it is not the pattern that I want. I cannot deny that I have been the recipient of the kindness of folk who did not know me and had no right to care. I am eternally grateful to them.

But I have another path I need to follow …

Lizzie's son John came back at intervals and stayed for a night, never more than two, as he would then be on another trip. He worked as mate on board a coal-carrying barge, and travelled as far west as Leeds and worked the rivers and canals that connected to Goole, York and Castleford. He used his mother's as a place to lay his head, sleep off too much drink or get a square meal before setting off again at first light. Their paths crossed infrequently and when they did, Laura found his language and his demeanour unattractive. In return, he showed his resentment that his mother appeared to have taken a shine to her. His mother was always easily swayed by a sob story and a few tears, or so he thought. He could never meet Laura's eye, in fact he avoided her whenever he could, preferring the alehouse to his mother's table. If they met on the stairs or in the doorway, he would freeze like a rabbit caught in a beam of light, then muttering some uncouth words, drag his gaze away and push past her roughly out of the door.

He is not worth bothering about. He is of little use to me.

It was a busy town, growing in size due to the docks that were expanding as coal came in on the railway carts that now wound in and out of the countryside to spew out their filthy freight into the shallow coal-carrying boats that would take it by canal, river and sea to the heartlands and far off ports where it was needed to power the industries and heat the countless homes of neighbouring towns and villages, as well as distant nations. The tracks ran on an embankment behind the house and if the wind was blowing in the wrong direction, sooty smuts would besmirch the laundry hanging on ropes in the yard, necessitating a repetition of all the morning's hard work. She soon learned to judge the wind direction and keep a weather eye out for clouds sweeping in from the south.

By and by she managed to gather a few shillings which she stowed in the leather purse which she hid under her mattress. Lizzie took a fair but not extortionate amount for her board and lodging, and if they did well on market days, a few more coins would be added to her purse. Occasionally her skill with the needle brought a few more shillings her way when she offered to make up dresses or petticoats for the better-off women of the town who were impressed with the quality of her mending. But it was a slow accumulation and was never going to free her from this kind of life. Yes, she thought again, money is a woman's only power in this life.

One dark and bitterly cold winter's night, John turned up at his mother's door. They had just sat down to their evening meal – a wholesome stew with some mutton chunks and some dumplings that Lizzie had made – when the door burst open and John entered, shouting greetings to his mam. Laura could just make out the shadowy form of another man behind him, who was hesitating in the open doorway. John turned and hauled at the man's arm, dragging him in and shutting the door against the cold blast.

"Mam – this is George, me master. 'E's needin' a bed for t'night and ah tol' him 'e could bunk up wi' me. 'S'awreet in't 't Ma?" Without waiting for any answer, he pushed George into the room and manhandled him into one of the chairs at the table.

George had the good grace to look somewhat shamefaced at such an intrusion. Making to stand, he said, "Ah'm sorry for intrudin' like this, missus. But John wouldn't tak naw for 'n answer."

Lizzie interjected quickly, bidding them both to sit and going to get extra dishes. John slapped George upon his back as if to say, 'I told you so' and leant back in the chair he had just slumped into.

The food was shared between the four of them, and Lizzie added some slices of thick rough bread to eke it out. Laura kept her head down and said nothing, glad of the food but repulsed by the way John treated his mother. No-one spoke until the scraping of the mis-matched cutlery had all but ceased. A large teapot was brought through and mugs of tea washed down the last of the bread.

George was sitting opposite Laura and she had barely looked in his direction throughout the meal.

"So – George, tha's me lad's master? Where are tha headed? Coal is't?"

"Aye, missus, 'tis coal we should'a been takin' up t' York but t' river's so iced that we'll 'ave t' wait till t' mornin' an' they break a channel through."

"Well, ye're welcome t' bed up wi' John. There's a room upstairs for ye."

Laura lifted her head and for the first time really looked at George. He was in a dark woollen jacket with a brightly coloured neckerchief tied at the open neck of his shirt. He had discarded the coat, the woollen muffler and the fingerless gloves he had arrived in, which now lay on the floor beside him, alongside his cap which he had removed upon entering. He was older than her, she surmised, perhaps his middle thirties. His brown hair was trimmed and neat, the sides growing down each side of his strong jawline to meet a clean-shaven chin. His eyes were brown and his nose was long and thin but with a pronounced bump on the bridge. The shadow of a scar broke the line of his otherwise well-shaped lips. He was broad but not bulky, the build of a man used to physical labour.

Lizzie carried on prattling away to her son and anyone who would listen, talking about the weather, the poor market day she'd had, the hardship of trying to dry laundry on days like these, the price of tea, in fact anything and everything. She was always happy when John was home but always a little too nervously excited, thought

Laura. Nods and muttered responses kept her chatter going for a while until even she was running out of topics of conversation.

In a pause George looked at Laura and asked, "Are tha John's sister?"

Laura heard John give a derisory snort. "I am lodging here with Lizzie. No, I'm not her daughter, though she has been treating me as kindly as if I were."

Another snort from John and some unintelligible comment under his breath. Even Lizzie had the good grace to look sharply at him as he half sat, half sprawled in his chair.

"Where are tha from? Laura is 't?"

"Yes, Hull-a-ways," she replied, non-committally. She was not one to share all her business with just anyone. "And you?" she ventured.

"York ah s'pose is home, but ah tak m' boat roun' half o' Yorkshire. Hopin' to run another 'un soon when ah hire me a couple o' reliable men."

For the first time Laura lifted her gaze and looked him in the eye. He returned her look and it was as if everything seemed to fade in the room around them. Sounds became muted and colours seemed to become dull and monochrome. He felt enclosed by something but he knew not what.

"Well ah'm fer bed! Tha comin' George? Ah've a couple o' bottles of beer we can tak up wi' us. Early start, eh?" And with that, the scraping of a chair brought George back to the here and now. Shaking his head as if to clear a fog, he followed John up the stairs after bidding the women goodnight.

They were gone by the time Laura became aware of the muted light of the morning creeping into her room. Lizzie had left them a snack bundle each to send them on their way and by now they would be manoeuvring their boat out of the freezing dock.

He owns a boat – soon maybe two …

10

I t was a few months before she met him again. The first bit of warmth was being felt as the early spring sunshine lifted everyone's spirits. John headed home to his mam when he was in port but he was always on his own. Laura never ventured down to the dock area. She had no need – and no inclination to be so near ...

But fate took a hand. Lizzie asked her to deliver a bundle of laundry to one of the captains who was berthed in the Ouse Dock. He was a regular, she explained, but he wasn't often in port as he hailed from Hamburg. It was one of the larger vessels, a masted sea-going sailing vessel, and he sailed with his wife aboard. They always sent their laundry to her when they were here – and they paid handsomely, especially if any mending needed doing. In fact, Laura had darned a worn cuff and repaired a tear in one of the petticoats before folding and making up the bundle she now carried.

She had to ask at the dock master's office where the boat was berthed and hoped that it would be in the inner dock. However, because of its size it had been moored at one of the quays that ran parallel to the river as it left the dock area and flowed seaward.

She felt the bile rise in her throat and her heart started to race as she crossed the rail track and headed downriver. While in the dock area all that was visible of the water was huge basins of grimy water in the gaps between the various vessels – barges, coal carriers, cutters, all loading and unloading their cargoes accompanied by the cacophony of sounds that accompanied the frenzy of activity. But further out the river sprawled in all its grimy glory, silted and muddy but always moving. The occasional glint of sunlight as it reflected off the surface made her shield her eyes with her hand, the better to see her footing and where she was headed. Soon the masts of the ship she had been directed to appeared at the end of the quay and as she approached it, her legs started to tremble. She could see across the stretch of water to the other bank which had a large curved area of sand and mud spread out in a half moon shape where the wash of water had laid it down. Turgid and brown, the merest flow could be seen as the tidal current pushed against the hulls of the vessels nearby.

Her walk became almost a run as she strained to reach the gangplank of the ship she sought. Its sails were furled and she could make out the figurehead pointing towards her, the direction the ship would be sailing to leave the dock area behind and head out along the river and out into the Humber estuary. A few men stood about while others were carrying items up onto the deck – barrels, sacks, small crates. A man in a black peaked cap stood nearest the end of the plank and she approached him, breathlessly explaining her mission. He called out a few foreign words which were answered by another on deck. A few moments later a woman's head appeared over the rail and beckoned her to come aboard.

"Danke," she said, as she accepted the bundle from her. Opening it she held up the petticoat that Laura had mended and inspected the hole in the shirt cuff that had been darned. "Das gut," she nodded and smiled at Laura. Handing her a small bag in payment, she thank her again and, collecting up the bundle, made her way below deck. As Laura's feet reached the cobbled quayside, she held onto the rope that hung from the gangplank to steady her. Averting her eyes from the water, she took a deep breath and made her way back the way she had come.

I have heard of you. I know who you are.

I will make your acquaintance – sometime.

Maybe sooner than you think.

I don't know you. You don't know me.

I paid my debt.

Leave me alone.

But we are family …

That one was but a smaller cousin of mine.

We all meet up and mix.

And we tell our stories. And make our journeys. And then our atoms mingle again and we make our way once more from small beginnings to our great reunion.

We keep secrets. We hide lies. We hold what was given and bear witness to its history, its life, its passing. Its death.

It is a testimony to the continuance and never-ending orbit of our fluid life.

I don't need you. I don't want you.

It is done.

She was gasping for breath as she came to the end of

the quay and turned her back on the brown sweep of the river, heading back to a world of certainties. Passing through the dock gates at a run she all but collided with a group of men coming up from the other dock. As she stumbled, a hand shot out and grasped her tightly by the upper arm, preventing her tumbling face first onto the cobbles. Scrabbling to find her feet, she flailed about with her other hand until she grasped fabric, enough to pull her upright and gain her balance. The hands let go of her and then she felt them grasp both of her shoulders so that she was facing her saviour. Silhouetted by the low sun, at first she couldn't make out the features but then her eyes adjusted and she recognised George, the master of the boat John worked on.

"T'were lucky ah caught 'ee! Tha'd a 'ad a pair o' skint knees an' goodness knows what else, t'otherwise!"

Smoothing down her skirts and readjusting her bonnet, she thanked him and made to head off in the direction she had been going. But something made her hesitate. She turned again to face him and smiled, holding his gaze for a few moments longer …

He was held by the looking-glass eyes. They seemed empty and bottomless, yet all-knowing as they seemed to reach into his very soul. So light, almost clear. It seemed like he saw her properly for the first time. The couple of hours they had been together at Lizzie's seemed like nothing. He needed more time. He needed to see more of her. Touch her. Hold her. But as soon as she had tumbled almost at his feet, she had turned and started walking back up to town. Had she spoken? He was not sure. His feet seemed like lead and if his mate hadn't slapped him on the back with a guffaw, he would have been standing there like that for who knows how long.

"Cum 'head ye daft bugger! Ye're a married man, dinna forget!" and a few laughs followed as their boots carried on down to the dock area. As he focussed on where he was and shook the fug from his head, he knew he had to see her again. But he had a boat to load and a job to do.

It was over a week before he was back in Goole. It was a damp drizzly day when they docked and unloaded the coal from near Castleford, brought down the rivers Calder, Aire then Ouse. By the time they had unloaded the cargo and handed it over to the porters and dockers to send it on its way, he was filthy and covered in coal dust. John wasn't with him. He'd gone on George's younger brother Robert's boat on a trip up to Selby. The other mate he had brought downriver was already touching his cap as he set off for his own home and waiting family here in Goole. George had planned to pick up another load in the morning to head up the Ouse to York to where his wife and family would, no doubt, be pleased to see him after nearly two weeks away. But that was the nature of his business. Long gaps and short reunions.

Heading out of the dock gates and up towards the narrow back to back houses that ran behind the railway embankment, he stopped at Lizzie's door and gave a firm knock. When she opened it she let out a guffaw of delight at seeing him.

"'Ave tha a bed for t' night Missus? John's no wi' me – 'e's off to Selby wi' me brother Robert. Ah've a trip home t' morrow but a place t' lay me head would be welcome."

"Off course, ye're welcome – but," and here she stopped him in his tracks with the palm of her chubby hand towards him, "tha'll get thesen cleaned up first! Out round t' back an' ah'll fetch a bucket an' tha can get that filth washed off 'ee."

Entering from the ginnel, George stood in the small backyard under the roof of the lean-to where the laundry was done. Luckily no washing was hanging to dry, the weather being so damp, else Lizzie would have been exhorting him to mind where he put his hands. She appeared from the back door with a pail of steaming water and poured it into the tin basin, hanging up a cloth for him to dry himself with afterwards.

"There's a bit o' soap there for 'ee," she added, pointing to a slab of pink carbolic on the wooden shelf. "There'll be a brew for 'ee when yer finished."

Removing his battered cap, George peeled off the grimy muffler tied in a knot at his chin, then his short coat, neckerchief, waistcoat and stained linen shirt. Around his waist was a thick leather belt buckled tightly, with the hanging end wound through the loops on his moleskin trousers, which were gathered round his trim abdomen. His body was pale, never seeing the sun, but it was broad and muscled across the shoulders and arms. Beginning to rub the cake of soap over his arms and neck, he was aware that eyes were upon him but looking round he could see no-one.

She stood back from the grimed glass of her bedroom window and watched from behind the thin curtains as he soaped and lathered his strong body. Finally sloshing the water over his head and hair, he reached for the cloth and towelled himself dry. His damp hair clung to his head, the straggly curls snaking down the back of his neck, the only part of him whose shade matched that of his forearms, face and hands. Running his fingers through his damp hair after he had pulled his shirt back over his head, he turned and she fancied that he almost saw her from the yard. Stepping back into the room, she turned to head downstairs.

Someone was watching him, he was sure of it. But he could see no-one nor any movement to give away someone's hiding place. Glad to get his waistcoat and neckerchief back on, he left his coat, cap and muffler hanging on a rope under the lean-to rather than bring the coal dust into the house.

By the time he had entered the house, Laura was already in the kitchen, setting out mugs while Lizzie poured the strong dark tea from a brown earthenware teapot.

"Sit tha down," Lizzie exhorted him. " 'ave thesen a bit o' bread an' cheese."

Laura pushed the plate with thick slices of rough bread towards him while he sat down and accepted the steaming mug that Lizzie passed to him.

"John'll be back in a couple o' days. 'e said to tell 'ee."

"Then tha'll have room to thesen. Eat up lad! Tha need some meat ont' yer bones!"

Later that evening, when Lizzie had gone to visit her daughter and brood a few streets away, he and Laura were left in the house. Few words were said, but his eyes were always on her whenever she turned around or looked from the corner of her eye. He said a few pints of ale would go down well. Where was a good place? She told him of the place a street away and he asked if she would come with him. She declined, saying she had some mending to do so he went out the back way, picking up his coat and cap, and she heard the latch of the gate drop as his boots clattered up the ginnel.

A couple of hours later she heard steps in the yard and the door opened. Lizzie was still at her daughter's so Laura knew who it would be. Standing up from the table where she had spread her sewing by the oil lamp's soft light, she went to put the kettle on the range. Her back was to him by the time he had shut the door behind him.

From behind she was nothing remarkable. A bit on the skinny side, her waist accentuated by the strings of her apron. Her dark hair was loosely wound into a bun and held with some pins. Her skin was pale, even more so in the light from the lamp. Why did she captivate him so? But when she turned and looked at him, he knew. Those eyes. It was those eyes that had some kind of effect upon him that he could not comprehend. But he knew what he wanted.

She could smell the ale upon his breath, the tobacco smoke on his clothes. She knew what he wanted.

See what I brought you ...

Can we be friends?

I don't need to bargain with you.

Oh but we do. You know what I can do.

You know what I can bring you.

You know what I can take.

He is a good catch. I brought him to you.

We all did.

The rivers.

You want him, don't you?

Yes.

11

S ue had written down what little she knew about her ancestors – which was precious little when she came to look at it. Others in the genealogy class seemed to have files and folders of documents, research notes, certificates and photographs. She had unearthed a photo that her father must have taken of her and her mother Maud in the early 60's. Sue looked about eleven or twelve and was tall and gawky, squinting into the sun and standing beside a garden bench on which her mother sat in a floral summer dress. A book lay opened and face down beside her on the seat. The only image of her father was the shadow he cast while taking the photo. The only other thing with it, in a crumpled envelope unearthed from the back of a drawer, was a creased and faded newspaper clipping about the death of a local boy while on a training exercise. He was named as George Watkins, aged 19. In very faded pencil were the numbers 13.11.44, which Sue assumed was the date of his death or the newspaper article. The name meant nothing to her but she smoothed it out and put it in a plastic wallet with the photo and her course notes.

The first and most important thing, according to their tutor for the genealogy class (a rather hearty middle aged woman named Doreen) was that they must always start from the known and work backwards. "Hatch, match and dispatch them!" she announced cheerfully. In other words find their birth, marriage and death records or certificates if possible, or deal with known facts from still living family members. Sue started to feel uncomfortable as she had hoped they could start by delving into early 20th century records and working backwards, but Doreen insisted that they draw a tree starting with themselves and add any children (and possibly grandchildren) then going backwards, work from their own parents. For privacy Doreen also suggested that if they wished they could just indicate whether their children and grandchildren were male or female and not add names or dates of birth, etc.

Sue laid out a sheet of blank A4 paper and wrote her maiden name in a box about two thirds of the way down – Susan Martha Miles b. 10 June 1950. Beside it to the left she wrote in another box the name of her husband, Geoffrey Steven Innes and b. 1948 d.2001. Between the boxes she wrote m. 1978 Lincoln. From this she drew a vertical line down and drew another box. In it she wrote the name Deborah Katherine Innes b. 1975 d. 2000. From that box she drew another line down to a box in which she wrote the name Kate Laura Innes b. 1998.

Returning to the first box she had drawn containing her own name she drew a line upward and on either side drew a box. In the left hand one she added the name of her father David Roger Miles b.abt 1922? d.1992 (aged 70). In the right hand box alongside his she wrote Maud Watkins b. abt 1925? d. 1987 (aged about 63). Between the two boxes she added m.?

From Maud, her mother's box, she drew another line upwards and two empty boxes on either side, which she left totally blank. She sat back and pondered the results.

As Doreen walked past her desk, she looked over her shoulder and cheerfully quipped, "Well, you certainly have plenty to find out! Fear not! It's out there waiting to be unearthed."

Giving Doreen a weak smile, she looked back at the paper in front of her. Debbie's name looked back at her and the stark dates of her birth and death. Just 25, and when Kate was not yet two years old.

Doreen clapped her hands to draw the attention of everyone back from their tasks and discussions and suggested that those who had information further back might like to start looking for their ancestors in any censuses from 1911 backwards but for those whose search had not yet reached that point a look at the free online site FreeBMD might be a good starting point to confirm birth, marriage and death dates and places, reminding them that it was only the quarter of the year indicated not the exact month. Scribbling down the URL on her notepad, Sue gathered up her slim folder and joined Sally as they headed out of the building into the car park, pulling their collars up round their necks as a gust brought a spattering of rain into their faces.

Driving back home in Sally's car, they chatted about what they had found and next steps. Sally was already ploughing ahead, having taken out a subscription for Ancestry and she was already dropping hints that a subscription for Find My Past might be welcome in her Christmas stocking. Sue had more modest hopes – she would just try to pin down the dates for the ancestors she knew.

12

I t was a couple of days before Sue sat down at her laptop and brought up the Search page for FreeBMD as Doreen had suggested. She entered the name of her mother, Maud Watkins, ticked the box for marriages and entered start and finish dates 1948 and 1949, knowing she had been born in 1950. The page reloaded with the message 'Sorry, we found no matches'.

Sitting back with a frown, she returned to the search page and took the start date back to 1945, way before she expected to find them getting married. This threw up two possibilities – one in the June quarter 1947 in Swindon married to a man surname Flett, and one in the September quarter 1947 in Surrey to a man surname Winterton. Another blank.

She knew her own date of birth had been 10 June 1950 so she fully expected that her parents would have married in the late 1940s. But just in case she broadened the search parameters to 1950. And there it was in the March quarter – Maud K Watkins married to a man surname Miles in Lincoln. Beside it were the letters and numbers 3b and 326. Looking at the top of the list she found these referred to the Volume and Page number for that entry. Seeing the link 'Has our search engine found the record you are seeking? Click here to learn what to do now' she followed the link and found a whole page dedicated to helping researchers send for certificates. After trawling through it for a few more minutes, she had found the link to the General Record Office and completed the online application and paid the fee online.

Then she sat back and exhaled, realising that she had become absorbed in this for over an hour.

Looking again at her notes she realised that she would be able to discover quite a bit of information from the marriage certificate, when it arrived. She would find out what the K. stood for in Maud's name, where and when her parents were married and who their fathers were and their occupations. That should help her extend her tree by another generation.

When the certificate arrived the following week she couldn't wait to see what it contained. Laying it out on the dining room table, having cleared a space by her laptop, she pulled out her embryonic family tree and prepared to add some details. Firstly she could see her father's name David Roger Miles aged 27; bachelor; profession engineer; residence 17 Chambers Road, Lincoln; father – Robert William Miles (deceased), profession grocer. Below that was her mother Maud Katherine Watkins aged 25; spinster; profession dressmaker; residence Cranfield Cottage, Skelthorpe, Lincolnshire; father – Henry Cecil Watkins, plumber. Her eyes then went to the date and details of the place of marriage. 23 March 1950 at the Register Office, Lincoln. Below were their signatures and those of two witnesses, neither names Sue recognised. The marriage was recorded 'By Licence'.

Sue added in the names and dates into the blank places on her chart but it was only as she added the marriage date that she realised that she had been born less than three months after her parents had married. She sat back and thought about what that meant, musing that history certainly seemed to repeat itself.

After all, she had had Debbie in 1975 when she was twenty-five years old, and was bringing her up on her own until she met Geoff and fell in love, marrying six months later in June 1978. Her parents, Maud and David, were not pleased but they were supportive and of course, doted on their granddaughter. Debbie was such a pretty little thing. Pale grey eyes and dark hair gave her a striking appearance that often made people catch their breath and look twice. But who her father was – well, that was another matter. Sue had definitely been swept up in the mood of the times – the early 70's. She and her friends went to quite a few gigs and festivals and yes, she mused, it was all a bit of a blur. At the time she was smoking grass and enjoying the effects. Everyone did. And it was a few weeks after one of the gigs – she could hardly recall which one now – that she discovered she was pregnant. Who the father was, she had no idea. In fact, at the time she couldn't even recall half of what had gone on but seemed to think they had all piled into someone's VW campervan and headed up to York, sleeping under the stars on the river bank on the outskirts of the city.

And then her daughter Debbie fell pregnant when she was twenty-two. All through her teenage years she seemed to have something worrying her, something she wouldn't share with her parents. Geoff tried hard to get her to open up; she was such a Daddy's girl, but she would close down if he tried to ask her directly. She became anxious and depressed in the last year of College and would shut herself away in her bedroom for hours on end. In the hope of cheering her up, Sue and Geoff hired a cottage for two weeks for a family holiday near Naburn, on the River Ouse south of York. All seemed to be going well and they enjoyed car trips to local beauty spots – Rievaulx, Helmsley, Harrogate and the like.

Then one night Debbie had a terrifying nightmare and woke them up howling and tearing at the bedclothes, drenched in sweat. They returned home a couple of days later and Debbie seemed to shut herself away even more on return to their home. And then a few months later she broke down crying at the breakfast table when Sue spotted that she had recent scars on her arms. It all came out and she said that she thought she was pregnant. They could only assume she must have been raped but they could not work out where or when, or by whom. Debbie eventually gave birth six weeks early and baby Kate was promptly put in an incubator. Debbie refused to see her. When they eventually brought Kate home, Debbie became more and more troubled. Their GP put her on anti-depressives but the next year or so saw no improvement in her.

Then one night she left the house and never came back. Sue and Geoff were frantic and a police search began the next day. Forty-eight hours later her body was pulled from the river Witham, south of Lincoln. Kate was not even eighteen months old. And so Sue and Geoff became both parents and grandparents to her.

13

G eorge looked at his wife, slumped in the chair with their youngest girl on the floor at her feet, chewing on a crust of dry bread, her hands and face smeared with dirt and a trickle of snot running from her nose.

"Dear God – Sarah! Can tha not look t' child!" But she hardly stirred, and started to breathe more heavily as the drink took the remnants of her consciousness.

In a corner of the one-roomed hovel that she called home another child stirred from a heap of ragged blankets on a mattress in the corner. Picking up the girl from the floor, he laid her under the blankets with her sister and tucked them in as best he could. Turning back to look at the room, he saw the leftovers of some meal upon the boards that served as a table. A cracked cup and a bent fork lay beside a mouldy lump of bread.

Disgusted, he stormed out of the room and into the courtyard which reeked from the smell of the open drains and flow from the privies and ashpits further up the lane which drained into the river, untreated and unrestrained. The Lanes were where the dregs of humanity ended up. He spent so little time in York now – for a good reason. Since the loss of their oldest, their son Henry, she had become morose and took to drink. Although his father lived across the river, he had not been able to help his daughter-in-law, having lost his wife, George's mother, a year or so ago. Keeping a roof above his own head and his business going took all his strength and even though one of George's sisters looked in on him when she could, his father was obviously struggling. No-one could keep an eye on Sarah as well. They all had their own families and occupations, working to keep their heads above water. What money George had given Sarah, she had obviously spent on drink. When he had gone to find her at their usual address, he discovered she had done a moonlight flit and left owing rent. It didn't take long to guess where she might have ended up. The building he found her in was rented out as single rooms, and the poorest and meanest would crowd whole families in to eke out the rent. But there was another way to find the rent money. It was a notorious haunt of prostitutes. By day some women called themselves seamstresses, charwomen or lodging house keepers but by night they were prostitutes and brothel keepers.

He couldn't be there all the time. He had to work and build up the business. He knew if he left her money, she would only spend it on drink but if he didn't work the boats, there would be no money at all. Married twelve years and so little to show for it. While he worked hard, she sank lower and lower. She was lost to him. He could find so little compassion for her now. All he cared about were the two girls. Unlikely she'd bear him another son now. No lad to learn the trade, to show the ropes to, to accompany him on trips along the waterways of the East Riding. No-one to leave the business to when he was no longer able to do the work.

He set off across the Ouse Bridge, brushing aside the attentions of one of the common sluts that touted for trade along the staith. "Think yer too good fer me, eh?' she spat after him.

For the next hour or so, he sat in front of the fire in his sister and brother-in-law's house, while the three of them tried to work out a way to look after Sarah and the children.

"Mebbe yer Father could have 'em at his?" suggested his brother-in-law, but his sister soon quashed that idea, having seen the state of him and his creeping senility. He was not a well man and having the responsibility for her and the two children would just make things worse.

"Would tha take them in 'ere for me …?" began George, but before he could say any more his brother-in-law quickly interjected. "We've no room. Tha can see that wi' our five an' n'other on't way. Money's tight. Look t' yer own lad. Sorry, but that's just t' way 'tis."

So George returned to the one-roomed hovel where his little family slept and slumping on the floor against the wall, attempted to get some sleep before he had to leave the next morning.

As the first fingers of the early summer dawn crept across the sky, George pulled himself upright and un-knotted the stiffness out of his muscles. A whimper from the corner signalled that the girls were stirring and soon Hannah had crawled out of the heap and over to put her arms around him, snuggling her head into the crook of his neck. He could feel her little ribs through the thin fabric that clothed her. Annie began to emerge from the insubstantial covers and seeing her da, came over to embrace him as well. She was already eleven but could easily be taken for a child of eight or nine, so poorly nourished and looked after was she. As for little Hannah, barely three, she was as light as a feather when he hoisted her onto his hip and pulled Annie to him. Sarah hadn't stirred. A thin sliver of drool ran down her chin onto the thin shawl about her shoulders, while her skeletal fingers twitched occasionally, the only sign of life besides her shallow breathing.

Taking the children with him, he left the hovel, covering his nose to block the stench of the effluent trickling down in rivulets towards the staith and into the river. Neither of the girls had said a word, their eyes sunken in their sockets. Heading over the bridge and into the streets of shops just awakening for another day's trade, George collected some bread, cheese, milk, tea and sugar. Seeing the look of longing in Annie's eyes as they passed a confectioner's, he relented and spent a few pence on a barley sugar twist for each of them to suck on the way back home.

Sarah was just rousing on their return. She could hardly comprehend who was there at first but then walked a few steps, stretching her arms out to him. Pulling them down to her sides, he pinned them to her body and tightened his hands around the scrawny limbs. It was all he could do not to shake the life out of her, God knows it would be so easy – there was precious little of it left in her. As the force of his grip broke through her befuddled mind, she started to struggle and find her voice. Her mouth opened in a slack leer and with horror, he saw she had lost two of her front teeth, the rest of which looked in a poor way also.

Seeing his reaction, Annie piped up, "She fell – on t' staith t'other day. She … slipped."

He couldn't help but admire the child's loyalty to her mother, but nevertheless he couldn't help but blurt out, "Wi' drink ah'll be bound!"

Hannah started to whimper and Sarah tottered towards her, arms reaching out in an attempt to comfort her, but instead the child clung to her father's leg, looking out from behind it with large tears forming in her eyes. One soon tumbled over the lip and coursed through the grime on her face leaving a pale trail though the dirt.

"When did tha last go to t' school?" he asked Annie.

She merely shook her head, then said quietly, "Couldn't leave Hannah wi' mam."

In sheer exasperation he thumped his fist down upon the table, causing the few items on it to jump, the bent fork clattering to the floor. He had to do something …

14

K ate pulled her padded jacket over her shoulders and fastened the belt tightly round her narrow waist. Throwing a brightly coloured scarf around her neck in a couple of loops, she joined Jen as she went through the door of the flat. Mentally checking that she had her keys in her pocket, she pulled the door behind her and followed Jen downstairs and out into the car park area. The chill wind caught her and she snuggled her chin into the folds of her scarf and dug her hands into her pockets.

"Where are we meeting them?" she asked Jen.

"I said we'd meet them down at Nandos and then go from there," answered Jen over her shoulder.

"Hope I've got enough cash with me."

"Oh don't be such a worry. I've got my card if we need it but we're not going to be late," Jen replied.

"Just as well. I've an early tutorial tomorrow, then an assignment to hand in later. What time is the train back?" Kate asked.

"Good grief, you are a worrier! Chill, won't you!" remonstrated Jen. "The train's at 6.30 with the usual change at Newark and we'll be in Lincoln by quarter past eight – Dad's picking us up – he said he would as he was going to be there with a client and it was stupid for us to drag your Gran out when he was going to be there anyway."

"Fine, fine," sighed Kate. Fond as she was of Jen, all the weeks living on top of each other was beginning to grate on her just a bit. A couple of weeks back home with family and doing their own thing would be good for both of them. But tonight they had arranged to meet 'the gang' as Jen called them, the group of student friends they had gelled with over the past months. To be fair, most of them were Jen's, all sporty and athletic types. But a few of those from Kate's course were coming along and Kate was glad to have their company as well. In all there would be about eight or nine of them, unless they met any others along the way – which in such a small city was always possible.

By the time they had all rendezvoused at Nandos, collected a variety of takeaways and made their way to the open area at the bottom of Coppergate Walk, there were about a dozen of them, all chattering and laughing. Kate hugged her meal tightly, glad of the warmth seeping through her fingers, but eager to start eating as the pungent smell tickled her taste buds. Squatting along the low wall, the students spread out and the noise subsided as they tucked into their takeaways. On either side of Kate were two of her course chums – Barney, a rather introverted geeky type – as Jen described him, and Sonja, a quiet girl with a twinkling sense of humour.

The chatter started up again as meals were finished and two of the sporty lads started challenging each other to push ups off the low wall.

"Show offs," murmured Kate under her breath, but Sonja heard her a giggled quietly.

"Where now?" someone shouted. "I need a beer!"

"Let's go down to the river!" someone else replied and before they knew what was happening, the group was on their feet, stuffing empty wrappers and paper cups into already overflowing waste baskets and heading up Castlegate and down King Street. Ahead of them the river glinted with the lights of the buildings on the staiths and the waterside pubs. Turning right at the corner of King Street, Kate looked up and saw she was standing under the swinging pub sign of the Kings Arms. She was carried along with the group as they passed alongside some low windows, from where some cosy lights shone and the smell of beer emanated. By the doorway was a sign announcing that *'The Original Ghost Walk – World's No 1 – Starts Here 8pm'* but the group was more interested in slaking their thirst.

As they entered the small doorway, Kate could see that it would be a case of standing for most of them as the few tables and nooks were already almost fully occupied. Soon orders were taken and a kitty put together as the group spread into the remaining gaps. A few older people left after a while and Kate and Sonja squeezed into the seats by a window.

"Have you seen this?" shouted Barney over the hubbub.

"What?" Kate replied as she craned her neck to see over and round the crowd standing shoulder to shoulder and lined up at the bar.

"There," shouted Barney. "It's a measure of how high the floods come. Can you see the numbers? The years are shown and the height the water came to."

Sure enough, against the wall near the front door there

was a tall wooden board stretching almost to ceiling height. At the top in gold letters was the heading 'FLOOD LEVELS RECORDED AT THIS INN'. Over the heads of the crowd she could see that the top line had the date 4.11.2000 and was perhaps two or three feet from the ceiling. A few inches lower was the date 26.9.2012 and below that were 5.1.1982, 30.3.1947 and 30.12.1978. She strained to see the lower ones but her view was impeded.

"Wow! That's incredible," she mouthed back at Barney. She tried to imagine where that water line must have come in times when the river was incredibly swollen. And what damage it must have done to the homes and businesses along the banks. From what she could see, this seemed to be a not-uncommon occurrence here.

She sat back, lost in thought and trying to imagine what it must have been like for the people who had to live by the river. She wondered what the earliest date on the board was and stood, ready to shoulder her way through the throng. Barney moved nearer and helped to clear a way, clearly as interested as she was. Eventually they were able to shuffle near enough to see that the board reached to floor level and the date about two feet from the bottom was 1988, then they continued upwards – 1976, 2000, 1992, 1958, 1931, 2013, 1933, 1995, 1965, 1940, 1968, 2012, 1945, 1991, 1968 and, the earliest one listed, 1892 which would have been just about lower than her head height.

"Wow," was all she could say as the enormity of what it meant swept over her. Barney was also similarly impressed. Looking over the heads she saw Jen was in the middle of a group of 'rugby types' (as Kate labelled them) and thought better of calling her over, pretty sure she wouldn't be as impressed as they were. A bell and a voice announcing, "Last orders!" shook her from her thoughts. The heat and the fug was becoming oppressive and Kate was never really one for enjoying the company of inebriated companions.

Catching Jen's eye, she mouthed across at her, "I'll see you back at the flat," then pointed to her watch and mimed sleeping putting her hands together under her head. This was met by rolling eyes and a thumbs up from Jen.

Sonja stood and joined her and Barney as they pushed through the last few bodies and all but fell out of the door, the cool clear air making them catch their breath. Kate stood for a few moments enjoying the fresh air, as Barney told Sonja about the board and the dates. As they all enjoyed history, there was an immediate appreciation of the significance of it shared between them.

They stood in silence for a few minutes as they each contemplated what it must have been like over the years when the river repeatedly flooded and inundated the low lying parts of the city and the surrounding areas.

"I've got an old map of York I got printed out for me at the Archives," said Barney, breaking the silence while pushing his glasses up his nose. "Must have a look and see what was here before."

This was met with mutual interest from the girls and Kate wished for just a moment that they weren't heading home tomorrow.

"I'll bring it to the tutorial tomorrow morning," Barney added.

"Oh that'd be great," both Kate and Sonja agreed.

As they turned to head along the front of the pub and up the steps onto the Ouse Bridge, Kate stopped in her tracks.

She could definitely hear something. She strained to filter out the muffled sounds coming from the pub and the rumble of traffic on the roadway over the bridge.

The hair on her neck began to prickle as she could clearly hear the sound of a child whimpering nearby. Her eyes flashed round, scanning the cobbled pathway, the benches with seats attached that spread along the length of the chained bollards by the water's edge, the dark waters slowly swirling past, causing the reflections of the nearby lights to shatter and break into shards of light and colour.

There it was again. She turned to her left, looking down the length of the river. On the far bank were the tall square brick buildings, once warehouses but now flats or hotels. A few stragglers were leaving a pub further down the pathway on the same side as they were but they were adults and headed away from her. She took a few steps away from her companions and found herself on the corner of King Street, the road they had come down earlier that evening. The corner of the pub was at her left side but the sound seemed to draw her round towards the street as it sloped gently up and away from the river. She took a few steps up the roadway but the sound seemed to become fainter. She felt disorientated and struggled to fix the direction of the quiet sobbing. She stood stock still, straining her ears. Then she felt a hand on her arm and jumped.

"What is it Kate? Are you alright? I turned round and you'd gone," Sonja asked her gently.

"Did you hear that?" whispered Kate, looking up King Street again.

"What?" asked Sonja, as Barney came to join them.

"Did you hear it?" Kate repeated, this time looking at Barney.

"No. What? I don't know. What was it you heard?" Barney looked at her, frowning and repositioning his glasses yet again.

"I – I definitely heard a child crying. I know I did. Help me look for them." Kate started to look around her wildly, trying to pinpoint the direction in which to go. Terrified there might be a child in the water, she darted to the riverside and leant over the chain, looking left and right.

They joined her but soon agreed there was nothing – or no-one.

"Can you still hear it?" asked Sonja.

Kate stood stock still and tried to catch any sound, however tiny it might be. But there was nothing, just the gentle lapping of the water against the stone staith. The moment was shattered as the pub door opened and a group of loud customers tipped out onto the cobbles.

"There's nothing Kate. You must have imagined it. Maybe it was a cat – or something," Sonja tried to placate her friend.

Kate shook her head and tried to summon up a weak smile, all the while knowing that she definitely had heard it, as clearly as anything. But maybe not here – or now …

15

I n the end he decided he couldn't leave the girls with Sarah. He would have to take them to his father's across the river on the other staith. At least they would be clean there with no vermin running across the floor. Annie was capable of keeping an eye on Hannah. He walked up to the local parish church and tried to get someone to come to help Sarah. He couldn't remain behind. He had customers relying on him, merchants awaiting shipment of their goods, contracts signed and deals he couldn't welch on. And he had the purchase of his second boat to complete on his return to Leeds. The family relied on him as breadwinner so he had no choice.

By the time he departed from York a day later the girls had been well fed, had clean clothes obtained from the pawn shop, their tattered hair had been washed and combed and each had a new ribbon to tie in it. Annie chose a blue one and Hannah wanted a yellow one. He delivered the girls to his father's house. The old man had aged much in the last year since the loss of George's mother, and the house showed it lacked a woman's touch. But Annie wanted to help and was keen to demonstrate that she could undertake some of the household tasks. George had no choice but to leave them in the grandfather's care, hoping his sister would look in a little more often. He also left some money with his sister to buy food for Sarah. He wrung a promise out of her to look in on Sarah although she was horrified at having to walk into the Lanes, saying she would only go in full daylight and with her husband at her side. He also made them promise not to leave any money with Sarah as she would only use it for more drink. He had seen the lost look in her eyes and knew that she was in a place where drink was the only way to soften the hurt and ease the pain. He would have to consider if she was in her right mind. He would have to think about the asylum if there was no way back.

George returned to Goole by the end of the following day, sailing with the current down the Ouse and mooring at the dock, ready to load up the following morning and set off for Leeds.

Once more he found his pace quickening as he walked from the docks and to the house under the railway embankment. He couldn't wait to see her again. He knew what he wanted. He was sure she did too – her eyes had told him even if her words had not.

As he neared the row of red brick houses he saw Lizzie leave clutching a basket and turning to head up the street and round the next corner. He was just about to nip down the ginnel when he heard John's voice from the yard beyond. His pulse pounded in his ears as he changed direction, going instead to the front of the house and knocking on the door. At first he thought no-one would answer but then he heard the lock turn and John appeared.

"George! Mate – tha's just goin' ta miss me. Ah'm off on 'nother trip wi' yer brother. Were tha wantin' a bed for t'night? Well ye're in luck. Mam's just gone out but she'll no' be long. She'll be reet glad o' yer company and yer money nah doubt! Gur awa' in."

And with that John set off down the street, having given him a hearty slap on the back. George hesitated, then stepped across the threshold. Was he alone in the house? He was sure John had been talking to someone. At the sound of steps on the stairs, he looked up and saw a pair of small booted feet and ankles coming down towards him.

She hesitated but for a split second, then continued down towards him as he pushed the door shut by stepping back against it, still facing into the hall. She took a few more steps until she reached the last tread, where she halted. Stepping forward he drew level with her in one stride and looked into her eyes, level with his. Those eyes. She held his stare without blinking and a thousand words went between them unspoken.

She knew what he wanted. She had been here before. And look how that had ended. This must be no casual affair. She must see to that.

He never gave his wife, or family, any thought. Only one thought pulsed through him. His hands were around her waist. His mouth came down on hers. With one hand he threaded his fingers through her hair and held it firm as she pressed forward, the other felt the side of her breast through the fabric of her thin blouse. Moving his hand up, he fumbled with the buttons at the high neck and sought the soft white skin of her neck. Raining harsher and harsher kisses upon it, he lifted her off the last step and moved her backwards towards the wall. His hand found the hem of her skirt and lifted it, seeking a way through her petticoats until it reached the top of her woollen stockings. The soft flesh was warm and leading him onwards. There was nothing else – just here and now. Pulling back from her to see her face, he was suddenly caught by her eyes. And he couldn't look away. Falling into an alien place. It was like arriving at an unfamiliar place but feeling you have been there before.

And he so wanted to go there … now …

The rattle of the latch startled them both. Lizzie's voice cut through the dream and suddenly they were a step apart and Laura was walking down the corridor, fastening her collar and straightening her skirts as she went. He was less composed but had just enough self-control to greet Lizzie, saying Laura had just invited him in to await her return, as he wondered if John was about.

"Oh lad, ye've jus' missed 'im. Did she no tell 'ee? Sure Laura – 'asn't John gone off ont' trip for t' next two days?"

" I hadn't realised. He didn't say much when he went out a few minutes ago. I thought he'd be back to say goodbye to you," she said, thinking quickly.

"Are tha after a bed for t'night lad? There's one goin' spare 'ere."

"No, no. I'll be reet. Ah've an early start so ah'll be sleepin' on t'boat t'night."

Lizzie waddled off into the kitchen and started rattling about putting on the kettle and poking the embers on the stove to set it boiling. While she was out of earshot he whispered to Laura, "Come wi' me. Come nah. Get away an' ah'll meet thee down t'road." The look of yearning in his eyes said it all. Her reply was but the merest nod.

"Tha'll have a brew lad?" came Lizzie's voice from the kitchen.

"No. Ye're aw reet. 'ave t'go. See tha sometime soon. Ta'ra!" and with that he went through the door and slammed it behind him.

"Well! Short an' sweet! Tha' wantin' a brew lass?" Collapsing onto a chair she removed her boot, complaining, "Oh me poor feet!"

"I've got mending to deliver. Better go before the rain starts. It was threatening earlier."

"Aye – yer reet. Gaw careful." And with that she proceeded to remove her other boot with a large sigh.

Fetching a bundle from her room, and putting on her bonnet and jacket, Laura left the house and headed down the road. Having just passed the corner, she was startled as a figure appeared behind her. Putting his arm around her waist, he pulled her close and together they fell in step as they walked towards the dock gates.

It was only as they neared the basin, that she began to feel uneasy. But this was the dock, enclosed. This was not the river. There were no … voices.

Row upon row of boats were moored together. Some were large and wide, with a cavernous hold for coal or gravel. Others were narrower, with a small locker at one end. The longest and narrowest ones had a cabin at one end that would house a family in the cramped but cosy interior. George's boat was somewhere in between these two. It had a covered deck and a cabin which was only a shelter and a place to stretch out.

Unlocking the hatch that opened into the interior, George took her hand and helped her aboard. Suddenly, unexpectedly, he felt ill at ease. What was he doing? What about his wife, his family? He had no wife to speak of now. She had been lost to him long ago. This was about here and now.

She saw and perhaps, read his thoughts, her eyes probing his mind and sensing his inhibitions. This had to be right. She had a future to consider. First she had to ensnare him, just enough so that he wouldn't feel the net around him. There was plenty of time to pull it tight.

The cabin smelt of tar and coal dust, metal and tobacco. Male scents. Perhaps that aroused her senses. Taking off her bonnet, she found a convenient hook upon the wall to hang it on. But before she could unbutton her jacket, he had stepped forward and held her face in his hands, his breath hot on her cheek. Looking in. Diving in. Sinking. Drowning.

Sweeping aside the clutter on the bench that served as seat, bed and table he pushed her down as she twined her arms around his neck. The buttons at her neck were soon parted and he journeyed lower to loosen her bodice. He lost himself in the soft fullness, all the while his hands reaching for the softness that travelled upward from her skirts. He could not look away from her eyes which were open, clear and in which he was swimming, drowning, naked and unashamed.

They awoke to voices and footsteps on the cobbled quayside, the clatter of hobnailed boots on wooden planks and chains rattling. It was dark but not yet night, the last light disappearing from the sky. Wanting to keep her here for ever, he had to give in to her when she said that she must go home.

He had to go too, he knew he had contracts to fulfil. But he would be back soon. And as often as he could. The nagging thought of Sarah's plight threatened to worm its way into his head but he pushed it aside, salving his conscience with the knowledge that he had done the best he could for her.

She knew this was but the first step. But much as she wanted to, she had to be patient and not throw away all she had gained until everything else was put in place. He walked her back to Lizzie's and she slipped inside as a faraway clock chimed eleven and the last stragglers were thrown out of the alehouse down the street.

I can help.

Have you a plan?

Be patient – there is a way.

Can you hear me?

I cannot hear you … yet …

16

December 2017
Lincoln

Following Doreen the tutor's advice, Sue next decided to look for the birth of her parents – Maud Katherine Watkins and David Roger Miles. As they married in 1950 she searched on FreeBMD for the interval of 1920 to 1930 in Lincolnshire. Sure enough she found Maud registered in the Dec quarter 1924 in Lincoln. Then she found her father registered in the March quarter 1922,in Peterborough. Noting the volume and page numbers, she sent off to the GRO for their birth documents.

Again there was the wait while she anticipated what she might find out and what new information she could fill in on her family tree. At the evening class that week Doreen had outlined how to use census information and Sue was dying to be able to delve into her family's censuses but was frustrated as the first available one was 1911 and her parents were not yet born. Hopefully from the birth records she could get back into the censuses and trace their parents back in ten year jumps.

A few days later the familiar flop of a large envelope sounded from the hall as the postman's cheery whistle disappearing down the path heralded a delivery. Tearing open the envelope two copies of birth records were neatly inside. With slightly shaking hands, Sue slipped them out and laid them side by side on the dining table. On the left was the one for her father. She carefully scanned across the columns.

When and where born: Twenty-eighth January 1922; 49

Grantham Street, Peterborough.

Name, if any: David Roger

Sex: Boy

Father's name: Robert William Miles.

Mother's name: Annie Beatrice Miles formerly Barford.

Rank and profession of father: shopkeeper, general goods.

Signature, description and residence of informant: Annie B Miles, Mother 49 Grantham Street, Peterborough.

When registered: 15 February 1922.

Signature of registrar: Henry B Chalfont

Looking at the name of her grandmother, she suddenly felt a quiver of excitement and began to realise how family searching became so addictive.

Next she turned to her mother's record.

When and where born: 12 November 1924; Cranfield Cottage, Skelthorpe, Lincolnshire

Name, if any: Maud Katherine

Sex: Girl

Father's name: -------------

Mother's name: Eliza Kate Davis

Rank and profession of father: ----------------

Signature, description and residence of informant: Eliza K Davis, mother, Cranfield Cottage, Skelthorpe, Lincolnshire

When registered: 23 November 1924

Signature of registrar: George Winton

Sue sat back and looked again. What stood out were the two blank columns, yawningly empty of information. How? Why? Her head buzzed with unanswered questions. Sue thought about what she remembered of her grandfather. A shadowy figure in her memory but not one she could put a face to. But she definitely had one. So had Eliza married him after Maud's birth? It seemed the logical answer so she opened her laptop and went back to FreeBMD, looking for a marriage for Eliza after the date of Maud's birth.

This time she entered the date parameters as 1924 to 1926. Sure enough up came the entry for the Mar quarter of 1926 with the surname of the groom as Watkins and place as Lincoln. Another certificate to send for, she thought. This could get expensive! But now she was well and truly hooked and she reckoned if she could collate as much information as she could it would be a great gift to give Kate in the future. In the meantime she recalled that Doreen had mentioned the 1939 register which gave information collected in wartime and which might be a useful clue in the absence of a census. By now she was beginning to appreciate that she would get further, and quicker, if she had a subscription to a family history site so for the next quarter of an hour she set up her Ancestry.co.uk account, telling herself that it was an early Christmas present from herself to herself.

Logging in with her newly set up password, she found the link for the 1939 Register and soon was looking at the image of a page of names in closely lined rows and columns, but with some heavy black lines where information was blanked out with the phrase '*This record is officially closed.*' Nevertheless she found Henry C Watkins and below him Eliza K Watkins living at Richmond Lane, Lincoln, then whether M or F (male or female), the exact date of birth – 'Great!' thought Sue, 'more details,' and their married status, occupation, and on the next page, any other comments.

Henry's date of birth was shown as 21 June 1890 and Plumber (Master) and on the facing page was written Air Raid Warden. Under Henry was Eliza's entry with her date of birth shown as 5 Aug 1901 and Unpaid Domestic duties as her occupation. Annoyingly the next two lines below that had been redacted. Sue recalled Doreen saying that would be because they could still be alive. The following line showed a new household so the two missing people had to belong to her grandparents' household. Another mystery. Back to FreeBMD and Sue started looking for any other children born to them after Maud. Sure enough she discovered that a son was born to them named George Frederick Watkins in the Dec quarter of 1926.

"So Mum had a brother!" mused Sue out loud. "I never knew I had an uncle. I wonder what happened to him?"

Now that Sue had made the discovery of an uncle

she knew nothing about – technically a half-uncle, she started to look for his marriage in the hope of finding cousins. She tried every year from 1942 up till 1970 and although there were a few possible men called George Watkins, she couldn't tie it down and didn't want to send for a fistful of certificates. It was only when she brought the topic up with Doreen at the class that Doreen suggested looking at WW2 records – after all he would have been sixteen when in 1942 and nineteen when it ended. Maybe he had served in the forces?

Suddenly it hit her like a bolt from the blue and delving into her now-growing file of information, she unearthed the envelope with the tiny, creased newspaper clipping in it. This time she looked at it much more closely and quickly realised that as the name hadn't meant much to her when she first unearthed it, it now most definitely was a part of her family jigsaw.

TRAGIC DEATH OF LOCAL LAD

George Watkins, aged 18, son of Harry and Lizzie Watkins, residents of Richmond Lane, Lincoln, was tragically found drowned while on a training exercise as an Army recruit. The precise location has not been released for security reasons but it is believed to have been near York. No funeral details are yet available.

In very faded pencil were the numbers 13.11.44, which Sue assumed was the date of his death or the newspaper article.

Ten days later as Sue opened the brown envelope from the General Record Office, she found she was holding her breath in anticipation. From her grandparents' marriage record she would be able to take her tree back another generation to her two great grandfathers. Sure enough as her eyes flicked across to the two furthest right columns she could see Thomas Watkins (dec), profession plumber and Herbert John Davis, profession gardener. Disciplining herself, she laid the record on the dining table and opened her file, unfolding the tree, now made from two sellotaped pieces of A4 paper.

"Must download a blank one," she thought, remembering Doreen had told them of sites where they could do that, or they could have one from the bundle she brought each week to the class.

So now she knew her grandparents had married on 8th February 1926. Henry Cecil Watkins was 36 and a widower. That surprised her and she made a mental note to try to find out about his first wife, and any family. He was a plumber, living at Richmond Lane, Lincoln. Eliza Kate Davis was 25 and a dressmaker, living as she had found before, at Cranfield Cottage, Skelthorpe. So she had still been living at home with her parents and her baby daughter, Maud. Again the marriage had taken place in the Lincoln Register Office by Licence.

So now she had discovered her four grandparents and already two of her great grandparents. The search was on!

17

1873

T he weeks passed and George found himself opting for trips to Goole whenever he could. He also avoided taking John as mate, asking Robert or another to do so whenever possible. But there were times he had to go to Selby or Wakefield or Castleford to transport coal to and fro as required. The waterways were busy highways and with the rail links being continually added, the movement of coal was a never-ending one. And it paid well. If a boat owner or master could fulfil deliveries on time, he got a good reputation – and that always counted for something with so much competition for trade. It was quite a small community though, the watermen knew each other and whole families often inter-married or were related to each other. So all the more reason that he kept his times with Laura private – there were plenty who knew he had a wife and family in York. Yes – he found he put off returning there whenever he could. Was it a guilty conscience? There were moments he felt shame but then he only had to see her again and soon he was swamped and drowning in her eyes and all they told him.

He completed the deal on his second boat, and already had hopes that he might start to build up a fleet in the future. He had ambitions and his family name was respected on the waterways of Yorkshire. His father and uncles on his late mother's side all worked on the rivers or dealt with the business of trade connected with that. He needed a son to join him and carry on building what he was starting. For now that was something he couldn't envisage happening with Sarah, but it was something he thought of when he watched others taking their lads with them and teaching them the ropes, managing the locks, tying off the boats, legging through the narrow tunnels or leading the horses along the towpaths.

Laura met up with him whenever he came to Goole. He would let her know his planned trips and she would listen out for his whistle in the ginnel. Finding an excuse to go out, she would collect a bundle or a basket and give some reason to Lizzie. But Lizzie was already beginning to suspect that she was meeting someone, she didn't know who but she could see the signs. She got no information from her casual questions or oblique comments. Laura was too circumspect for that. This was something she needed to keep close.

He gave the mate the night off and moored his new boat up river, away from the dock area and brought her there. He wanted to show off his new acquisition but of course, there were other reasons. It was not new, but not that old and in sound condition. He had struck a good bargain and his family name counted for much when he finalised the deal with a retiring coal dealer. The boat was wider and had a bigger living cabin than the other boat. There was a proper couch cum berth as well as a small area for cooking, washing and so on.

As they walked arm in arm down to the mooring, Laura asked about how much it had cost and whether he had paid outright or whether he would have to make payments to complete the purchase – which it turned out, he had. He was somewhat puzzled at her interest but she obviously had a shrewd head for business as she asked about interest rates and collateral. But when they arrived and he helped her aboard, there were more pressing matters to deal with. The water lapped at the hull as other boats passed up and down the grimy river, slapping a rhythm and rocking the craft gently as another rhythm was beaten out behind the closed doors of the cabin.

But already she knew what she had suspected. There were now three cossetted together in this cosy little space.

Aha – I see you have snared your prey.

Are you making plans now?
Do you need my help?

No.

I don't need you.

I think you do.

Just leave it to me.

There is a way ...

◆ ◆ ◆

As the last days of summer were passing, the weather turned unseasonably wet. The Ouse became full and as was its wont, it soon threatened to flood York and the surrounding area. As the water level rose, the staiths and quaysides were soon underwater, and the filthy water started to creep into waterside lanes and dwellings. The cesspits, privies and open sewers were soon inundated and the ordure flowed into the low lanes and cellars. And then as quickly as it had come, the weather reverted to an Indian summer of hot humid days with hardly a breath of wind. The result of these two phenomena was that the gases produced by the lack of proper sewers and sanitation crept insidiously into the poorer dwellings and up into the trading streets of the city, it rolled like a miasma under the bridges and through the yards, causing the residents to complain to the city council and demand some action. But there were others whose voices were not heard. They suffered in silence.

One of those was George's wife. Although he had asked his sister and brother-in-law to watch out for her, there would have been little they could have done to have prevented her demise. It was Annie who had found her. A dreadful ordeal for the poor child. She had walked over to see her mother as the water started to seep away from the flooded ground around the staiths and alleys that ran from it. The unseasonably humid air sucked up the vapours and fumes that rose up from the human and animal waste that collected in the lanes or was washed up from the river. The gas crept into the fabric of the buildings, through gaps in windows and door frames, through insubstantial walls and up through cellars, invading every nook and cranny with its insidious grasping fingers, searching out the weak and infirm, the young and the very old, those whose hope of escaping the hovels they inhabited was ebbing away. Coughing, shortness of breath, dizziness and nausea, drowsiness, torpor – and eventually, death. Sarah had no reserves with which to fight the menace of the poor who lived with the river as a close neighbour. Her liver was already damaged with drink and she was so malnourished that it was an easy battle for the gas to win.

Word reached George the next day when his brother Robert met him as he was headed back to York. Signalling him to pull over and lashing the two boats together, Robert climbed aboard his vessel and broke the news. At first George felt nothing. After a few moments he felt as if a weight had been lifted from him, then comprehension of the situation hit him. He grieved more for his motherless children and especially Annie who had surely experienced the worst thing a child could possibly have done.

Sarah was not the only unfortunate to have ended their life with sewer gas poisoning as the cause of death in the ledger that the registrar updated each day. George stayed on for a few days until her funeral could be held, but he had to feed the family and fulfil his contracts.

He left the girls with their grandfather again. The old man seemed to understand what had happened in moments of clarity, and then a few minutes later was totally unaware and would ask about Sarah. Annie had to shoulder a lot of the responsibility for looking after the house and her sister Hannah, even if her aunt did look in at times. George left some money for Annie to use for any immediate needs they had and felt guilty at putting such a responsibility on so young a pair of shoulders. But without his work, there would be none.

It was nearly a fortnight later that he once more docked in Goole. Part of him felt appalled that he could only think of spending some snatched hours with Laura while his wife lay cold under the earth of a freshly dug grave. And yet … and yet he supposed he could partake of those pleasures with a clearer conscious now.

Giving the usual signal in the ginnel, he waited to see if she would appear. It seemed an age but eventually he heard the rattle of the latch and the gate from the yard opened and she appeared with a bundle to deliver. His heart lurched and all earlier thoughts evaporated as he grasped her to him and kissed her forcefully. Pulling away from him, she looked into his eyes, questioning the ferocity of the embrace.

As they walked towards the dock area, he explained the reason for the time that had passed since their last meeting. She said nothing, merely letting him tell her the full account with the merest nod or shake of her head to acknowledge his comments. By the time they reached his boat and climbed into the cabin, all she wanted to do was to take him in her arms and console him. But was it consolation he wanted? He knew he wanted much more.

Later, as they lay in each other's arms, she turned and looked at him. Taking in his straggly brown hair, damp with sweat, his chin with a day's growth coming through, the full lips and dimpled chin, she fixed her clear eyes upon his and held them there, unblinking as she gave him her news.

"Are tha sure? 'ow far gone are thee lass?" he said, pulling himself upright to face her fully.

"Just over three months. By my reckoning you will be a father by March." Studying his face for a reaction, she was pleased to see that slowly a smile was spreading across his face.

"Tha'll marry me lass? Ah've no encumbrances now. Will tha be a mam t' me bairns? 'Tis a lot t' ask of 'ee, but ah'll be a good husband an' father t' child. Will tha 'ave me?"

She turned away from him, breaking the hold her eyes had for but a few moments, then turned again and nodding, drew him closer to seal the agreement with a kiss, before she left to return alone to Lizzie's.

I told you I had a plan.

Aren't you pleased?

I knew that it would please you – don't deny it.

No!

This was not of my making.

I did not wish her dead!

No?

Well, it has worked out rather well though, hasn't it?

Now, about some ... recompense for all my help ...

Don't you dare!

I did not ask for this.

I did not wish it. I made no deal with you!

No?

But you got what you wanted though, didn't you?

I can wait ...

18

K ate and Jen ran into the station and collapsed gasping onto the last seats in the carriage just as the doors closed and the train started to leave the station.

"Phew! That was close," laughed Jen.

"Did you make it to that lecture?" asked Kate. "You were very late back last night."

Jen answered by rolling her eyes and giving a smirk. "Not with the sore head I woke up with!"

"Serves you right!" Kate said, adding a laugh so that it didn't sound quite as dictatorial as it had come out.

"You're not my mum you know!" retorted Jen, but also burst into laughter to show that there was no ill feeling between them.

Jen sat back in her seat and shoved her Bluetooth buds into her ears, closing her eyes and signalling that she was all for a snooze and a blast of 'soothing' music.

"I'll give you a poke when we're nearly at Newark," Kate assured her, and sat back with her own thoughts. The light had all but gone outside and the bright lights in the carriage meant that all she could see were reflections of their fellow passengers and seats.

Digging into her capacious shoulder bag she pulled

out a clear pocket and unfolded the photocopied sheet within. After the tutorial that morning she and Sonja had grabbed a coffee with Barney and he had produced the map he had mentioned the previous night. He had made two copies for the girls. Each was of the part that interested them from last night – the part that covered the river, the Ouse Bridge and the staiths on either side. It was dated 1852. They had spent about ten minutes that morning talking about last night and the flood measure board but Kate didn't want to revisit what she had heard and neither of them broached it, sensitive to how she had felt and reacted afterwards.

Spreading their copies out in front of them, Barney's index finger had pointed out where they had stood last night and where the pub now stood. He had also put a Google Map image up of the street map as it looked today and they could quickly see that the street layout did not match exactly. The Coppergate still ran down towards the river but there was no mention of King Street, the street they had walked down and on the corner of which stood the Kings Arms pub. However, almost exactly matching the footprint of that street was a street named First Water Lane and in tiny writing on the corner with Kings Staith, the words The Kings Arms P.H. with, on the opposite corner, the words The Ship Inn P.H.

"Public House," Barney had clarified in answer to their puzzled frowns.

Now as she sat on the train, the glaringly bright lights helped her make out the other street names in the miniscule printing.

Directly opposite was the Queens Staith and running the length of the river parallel to it and behind it was

Skeldergate. She could clearly see the indication of the flights of steps at each end of the Ouse Bridge.

She allowed her gaze to wander up and down the streets of the old map, trying to match them to the city she was getting to know now. She loved 'reading' maps – she could spend hours doing it and as a child, she loved getting the atlas out with Gran and taking tours through all the countries, planning where they would go on adventures – 'one day'.

The jarring ping of the impending announcement brought her back to the present as the nasal, almost inaudible, message about their imminent arrival at Newark burbled through the hubbub of voices. Giving Jen a kick with her toe under the table, she folded up the map into the pocket and replaced it in her shoulder bag, her virtual journey through the old streets at an end.

19

George decided that he would have her with him on the boat. Many wives, and even families, travelled the waterways together. It was an arrangement that worked well. Someone to warm their bed at night and to look after them during the days, to lend a hand at the locks and be a companion on the long stretches unbroken by inns to quench a man's parched throat. He told her so at their next meeting.

She reacted in a way he had not expected. Instead of being delighted at having his company every day and in his bed every night on the rivers and canals, she turned pale and even began to tremble a little. He was not sure what that meant. Disappointment? Anticipation? But in the end, she took a deep breath and her lips parted in a hesitant smile, washing away his worried thoughts.

Dear God – on the river. Can I never escape its hold? Yet ... perhaps that is the best way. I can watch over him, keep him safe and guard against that debt being called in. And together we can plan for the future. I can steer his path in more ways than one. Yes, this is a way.

She told Lizzie the next day. However Lizzie had already suspected that she let that room out to more than one, and asked her outright when the child was due. Laura was surprised but then realised that Lizzie had had a brood of her own, and if anyone could read the signs, it would be her. Who was the father, she wanted to know. Laura hesitated, unsure if she really wanted to tell her, but then she presumed that it would only be a matter of time until word was out. After all, the watermen were a tight knit group and often interconnected by blood and marriage, and soon all would know their business. When she heard it was George, she was taken aback. After all, was the man not newly widowed? John had told her as much not more than a week ago. She could calculate the figures, she knew what had been going on while the man was still married. And didn't he have a family in York? Lizzie's face was becoming redder at every accusation. Laura could only placate her by saying that they would wait a decent amount of time before getting wed, but before the child was born.

"Ah thought 'ee a better lass than that, ah haf' t'say. Well, what's done is done. Ye can pay yer rent up till end of t' week. Ah can't deny ah'll miss 'ee, an' tha've been a reet good worker an' a welcome bit o' female company when John's away. But ah'll wish tha well. These things 'appen. Ah've lived long enough now that nothin' surprises me."

A few days later Laura packed up her belongings, reminiscing on what she had arrived with all those months ago. Lizzie had been a godsend, there was no denying and she did feel a pang of remorse at her having to find out this way. But life had to go on and her future had to be secure. Tying yourself to a man who had plans and ambitions was the only way forward for a woman in this life.

Clearing the cupboard of all her personal effects did not take very long. Folding her clothes around the few small personal items that she had purchased with the extra coins she saved in her leather bag, she tied a belt around them and carried them down the stairs. Giving Lizzie a heartfelt embrace and thanking her for all that she had done for her, giving her a roof over her head when she had nothing and nowhere to go, giving her employment, being a friend. As Lizzie wiped her eyes with the back of her hand, she closed the door behind the woman who had come into her life unexpectedly and who had fascinated her, as much as befriended her all these months.

Laura stepped onto the roadway, adjusting her bundle on her hip and turned to cross it and head towards the docks. As she tucked her hand under the cumbersome bulge, a piece of creased and yellowed newsprint fluttered to the ground behind her. Landing on the muddied thoroughfare, it lay half open momentarily, before the wheels of a passing cart ground it into the muck and its words were lost forever. Had Laura noticed, she would have hastily stooped to pick it up, glanced at the words with a shiver, refolded it and returned it deep in the folds of her pack.

TRAGIC DROWNING

The tragic death of a young child was reported Thursday last. The body of the three year old was washed up on the Humber mudflats off Humber Bank. He was named as Joseph Harrison. He was last seen with his older sister while they were out for a walk along the river bank. The ten year old sister said she was momentarily distracted by the shout from a friend and after talking to her for a few minutes she turned around to discover her young brother missing. No other witnesses to the tragedy have been found. A verdict of accidental death by drowning was passed at the inquest this Monday.

George was waiting at the dock gates for her, nervously shifting his weight from foot to foot. Taking her bundle from her, he offered her his arm and together they walked along the bank to where the boat was moored. As he helped her aboard and the boat shifted slightly at the change of load, she wondered if she was taking a step in the right direction or one which would lead her deeper in the tangled web that was her life – past and present. And the future?

That night they lay cocooned in the small cabin, for the first time at ease and not watching the time for her to return to Lizzie's through the darkening streets. They talked about where their different paths had brought them and where they hoped they would lead. George knew that she had come from a different, better background to the one he had grown up in, but she said very little about her past and always changed the subject when he tried to find out more. She had obviously had a better education than him. She spoke what he called 'properly' and in one way that was the attraction between them. The mismatch of their pasts drew them together like opposing poles of a magnet. There was always a nagging doubt at the back of his mind that she might find his way of life beneath her, but she had not objected so far so he hung onto that aspiration for the future.

The next trip he had to do was up the Ouse to Selby, where he would pick up another cargo and head to Leeds. Although Laura felt ill at ease being on the river, she knew she had to keep control of her fears and rely on having his companionship and security. If only he knew what a feat of willpower that was for her.

En-route they passed other watermen that he knew and shouts and greetings were traded. She kept in the background, unsure how much he wanted her to be seen to be with him but soon he brought her up beside him and said that they had nothing to be ashamed of. Weren't they betrothed, albeit privately, until a decent period had elapsed from the time of his widowerhood? Who could gainsay them? Her gently swelling belly was easily hidden in the folds of her apron or the fringes of her shawl, although the tiny being was now making his fluttering presence felt more and more each day.

From Selby they left the river and joined the canal which connected to the River Aire and thence to the Aire and Calder Navigation which brought them through Knottingley and eventually into Leeds. Normally George would have been wanting a quick turnaround and to be heading back towards Goole or York with another cargo – freight meant money. But instead he decided to have some time in the city with Laura, as she had never seen the vast metropolis that Leeds was fast becoming. Taking the boat as far into the centre as he could on the water, he moored up and they made their way into the busy streets lined with warehouses and factories. Smoke hung over the city and work and money were obviously the Gods here. Finding a small area of green that served as a diminutive park among rows of houses, they sat down on a bench and George produced a couple of pies and a bottle of beer which they shared. Although well into autumn, there were some shafts of sunlight struggling through the pall that hung over the metropolis and it was pleasant to enjoy the last warmth of the year before the harsher days began.

A few other people were also making the best of the clement weather and a mother was walking with two young children along a path which wound between the trees alongside the railings that surrounded the little oasis. As she came closer, Laura started to frown and sit forward, narrowing her eyes to focus better on the approaching figure. George was oblivious to her movement, half dozing, eyes closed and his breathing gentle and regular as he lay back with his hands clasped behind his head, savouring the kaleidoscope of colours behind his eyelids. She stood up as the woman came within a few feet and then took a couple of steps towards her, so that the woman could not help but turn to look at her.

The woman froze, then instinctively turned to check that her children were within sight, before turning back towards Laura. Taking another step forward her lips parted and the merest whisper escaped them as she uttered, "Laura?"

As Laura nodded, the woman's hand flew to her mouth as she let out a small gasp. Then having considered for a few more seconds, the woman took two more steps forward while stretching out her gloved hands towards Laura. At her smile, Laura reached out and clasped the offered hands, then found herself pulled forward into an embrace.

"Is it truly you? I never thought to see you again. Where have you been? What has happened to you? But ..." and then she paused in her flow of questions. Her eyes went to the man that Laura had left sitting on the bench, half asleep but now rousing as he became aware of the movement and voices nearby.

"Eliza. Is it really you? I knew you had gone to work in Leeds but after that, I ... heard no more."

"Are you well?" asked Eliza, her eyes now darting over Laura's shoulder at George, who had now stood and seemed uncertain whether to join them or remain where he was.

"Yes, yes, I am well. And you?", and looking over to the children who were now running towards them she continued, "Are these your children?"

Eliza drew the two children towards her and introduced Becky, who she explained was seven, and Frederick who was three. Laura felt obliged to introduce George at this point, and turning towards him, put her hand upon his arm and drew him nearer. "This is George, my betrothed. He is a coal merchant, and waterman with a fleet of boats to his name," she added expansively. 'Or soon will have', she thought to herself. "George, this is my older sister Eliza. We have not met since … well, for some time." At this she flashed a glance at Eliza which seemed to indicate that no more should be said on that subject.

After a few more minutes, as the sisters exchanged questions and answers, George gathered that Eliza was married to a builder, Charles, who now employed three men and that he was also intending to expand his business in the thriving atmosphere that Leeds provided for a man with ambition. He also gathered they had a modest house nearby and that both of them would be welcome to come and take tea there tomorrow, if that was convenient, and meet the rest of the family which comprised of baby Arthur who was only a few months old and in the care of the nursemaid cum housekeeper.

At this George felt compelled to interject, "Reet sorry lass, but we 'ave a cargo t' load this evenin' and then we leave int' mornin'."

"But I'm sure we will be back to Leeds soon," Laura quickly added, to save George having to make any further excuses.

Taking their leave of Eliza, Laura having secured an address for her, they retraced their steps. George seemed uncommonly quiet and his face was drawn into a frown. She could read his thoughts. He didn't want to share her with anyone else. And he could see that her family came from better than him and his. She said little and left him with his thoughts until they reached the boat and she climbed down into the little cabin. He remained on deck, restowing rope that was perfectly well stowed, tidying up tools that were already neatly racked and stored in their respective places. Removing her bonnet and shawl, she looked up at him through the open hatchway and waited until he turned and met her look. Her eyes pulled him towards her, although he felt himself pulling away. But it was no use. They always won their prize.

As if guessing at his thoughts, she reassured him that all she wanted and needed was right here, right now on this boat. If he wanted to ask about her and her sister's childhood and family, those questions were quashed as she took him in her arms and he was transported to that place she always took him where the present dissolved into a surfeit of responses to each of his heightened senses. The smell of her hair, the taste of her skin, the feel of her touch, the sound of her voice, the look in her eyes. Eyes that forever trapped him and drove all other thoughts from his mind.

20

Over the next few weeks and months George found himself on trips to Leeds more and more often, and Laura would walk up to the park to meet her sister, but there was always one excuse or another why they couldn't stay or come to meet Eliza's husband, or visit their home. It didn't bother George – he had plenty to do at the quayside, where he felt more at home among the other men he knew, exchanging exploits and near-misses, accidents and mishaps. And a few ales in the local hostelry was always welcome. But she was always there when he returned, growing ever fuller round the middle.

He asked her how she explained this to Eliza but she merely waved away the question with a change of subject or non-committal reply. But winter was approaching and the days were definitely darker and colder. Fingers became raw handling the ropes and clutching the tiller, even with gloves and a warming mug of tea passed up from down below.

One evening as they sat huddled together under the rugs in their cabin, Laura broached the subject of their marriage. The year would soon come to a close and the babe would be due in a few months after that. Then she surprised him by saying that Eliza had suggested that they marry in Leeds, at their local parish church. Her sister had spoken to Charles, her husband, and he was of the same opinion.

"An' what 'bout my 'pinion?" George shot back at her.

" I knew you would want to do this properly. After all, you have your name and reputation as well as mine to consider."

George frowned as he considered the implications of this. He hadn't really done the counting – to be fair, he would have been quite happy going along the way they were. There were plenty of babes born on the river and no-one asked too many questions about their legitimacy. A baptism the next time they were at a convenient church was all that was required when the time came, whenever and wherever that might be.

"And as your legal wife, things would be so much simpler – in the future." She stopped to let him mull that one over. "If something were to happen to you, at least you would know that we were provided for – of course, you would have to have made a will. You have, haven't you?"

At this George prevaricated and muttered something about 'all in good time', but Laura realised that she would have to help him focus his mind on these things sooner rather than later. Who knew what the future held? And she wanted security.

Laura managed to persuade him to allow their marriage to go ahead in the parish church that her sister had suggested in Leeds. But to do that, the banns had to be read on three consecutive Sundays – and at least one of the participants had to be living in the parish at that time.

George took a few moments to consider that one, then

asked her how they would manage that.

"Eliza has suggested I spend a few weeks living with them. Her nursemaid, who also takes on the duties of her housekeeper, is run off her feet as the youngest is now starting to crawl everywhere. She made the suggestion and frankly I see it as a good compromise."

George did not see it as quite as good a compromise, but in the end he agreed as he found he could not really deny her anything, especially when she held him close and he was held in her gaze.

And so, as the new year began, George carried Laura's belongings to Eliza and Charles' house. It was not far from the little park and not nearly as grand as George had been imagining. It sat amidst a short terrace of similar houses, brick built and of modest proportions. If Charles had ambitions then he was starting from unpretentious beginnings. Nevertheless the house was on three floors, the topmost windows being small and set into the slope of the roof. No doubt the nursery and housemaid's quarters, he surmised. The path to the door was clean and tidy, flanked by a bedraggled flower bed and a few shrubs past their best now that winter had arrived. The door was answered by Eliza herself and she welcomed them both in with nervous chatter and a shout for Charles to come and meet them.

After some tea was brought into the small parlour, Charles entered and strode across to shake George's hand. A firm handshake, thought George, while he appraised the other man whom he took to be about his own age. Well-dressed but not overly so, and with a fine beard and moustache which had hints of grey through them. While the two of them sat down upon the two chairs that flanked the fireplace, Eliza took Laura upstairs to show her where her room was. The two older children shared a room and the baby still occupied the nursery so the only other room was a small one beside it on the top floor which served as a storeroom for extraneous items. Next to it the housekeeper had her room so that she could be close to the nursery where Arthur slept. Eliza was rather apologetic about the lack of space but Laura assured her she had slept in far less comfortable places, before quickly noting the look of surprise on Eliza's face. Before she could probe further, Laura walked to the small bed that sat along one wall and laid her belongings upon it. Her sister apologised again but said that there was a small set of drawers there for her use and that she should ask the housekeeper, Mrs Grimes, for water for the basin that stood on the washstand in the corner.

Assuring her all was perfectly suitable, Laura took her arm and steered her back towards the stairs so that she could rescue George from her brother-in-law's questioning, should he be feeling uncomfortable. But she was pleasantly surprised to find upon their return to the parlour that the two men were to be found stooped over a small table upon which was unfurled a large drawing. Charles was at that moment describing his outline for a new building to be built near the docks and proudly announcing that his plans were in the shortlist for the contract. George had just been telling him of his plans for extending his fleet in the fullness of time and already they were making plans for how George could undertake the transport of the materials required. Seeing the women returning they both straightened up and Laura's heart warmed to see that George was beaming and Charles had placed a hand upon his shoulder in a gesture of camaraderie.

Eliza excused herself for a minute and was heard to call for Mrs Grimes to fetch a fresh pot of tea. When she came to the parlour door, Eliza went out into the hall with her for a few words. Laura took little notice of this until, as she went over to look at a rather interesting picture upon the wall by the door, she overheard Eliza.

" ... and she will be staying here for the next month or so. You may call her Mrs Cowper – she is a widow. She may play with the children, entertain them, read them stories or whatever, but on no account must she be left alone with them when outside, especially on any walks by the river, the pond or the docks. Do you understand?"

Laura assumed that the answer was given in the affirmative as Eliza entered the room almost immediately, by which time Laura had taken a few steps away from the door and resumed her interest in an item of minor interest upon the mantelpiece.

As the evening drew in, Laura accompanied George back to the moorings where he would load up and depart the following morning. They bade each other a fond farewell in the cosy cabin, after which he helped her clamber off the boat, her added weight and girth starting to impede her mobility and balance.

Night had fallen as she picked her way back up the pathway that ran by the water. A sound caught her attention and she stopped in her tracks as the sound grew louder and more insistent.

I have been waiting.

When will you pay?

I owe you nothing.

Nothing?

Have you so short a memory?

I paved the way for you, don't you recall?

It was going to happen.

You had no hand in it.

Are you sure?

Do you really think so?

Now … some recompense for the kind deed is outstanding, don't you think?

But you took her!

Ah, but I didn't keep her in my grasp.

They took her away and put her in the ground far from my reach.

I still hunger for payment.

There is nothing.

There is no-one.

We will see.

We will see …

Picking up her skirts, she broke into a run, getting as far away from the water as she could, her footsteps drowning out the whisper of the voices in her head.

21

Over the next few weeks George plied the waterways between Leeds, Goole and York carrying the cargoes to their respective destinations and loading up again almost immediately in order to fulfil the orders that were now pouring in. It was a boom time for trade on the waterways, even though the railways threatened to supersede it, the two linked together as the rail tracks were led into the dock areas so that coal could be directly loaded and unloaded and sent to the demanding centres of the industrial Midlands.

When George returned to York he visited his daughters at their grandfather's and always tried to bring them a small item to greet them with – a sweet confection or maybe a small coin. It also helped to salve his conscience somewhat when he thought about how he had not been able to look after his wife better and keep the girls from the horrific experiences they had suffered. He was pleased to see that his sister had been dropping in to visit them reasonably frequently, but he still felt guilty at having to leave them there. His thoughts turned to providing a secure home for them with Laura and their step-brother or sister in a few months. To that end he walked through the city, away from the river and the dreadful memories that it held, the tower of the Minster showing between the crowded rooftops of the Shambles and Goodramgate.

Passing through Monk Bar, the old stone gateway with its crenelated tower in honeyed stone, cruciform arrow slits set into the side of the tower and the larger archway which once held a heavy gate to bar the way, he was now beyond the old mediaeval walls of the city which once withstood the onslaught of invaders throughout the centuries. It seemed poverty and overcrowding were the biggest enemies of the inhabitants now. He turned along what was called Lord Mayor's Walk which was bordered on one side by the turfed ramparts of the old walls and planted with a line of elm trees, inside which the Minster gardens were ensconced, and crossed into one of the many streets that opened off the opposite side. The broad turfed ditch was dotted with a few sheep grazing, brought in from the winter fields before lambing started. The housing comprised long terraces of small houses, other streets connected with these at right angles, all close together but reasonably well maintained.

One of these was called Wheatley's Row and when he found the house he was looking for he was pleased to see that it was well kept and in good repair, at least from the outside. He had already collected the key from the landlord and walking up to the door, he let himself in. Laura had been mithering him about having a home for them to live in once the baby arrived as she was vehemently against them living on board a water vessel with a new baby. And, she assured him, as his business expanded he would require an address which would reflect the respectability of its proprietor. She appeared to have plans for him that he had not even considered, but he was happy enough to go along with them if it meant they could all be together somewhere safe and healthy while he was about his river business.

The house had obviously been recently vacated as a few items lay abandoned – crushed newspapers and a broken stool, but it was in good repair and had a small parlour leading off the hallway to one side and a kitchen and scullery at the far end. The narrow stairs led up to a small landing with two bedrooms, one on either side.

Through the scullery a door led out into a small yard with a privy at the end and a gateway out into the ginnel behind. Pleased with what he saw, he smiled to himself at the thought of bringing Laura here and watching her face as he swept open the door and ushered her in. More immediately he had to set about collecting some items of furniture and so with that thought in his mind, he locked the door behind him and returned the way he had come.

All Laura's plans were coming together. It had been a fortunate twist of fate that had brought her to Leeds and to meeting her sister. Eliza was three years younger than her and had had little recollection of the circumstances that had ripped the family apart and caused her to be ostracised from it. But from what she had overheard that day in the house, she realised that Eliza must have some idea of it, although she would never broach the topic with Laura. It was a long time ago and not for revisiting, even though it had stalked her ever since.

I must be on my guard. I must make every effort to resist its power and influence. Why me? Why did it choose me? How does it make these things happen? Just when I think myself free of it, new fingers reach out to me, no matter where I roam. But I know its thoughts and that gives me some advantage. I must never lessen my watchfulness.

The banns had been read for three consecutive Sundays and the minister had been assured of the lack of any impediment to their union. They were both widowed and at least one of them had been residing in the parish for over a month. He had been assured that the child she was most certainly expecting was the groom's and had been conceived after the passing of both of their previous spouses, something that George was reluctant to agree to, being patently untrue, but as they were away from his home town, no-one would be any the wiser. The date was set for the second Wednesday in February. Although Laura was a widow, she had not expanded on the circumstances or the details of her previous marriage to Eliza. And she certainly did not wear mourning, so Eliza assumed it had occurred more than two or three years previously. Eliza insisted that Laura get a new bonnet and velvet cape for her wedding as the weather would be bound to be chilly and certainly St Simon's Church always was. They went shopping together and choose a cape in deep burgundy with a little matching fur muff which would go in some way to cover her swelling belly. A velvet ribbon in burgundy was fixed in a floppy bow at the back of the bonnet and the upswept brim and crown were adorned with small flowers. Other than that Laura did not expend a lot of expense on any more outfits. As befitting a good Yorkshire woman, she knew the value of money and preferred to conserve rather than spend her hard-earned savings.

George had asked Robert, his brother, and a few of his friends from the waterways to attend the wedding and Laura had Eliza and her husband as her guests. The day dawned cold and breezy, but bright and thankfully with no threat of freezing temperatures so that by midday the low sun was blessing the city with weak lukewarm beams of light. George and his friends walked up from the river where they had berthed their boats and Eliza's husband Charles had hired a handsome cab to bring them to the church. As always when George saw Laura, his heart raced and he found himself lost in her gaze. The service scheduled for early afternoon was over quickly, a minimum congregation attending, and after a hymn the minister, Reverend Ambrose, conducted the marriage ceremony and then pronounced them man and wife after George slipped the slim gold band onto Laura's finger. A final prayer and blessing followed and then they entered the vestry where they signed their names in the marriage register – George in a strong, firm, sloping hand and Laura in a neat, efficient script, while Charles acted as one witness and a friend of George's as the other.

George would have preferred to have taken Laura there and then to the boat and sailed her back to York but Eliza insisted that a little celebration should be held in a small local hotel where some food and drink had been laid on for the gathered guests. George was a little overcome at Charles' largesse and hoped that they could in time become good friends, if not, as Charles had hinted, business partners. It all seemed to be working out very well for them and he was looking forward to married life and many years together as Charles toasted the couple and everyone cheered and wished them well.

I haven't forgotten ...

22

I n York, with the threat of freezing temperatures having abated, the waters by the staiths and quay-sides were running freely and boats of all descriptions and sizes were moored, awaiting cargoes, journeys in the offing, journeys completed. They were moored three or four deep, their bows and sterns lashed together to stop them floating about in the current as the river flowed through York, meeting up with its lesser cousin the Foss as it departed the city and together joining to flow to-wards the Humber estuary and beyond. It had already come from higher parts where it had been formed by the Ure and Swale, giving them a new name and iden-tity as it swirled and flowed under bridges, over weirs and through valleys to find room to spread as it swept through the city and on to its final destination. It brought with it many stories, many experiences, it had taken many on journeys and caused many a journey to end. It had slipped along soundlessly to remain incon-spicuous or else thrashed about in fury to make itself noticed. It had many moods – some capricious, some more menacing and it harboured many grudges as it was ignored, abused and taken for granted. Some paid it trib-ute – but not enough to assuage its thirst. To be used thus it demanded, nay expected, fair recompense. It had ever been thus for millennia – and it still was ...

As the day dawned fair after a few frosty mornings and bitter cold days, the children of York donned gloves and mufflers and broke free of the shackles of cramped rooms and oppressive dwellings. At the same time in Leeds, George and Laura had been making their respect-ive ways to the church where they would bind them-selves together in matrimony.

Down by Queens Staith, in Sampsons Yard, Annie collected her basket and donned her gloves and muffler too. Her aunt had brought them some provisions early that morning and she was grateful that she could make something nourishing for her grandfather. At times he was a jovial grandparent, pulling Hannah onto his knee and telling them tales of when he was a lad and the pranks he would get up to. He would tickle the child and she would giggle until she wriggled and writhed so much that she would end up on the floor laughing so hard that she would end up with the hiccups. Annie, too old for sitting on laps, would nevertheless be holding her sides at the sound of Hannah's laughter, bringing back memories of happier times with her parents before everything had gone so wrong.

But at other times, her grandfather would lapse into long silences, his eyes vacant and staring into space, seemingly oblivious to their presence in the room. At these times, he would not eat and seemed not to recognise them, he would ask the same question of Annie time after time, never remembering the answer or else think that she was Ann, his wife, who had departed this life just over a year ago. Annie had learned to be patient and hope for the next time he would be lucid and her funny grandfather again. She washed his clothes as best she could, and made the simple meals that she could manage. Hannah seemed to notice these lapses less – but then she was not yet four years old and only noticed the here and now.

Pulling Hannah's hand, Annie went out and shut the door behind her, heading up towards Ouse Bridge and into the streets which led to the market where she would get a few things with the coins that Grandfather kept in a tin box in the back of the dresser. When he was alert he had told her to use these if she needed. Hannah was in a mood and squirmed at being held so firmly by her bossy big sister.

"No. No! Ah want t' play 'ere!" she wailed, tugging her hand from Annie's grasp. "Look, there's Mary an' Joe – ah want t' stay here an' play wi' them. Lemme go!"

Annie took a deep breath and thinking that getting to market and back without her little sister having tantrums beside her would be far easier, she relented. Noticing the children who were now appearing from various yards and doorways, she told Hannah to stay with them and behave. "Be careful an' ah'll be back soon. Mind tha stay wi' t' big children an' keep 'way from t' water as tha've been told." With a final nod to John, who was the oldest there, she headed over the bridge and into town.

At the very moment that George was putting the ring on Laura's finger, it happened.

A little yellow ribbon tugged free, drifting and swirling about in the water, gently captured by the undercurrent, then funnelled by the flow between the hulls of the boats. A splash of colour among the dark wood, work-stained hulls and murky water. Catching the low sunlight as it bounced on the surface and reflected on the ripples.

I told you.

I could wait – but I have not got infinite patience.

So pretty.

So small.

Not unlike another one, another time …

The report in the paper a few days later read:

On Friday an inquest was held concerning the death of Hannah Shipton, daughter of George Shipton a waterman from the city of York, formerly living in Water Lane, aged 3 years and 10 months. On Wednesday afternoon, the deceased along with a number of other children, was playing on the vessels lying alongside the Queens Staith, and they were ordered on shore by the master. As deceased did not come home at five o'clock for tea, her sister became alarmed, and, on the river being dragged about half past eight the same evening, her yellow ribbon was spotted floating nearby and her dead body was found at a spot about 30 yards lower down from the keel on which she had been playing. A verdict of "Accidentally drowned" was returned.

<u>Yorkshire Gazette</u>

By that time George had sailed back to York, word having come downriver the way it always did, mouth to mouth, messages passed and sorrows shared. It was a bittersweet arrival to their new home and he spent but a few moments with Laura, having led her there through the bustling streets and left her with the key, while he turned about and headed for his grandfather's. Arriving there he found his sister already waiting for his arrival, her arms around Annie who was wide-eyed and who burst into tears at the arrival of her Da. Enfolding her in his arms, he broke down in silent sobs, while holding his last remaining child close. Grandfather was oblivious and kept asking what was wrong. Everyone ignored him, after all they had told him innumerable times now.

George told Annie to pack up her belongings and collect Hannah's few bits and pieces, while he gave his sister their new address and told her that she could find them all there from now on. In fact, she should come and meet his new wife at the soonest opportunity. His sister was visibly shocked at the haste in which he had taken a new wife but, as he said, "Me girls needed a Mam."

Leaving them in the house by the staith, he shuddered as he crossed the Ouse Bridge, and Annie pointed out where Hannah had been found. "It weren't me fault Da. Ah tol' her no' t'play on t'boats. Ahv'e tol' 'er loads o' times. Honest …" and here she broke down again in sobs.

"Ah know, ah know lass. 'Tis a dreadful accident. Tha's no' t'blame. Ah should never 'ave left ye both for so long but brass 'ad t' be earned. An' ah 'ave a new home for 'ee t' live in. Not like yon hovel tha had wi' yer Mam, God rest her soul." At this Annie threatened to burst into further sobs so he hastily continued, " – an' tha can meet yer new Mam."

"Step-mam," interjected Annie defiantly.

"Aye, yer reet, but she'll tak' guid care o' 'ee – an' tha'll soon 'ave a wee brother or sister to cheer thee up!"

This did not have the desired effect, and Annie once more broke down into sobs. "Ah jus' wan' Hannah!"

He gave up trying to say the right thing, and together they walked through the streets to their new home as Annie snivelled and wiped her nose on the back of her glove.

◆ ◆ ◆

That night as they lay together in their new home, they could hear the muffled sounds of Annie crying.

"Give it time," said Laura, "She will be alright soon. We will take good care of her. Tomorrow is the funeral and after that we will be able to move forward, together, as a family."

"Ah hope so lass," he replied, with less conviction than he felt. So many losses in such a short time. Life was so fragile. He just hoped that the new bairn would be strong and healthy, and that Laura would be spared any complications from the birth. After all, it was her first. She seemed so calm and confident. Women were definitely stronger than men, he thought wryly.

"There is something we – you – need to think about George. Have you made a will yet?"

"Well … no, ah never really thought about 't."

"You have a child to think about, and another on the way. And a wife, remember. And you have all your business ventures. We should need some security … if anything were to happen. God forbid," she added hastily, leaning on her elbow as she moved her cumbersome form to lie facing him in the soft glow of the oil lamp by their bed.

"Ah, lass, ye're ever th' practical one. But let's no' think about that jus' now."

The soft flickering light reflected in her pale eyes, and he reached out to pull her close and laying a hand on her distended belly, began to stroke and caress her pregnant form, every part of her seemed to be softer, fuller and inviting exploration and further contact. Burying his face in the folds and mounds of her body, he once more lost sense of time and place.

She let him have his way. Although the touch of him always heightened her senses and gave her a sense of power as she bent his mind and body to her will, she remained a place apart, her mind alert to the future and what plans she still needed to make.

23

"Give over! Stop mitherin' me woman!" he reproached her, but with a smirk and a laugh in his voice. "If it'll make tha quit yer naggin' I'll go t' lawyer this afternoon and set me affairs in order."

With a feeling of triumph, she merely smiled sweetly as she coquettishly turned her back on him and continued stirring the pot upon the range, arching her back and pressing her hand into the ache that seemed permanently there. The babe should not be long in making an appearance now, she felt, and she would be grateful to shed the cumbersome weight that she was carrying about with her.

Annie sat opposite at the table and despite saying that she didn't want another Mam, she grudgingly had fallen under Laura's spell and found that she enjoyed the care of another woman again. But she would never forget her real Mam, she asserted, to which Laura replied, "Of course. You should not. It is important that you never do. Now will you read to me and let me hear how you are doing? I know you missed a lot of schooling and I would like to make sure that you have the skills you will need in this life."

Annie went unwillingly to fetch the bible from the shelf and prepared to continue from where they had left off the other day. Laura planned to get some other texts for her to broaden her experience of literature, but for now that would have to do. George went out, bidding them both goodbye and placing a peck on each of their cheeks.

Leaving the pot to simmer, Laura lowered herself awkwardly into a chair opposite Annie as she started to read from where the ribbon marked the place. She was doing reasonably well, Laura thought to herself, but she would continue to encourage her efforts. A woman needed every skill she could possess to succeed in this world. She knew that better than anyone. Her early life had been one of schooling and a broadening of her horizons. Unusually she attended lessons up until she was well into her middle teens, alongside two of her older brothers, and the family's tutor had found her to be a receptive and able pupil. She could have been destined for greater things. What might have been.

But then …

George left the next morning, walking back through the town to the staith near his father, where he had moored the boat he was taking down to Selby. First he wanted to look in on his father but every time he did, it saddened him more and more. Should he bring him to live with them? But the old man was so confused as it was, that a new place would only make things worse. And there was the arrival of the new baby to consider. No, he would leave the old man under his sister's care. But before he left on today's trip he would look in on him and see how he was faring.

Less than an hour later, feeling immeasurably saddened to see his father so frail and confused, trying to eat the broth his daughter had brought him with a fork, George slipped his moorings having been joined by one of his regular crewmen and they felt the pull of the current as the river caught them and pointed them south. Soon they passed the confluence of the river with the smaller Foss and then headed out into the open countryside, passing Naburn, and waving a greeting to the familiar figure of the ferryman that took the ferry across from shore to shore at this point. All he could think about was when he would be back again with Laura and his mind turned to memories of midnight caresses and drowning in the bottomless pool of her eyes.

Passing through the Selby Lock the boat left the Ouse and joined the Selby Canal. Then they headed through the Haddlesey Lock and it was taken by the River Aire. Through further locks, passing through Knottingley and then arriving at Ferrybridge, they moored up for the night. He spent the evening with watermen he knew at the nearby inn and caught up with all the stories he had missed being off the waterways for the last few weeks. The next morning, having walked somewhat unsteadily back to the boat the night before, he untied the mooring ropes and headed for their final destination of Wakefield.

Meanwhile Laura was preparing to head into the town. Walking now was becoming an effort but she still enjoyed the opportunity to stretch her legs. Taking Annie with her, they turned out of Wheatley's Row, nodding to a few of the neighbours as they passed and faced the tall embankment of the old city walls. The trees were still bare branches but in another month there should be the promise of spring and new life. Turning through Monk Bar and heading down Goodramgate Laura was making for a bookseller she had seen before in Petergate. With the huge edifice of the Minster to their right, they turned down into Stoneygate and soon saw the sign over the doorway of the shop she was in search of. A bell tinkled as they entered and she was immediately transported back to times in the schoolroom as the smell of paper and print assailed her nostrils. Closing her eyes for a moment to savour it more deeply, she was aware of a hand upon her arm.

"Madam," the voice came from an elderly gentleman with a pair of glasses perched on the end of his nose. "Are you quite well?" Seeing her advanced state of pregnancy it was not surprising that he mistook her moment of rapture for something more worrisome.

"Quite, thank you for your concern. I was just enjoying the smell of books. It takes me back to …," but here she stopped, and bustling over to some shelves, began rifling through the titles in search of something she deemed suitable for Annie. Letting her fingers caress the leather bindings, she was momentarily lost for words as memories flooded back. The texture, the lettering, the tang of fresh print wafting from the back of the shop, the mustiness of old volumes about to pass through a second or third or more set of hands. It was intoxicating. Annie did not seem quite so enamoured however and began shuffling her feet and looking longingly at the door.

"Of course, I see we have a similar passion then perhaps? What may I help you with? Are you looking for anything in particular? Pray, take a seat." At this he pulled forward a wooden chair, plainly concerned at her condition.

By the time they left the shop, Laura had purchased half a dozen volumes she thought would be appropriate for Annie and, in a rare moment of self-gratification, one for herself which she had enjoyed in times past. She had mentioned it to him and after rooting around on some low shelves at the back of the shop, emerged triumphantly holding it aloft. Curling her fingers round the brown paper parcel he had tied with string, she could not wait to return to reading 'Cranford' by Elizabeth Gaskill, if she had any time to herself she thought ruefully. Maybe she and Annie could read it together. She must ask George to get a small bookcase which could sit in the front room.

"Can we go an' see Grandfather? Ye've not met him yet. 'e may be in good fettle t'day," piped up Annie, as they departed the shop, the little bell tinkling as they closed the door behind them. Laura pulled up short as her thoughts returned to the practicalities of the here and now. She knew the child missed him but as their steps led them down Coney Street and towards the Ouse Bridge, her heart began to race at the sight of the broad river between the buildings. Pausing at the church perched on the corner of Spurriergate and Ousegate, she leaned against the railings and her breath came in short shallow gasps.

At last – I thought we'd never meet again.

Did you find my recompense – appropriate?

You are despicable.

She was only an innocent.

Not even mine to take.

But I helped you get him.

So someone had to pay – and you had so little.

But he could pay instead.

You have him trapped, don't you?

He came to me willingly.

Do not accuse me thus.

Accuse?

Oh my dear, we know each other better than that,

do we not!

I have no more debts to pay.

Well, it never really ends, does it?

One good turn deserves another.

Our debts are settled.

Leave me.

We

shall

see …

"I'm sorry Annie. I can't go today. I – I am feeling a little faint. We should return home. The noxious miasma from the river makes my stomach heave."

Annie made to continue on her way but torn between her wish to see her grandfather, and her newly discovered care for her stepmother's welfare, she turned and took Laura's arm.

"Maybe another time," Laura added in the hopes of placating her stepdaughter. "Thank you. Let us have a drink of chocolate when we get home. I think it is the restorative we both would enjoy, don't you?" And with that, they turned back towards the busy streets and headed away from the river, leaving the ripples to chatter and tinkle unheeded.

24

E xactly eleven days after she had stood in the church in Leeds and made her marriage vows, Laura was gripped by a pain that was unexpected but familiar. She had been out in the yard, washing linen in the tub, steaming with hot water that she had filled with kettles from the stove. Her hands and forearms were red with the heat of it and the cold air that marked the last day of February. The shock of the stabbing pain caught her breath, and she involuntarily bent over and gripped her belly. Leaning against the cold bricks of the wall she took a few breaths until it passed, only to be followed a few moments later by the trickle of warm liquid down her legs. Making her way to the scullery door, she called out for Annie but then remembered she would be attending school, having resumed her modest education. She would not be back for an hour or more to have her lunch. The knowledge that she had been through this before gave her some resolve, although the conclusion of that previous time was hopefully not what would be the result this time. This time she was better nourished. Better cared for. Made better plans. She would never be so insecure again. She had learned the hardest lesson in this world. Look out for yourself – don't rely on anyone else.

Another grip of pain stabbed through her and she hung on the banisters taking a few breaths until it passed and then pulled herself up the stairs. Laying an old sheet over the bed, and taking off her soaked petticoat, she lay back on the pillows awaiting the next onslaught.

Annie ran down the ginnel and through the gate into the yard, noting the tub of water, now scummed with soap and cold with the unwashed linens lying untouched. Nothing hung on the lines stretched across the yard and she knew that today was washday. Feeling the first prickles of unease, she went through the scullery door, left slightly ajar, and listened for any sound. When she heard nothing she froze, uncertain whether to go any further. The stove was cold, no soup bubbled in the pot for her lunch this chilly day. No bread lay warm and cut into thick slices ready to have the golden butter spread upon it. Just when she made to walk further into the kitchen she heard the first howl, deep and primeval, coming from upstairs. After a few moments passed she heard Laura's voice. "Annie! Is that you?"

"Ah'm 'ere, Mam," she called, without realising what she had said. "Ah'm comin'." And with that she dashed through the hall and ran up the stairs to be met with the sight of Laura on the bed with her knees pulled up and her stockings half down her legs. Over her middle and thighs she had pulled a blanket.

"Go and fetch Molly. It's the baby. Run!"

They had already discussed what Annie should do if George was not here when the baby came, so Annie spun on her heel, her face ashen and raced out of the house and over the few streets to the door of Molly, who was known as the local midwife. Thankfully they had learned of her proximity within a few days of them moving into the house and Annie knew what to do. Hammering as loudly as she could, she was relieved when it opened and Molly stood there, apron tied around her rotund midriff, sleeves rolled up and her hair scraped back under a linen cap. "Yer mam, is 't?" she asked without any prompting from Annie. "Go back 'ome lass and ah'll be there d'rectly."

Annie needed no further bidding and by the time Molly arrived she had already put the kettle on to boil for hot water and got all the other things that Laura had directed her to when the time came.

"Go back to school Annie. No use you staying here," Laura urged her. "These things don't happen that quickly," she added, hoping she was right.

Molly waddled up the stairs bringing the kettle of hot water and laying it on the floor by the washstand. "Now, missus. Let t' dog see t' rabbit! Yer first ah hear?"

Laura nodded but as the minutes went by Molly gave her a look and asked her again, "Sure it's yer first? From what ah can see … But hey, lass, tha'd not be t' first t' 'ave a secret from yer man. Ah'll say nowt, tha can be sure o' that." Laura gave a weak smile in response and then grimaced as another pain gripped her.

The hours seemed to blend into each other. This time it was different. This time the babe had gone full term, not like the other time when its time had been cut short and it had not gained maturity and fullness of form like this one. And it was far harder work. It might be a second time, but it seemed to her that it would never end and she could bear no more. And then, at that point she was asked to make the added effort to push. And push she did with all the force that she could muster.

Annie was hovering around the hallway, then sitting on the stairs chewing at her nails. It wasn't as if she didn't know what was happening. The hovel they had inhabited had been witness to many a birth, and not all ended well. The groans and yells were not new to her ears. But nevertheless she was torn between running outside and covering her ears with her hands to muffle the tortured howls from upstairs, or else going up to be with the woman who had begun to supplant the place in her heart that had belonged to her mother. But Molly had said quite firmly, "No place fer 'ee lass. Tha'll know when 'tis time t' come up."

It was already well into the evening. No meals had been made and Annie started to feel the gnawing pangs of hunger in her skinny belly. She found some bread and smeared some butter on it, while she debated if she should stir up the stove, which had all but gone out again, and boil up the broth that sat in a pot.

Then it seemed like two things happened simultaneously. The lock rattled and the door swung open, as George shook the rain off his hat and strode into the hallway. At the same time a loud and long yell came from upstairs, followed by silence. As George froze, there followed the sound of a whimpering cry. Looking at Annie who was standing straight ahead of him in the kitchen, a mouthful of bread half-chewed, he headed up the stairs two at a time, arriving to find Molly wiping the newborn clean. Laura lay back upon the bed, strands of her hair, dark with sweat, stuck around her forehead in curly tendrils. Not sure who to look at first, he was preempted by Molly stating, "Tha 'ave a fine lusty son, Mister."

Striding over to look at his new son, George was overcome. A son! Turning to look at Laura, his smile all but split his face in two as he turned to sit on the bed and grasp her hand in both of his. "Tha've done well lass. A son to carry on t' name." Molly's tutting broke the moment as she shooed him out of the room, saying she would call for him when all was done and tidied up.

Returning to Annie, he found her sitting on the bottom step of the stairs. Sweeping her into his arms he gave her the good news.

"What'll 'e be called Da?" she asked.

Without a moment's hesitation he replied, "Henry. Like yer Grandda."

25

Over the next few days, life settled into a new rhythm around the newborn baby. George stayed home all the next day but then he left that evening to go back to the river. Annie stayed away from school for the next few days, insisting that her new baby brother needed her. Laura was soon up and about, the luxury of lying in bed for a fortnight after the birth not for the likes of them. And anyway she was fit and healthy and she soon resumed all the duties of a household – after all, wasn't that her place as a wife and mother? Annie grudgingly went back to school but was sure to run all the way home, coming through the back yard and making straight for the baby's crib, if Laura was not already nursing him in the kitchen by the stove. He was thriving and it was with relief that Laura could put the previous outcome of her first pregnancy out of her mind. She could give George many more babies, healthy sons and pretty daughters. For the first time in many years, she felt a sense of peace and contentment. They had a secure future ahead of them and she pushed any other thoughts to the back of her mind.

Annie wanted to show grandfather the new baby, and Laura knew she could not avoid going over the bridge to the yard that backed on to the river any longer. She had Annie with her, and George's sister Frances said she would try to meet them at the house, or else she would see them when she brought the old man's dinner down later. It would be their first meeting and Laura was a little apprehensive, knowing what George had told her of Frances. Approaching the Ouse Bridge, Laura found her chest tightening and her breath becoming fast and shallow. It was only Annie's excited chatter that kept her mind focussed on making her feet keep moving. Avoiding looking at the river and keeping her eyes on the baby and then looking up at the church that sat at the top of Skeldergate, she forced herself to cross the bridge, dodging the people that were crossing in either direction and the clatter of horses hooves and rattling carts.

Turning left to walk along the staith that ran parallel to the river, Annie slowed her steps and whispered quietly, "That's where Hannah were drown'd." Tears started to fill her eyes and Laura had to push the thoughts of other times, other drownings to the back of her mind. Taking her hand in hers, Laura lifted her head and taking a few deep breaths, headed for one of the yards that lay behind the staith. Here was where grandfather lived and where George had grown up, next to the river, with his siblings. His father had been a waterman, and most of the sons had followed in his footsteps. It was as inevitable as the river flowing to the sea. It was in their blood and the river was their livelihood. And now it had to be hers. This was not something she felt at ease with, but she would be strong and vigilant.

I know what you are like. When you took him from us, you were vindictive and cruel. There was no need. I did not know any better. You took advantage of me. Now I am older and wiser. I will keep my little ones close. They told me I must have lost my mind. Maybe they were right. You took my sanity – albeit for those few moments. Papa saw something in me – something he recognised but would not admit. Pushing me away was his way of denying what he himself knew. And I paid the price ...

Annie ran ahead as the door to the small waterside dwelling came into view. The house had a small yard at the back which was bounded by a wall. Behind it there was a slope down to the staith and the river, but at times when the river flooded, the water could rise and flood into the yard. There was always a dampness about the place and it proved an unhealthy area for families to grow up. But these were the dwellings of the men who plied their trade on and by the water. It made sense to live next to your source of income. And it had ever been so.

Shouting out as she opened the door and ran in, Annie announced their arrival and then came back to bring Laura into the dark interior. The room was small and dark, only lit by one small window which faced out onto the walkway. In a corner in an old threadbare armchair sat the hunched figure of George's father. He was struggling to wake from slumbering, the fire in the grate barely giving any heat, having been ignored for an hour or more. Annie knelt at his feet and took his hand gently, encouraging him to consciousness. As he began to focus more clearly, he took in the figure of Laura as the baby started to waken in her arms.

"Ann – is't you 'ome? An' t' babby 'e be needin' fed," his voice feeble and cracked.

"Grandpa – 'tis Laura that 'as married Da, your son George. Remember? 'Tis no' Granny Ann. She's gone Grandpa," Annie explained while patting his hand to encourage further attention.

He struggled to rise from the chair, Annie taking his arm, and straightened slowly, while peering through the gloom to try to focus on the figure he saw through eyes grown dim with the passing of the years.

"Is't George's wife – is't Sarah?" he croaked.

Taking a step forward, Laura spoke in a clear voice, "I'm Laura. George and I are married. We married – a while ago – in Leeds and I have brought your new grandson to meet you. He is called Henry, after you." Unwrapping the shawl from around the bundle she held, she turned sideways so the old man could gaze upon his namesake.

"Henry," he whispered, "Ah had a son called Henry. 'e drowned."

"This is your grandson and he is strong and healthy," Laura explained, pulling down the folds to further expose the baby's face.

"A bonny wee babby," he agreed. Moving towards the back of the house he added, "A cup o' tea t' wet t' babby's head, or mebbe summat stronger?"

"Tea will be lovely, thank you," Laura hurriedly replied.

And with that, Annie piped up, "Ah'll help 'ee Grandpa," as she darted ahead of him into the kitchen as Laura recalled that of course, she would know where everything was, having lived there for the few months after George brought his daughters here.

Laura laid the baby on the chair that Grandpa had vacated, it being the only soft or padded surface in the room. Following them into the small kitchen area she found Annie already putting the kettle on to boil, having raked the stove embers to life. Looking round for cups to help lay the table, Laura was dismayed to see the piles of unwashed items in the basin and leftover crusts and peelings in a heap at the side. Rolling up her sleeves, she could not help herself beginning to start to tidy up the hovel.

After some semblance of order was brought to the place, Annie poured tea into the mismatched cups laid upon the scarred and worn table at one side of the small room. Laura had baked some scones and had the fore-sight to bring butter and jam with her. Lying them on a cracked plate, she sat on the other side facing Grandpa. He was more interested in the treat of scones with thick strawberry jam upon them to pay anyone much attention. Laura wondered when he had last eaten, as he made the best effort he could to chew with the few teeth he had left. Slurping his tea in between vigorous sessions of mastication, he dribbled more down his chin onto the tattered woollen waistcoat, already witness to many other missed mouthfuls. Annie dabbed ineffectu-ally with an old rag that seemed to be used as a drying cloth, obviously having done this on many an occasion previously.

At the sound of the baby stirring in the other room, Annie announced she would go and see to him, while Laura could talk to Grandpa. Leaving the two of them in the kitchen, she walked through the open doorway and knelt by her little half-brother, cooing and sooth-ing him. Having finished the small confections that they had brought, Grandpa leant back and attempted to straighten up his stiff and arthritic back. For the first time since they had arrived, he looked directly at Laura, as if trying to recognise who was in front of him. Screw-ing up his eyes and leaning forward to try to bring her face into focus, his eyes suddenly grew wider and his hand flew to cover his mouth as he took a gasp. Laura's smile did little to reassure him as he started to visibly shake, his rheumy cloudy eyes fixed on her pale clear ones, with their dark ringed irises.

"No. No! Go 'way!" his voice grew louder and more agitated as he struggled to get to his feet. Staggering back and trying to get his balance, he reached out for the wall and followed it, backing away from her.

"What is wrong Grandpa!" Annie shouted as she came through from the other room. "'Tis alright. 'Tis Laura, Da's new wife. Me stepmother. Tha remembers." Taking his arm she helped him steady himself but he found it impossible to tear his gaze away from Laura's face – and eyes. Eventually Annie managed to get him through to sit in his armchair, having handed the baby to Laura.

"I appear to have upset your Grandfather. He must have thought me someone else."

"Don' fret, it 'appens sometimes. 'E gets confused," Annie tried to reassure her. "'e'll sit 'ere in his chair an' 'fore ye know it, 'e'll be dozin' again an' when 'e wakes up, 'e'll 'ave forgot all about 't."

Leaving the old man sitting in his chair, already beginning to calm down, they collected their things and prepared to leave. As they did so, he looked towards them and said, "Is that you Ann? Tha makin' a cup 'o tea?"

"No Grandpa. 'Tis just us. We'll be back again soon." And with that Annie put her arms around the old man's neck and planted a kiss on the sunken stubbly cheek. "Aunt Franny 'll be along wi' yer dinner soon. Bye fer now."

But as the door closed behind them, the old man stirred again and looking out into the distance he spoke to an invisible terror. "Tha said we were all square. Tha said ye'd never come again – until ..." but any other words were lost as the sound of their footsteps echoed off the walls of the brick built dwellings that led up the lane to the staith.

As they reached the church on the corner, Annie said, "There's Aunt Franny!" and waved at the approaching woman who was carrying a basket with a cloth over it. Under her bonnet there was a pinched face with a distinctly beak-like nose and small dark eyes. Laura's first thought was how unlike her brother. By the time they grew level, each woman had had a few moments to appraise the other and Laura was not sure if she had passed muster.

Acknowledging her with a thin smile and a nod of her head, Frances piped, "Good afternoon Laura. We meet at last. An' ah see that we 'ave a new member t' family. George tol' us tha gave birth t' a fine son." At that Laura uncovered Henry and let his aunt see him. "Bonny lad," was her only response. Looking under her bonnet up at Laura's face, she was immediately mesmerised by her eyes, finding herself both transfixed and yet uncomfortable at the same time. She had never seen any like them. It was the sound of Annie's voice that broke the spell.

"We've been t' see Grandpa but 'e's in a muddle again," Annie informed her. "But we 'ad some tea an' scones t'gether. We left him in 'is chair."

"Ah see," replied Frances, "Well ah'll see how 'e is an' leave 'is dinner wi' 'im for later. Ah look forward t' seein' 'ee again Laura. Perhaps tha'll find time t' come for tea someday." The last was a statement rather than an invitation and Laura had the distinct impression that Frances was far from pleased at the new wife George had acquired. As for looking forward to another meeting, Laura was similarly unconvinced about that.

Frances continued on her way, picking her skirts up to avoid a heap of horse dung on the road way and turning down the staith. Pulling herself upright and examining her thoughts about her first impressions of her new sister-in-law, she found herself ambivalent – unlike her, who usually had an opinion about every-thing – and a strong one at that. Wondering what her father had made of Laura, she approached the battered old door of the small dwelling where he lived and she wondered whether he would recognise her today. From what young Annie had said, he appeared to be in one of his confused states. Pushing open the door after a per-emptory knock, she walked into the gloomy interior.

Time for waiting is over.

I see you met my ... envoy, shall we say?

Are you listening? I know you can hear me.

Come closer ... listen ... listen ...

26

AWFULLY SUDDEN DEATH

On Monday last, an inquest was held in Skeldergate, in this city, by J.P. Wood, Esq., coroner, relative to the sudden death of Mr Henry Shipton, a coal dealer living in Simpson's Yard, Skeldergate. The deceased was 62 years of age. On Saturday afternoon he went into the yard adjoining his house and looked over the wall upon the river Ouse, he being at the time in reasonably good health. According to his daughter who had just arrived with his dinner, he returned into the house, having been suddenly seized with illness. He placed his hand upon his chest, and was seen to stagger. Assistance was rendered to him, and he was placed upon a couch. Observing his daughter present he exclaimed "Oh Franny," and died almost instantly. Dr Arthur was called in, and it appeared from the evidence he gave before this Coroner that sudden death had occurred within minutes of his arrival. He examined the body after death, and was of the opinion that the deceased had died from a severe paroxysm, or attack of neuralgia, which caused reflexed action of the nerves on the side affected, which in turn produced spasmodic contraction of the heart and death. The jury returned a verdict in accordance with the opinion expressed by Dr Arthur.

Yorkshire Gazette

Another funeral, and so soon after the last. Laura and George once more stood in the chilly church together, while the family said their farewells to the old man. In these times funerals of young and old were frequent but it did seem that George was suffering more than most. In the space of nine months he had lost his wife, his daughter and now his father. The Lord was not being very merciful in watching over his family, he thought. A darker thought crossed Laura's mind. Once more she seemed to be the link that bound them together after her acquaintance with George had been made. She shook those menacing ideas from her mind, thinking of the future instead and hoping they could continue their life together with brighter prospects. After all, none of it was her doing.

Did he see something in me? It was all kept quiet but I heard the hushed voices and the mumbled discussions behind closed doors. I heard the housemaids whisperings. At first I was too young to understand, but as I grew I was treated differently by my oldest siblings and my father. Once I heard him shout at my mother, 'She is different to all the others. Where does she get her looks from? Not from my side of the family I'll be bound!' But Mama merely said that often one of the family would inherit their appearance from a long gone member of their lineage. Papa was always distant and cold with me. I never really understood why. Not till a lot later ...

Little Henry was thriving, Annie was settling into her schooling and Laura was enjoying the routine of being mistress of her own home, albeit a modest one at the moment. In time she hoped that she could encourage and support George and that they could build a secure future for their family – if she was blessed with more children, which she hoped she would. Ambition was not a bad thing in this life. She felt a jolt as she realised that she could almost hear her father's voice, his bombastic tones as he laid forth at the dinner table. A shiver came over her as she pushed those thoughts out of her mind and scrubbed harder at the collar she was washing, her arms up to their elbows in hot soapy water in the yard behind the house.

George would be home that evening, if his trip went to plan, and she was well aware that he needed her comfort as well as her support, especially now. He was not a man to think much of the future, the present was of more concern to him, but nevertheless he was biddable and had a gentleness about him which she was thankful for. And he was willing to listen to what she had to say. Something not all husbands are keen to do, she thought wryly, her thoughts flitting back to her overbearing father again. A good team, that's what we make, she thought to herself. Yes, a good team, and with that she set to again, scrubbing the grime out of the work shirt she held in her hands.

Annie's schooldays would be coming to an end soon. Already she was attending beyond the age of many of her contemporaries. Laura wanted to give her the best chance but even she had to agree that Annie was not a particularly gifted or able scholar and that convention dictated that her next step would be to seek a position for her in service locally. For now, she was happy to undertake some of the household chores and look after baby Henry when Laura's hands were full. It saddened Laura to think that Annie's lot in life would be much the same as many generations of women who went before her. Time in service, followed by marriage to someone of their own class and a hand to mouth existence, never rising above the level they had started at.

Laura was fortunate in that her family had been in trade and therefore elevated her to a class above. And when her father's business acumen enabled him to climb even higher up the social ladder, his children benefitted from that escalation, making better marriages than they might have previously. Of course, for the girls this was merely a way for her father to ally his with other families with prospects. Laura decided that she would broach the subject with George soon. If his business could be made to succeed, perhaps in a few years he too might be able to unite his family with another of similar standing through making an advantageous marriage for Annie.

My father made investments, so my brother told me. The railways, the docks, trade. He had an eye for a good deal. He made his money by being shrewd. I did not appreciate what that meant. Did shrewd mean 'distant and uncaring'? For that is how he appeared to me, a child looking for approval. Later I found out that he had started life as an apprentice bootmaker. Learning his trade from his uncle, who then died childless, leaving him the business. From there he never looked back, acquiring another shop for far less than its worth from a local tradesman who made some bad investments and went bankrupt. And he never looked back. Always mixing with others who had their ear to the ground and knew where a good bargain might be struck. His family were of secondary importance. And I fear his wife, my mother, was further down the line in importance.

Annie was in bed and little Henry had had his fill at her breast. The rattle of the door handle made her look up from the mending she was doing at the kitchen table by the light of an oil lamp. As she laid it down, George came in and his face broke into a grin as he swept her into his arms and planted a kiss upon her upturned mouth.

"'Ee lass I've missed 'ee," he mumbled as he buried his face into the crook of her neck, his stubble rubbing against her skin.

Pulling away enough to look at him she asked, "The trip

went well?"

"Aye lass, indeed it did. An' there's promise of 'nother customer. Robert put me wise."

"That's good news indeed. You are doing well George. You will soon have a fine business for you and your sons to work at," she smiled back at him, catching his eye while she smoothed back a wayward lock of his hair.

"Aye, sons. More sons – that's what ah want. Cum 'ere," and with that he pulled her to him, his kisses more urgent and demanding. Absence always increased his passion – and hers if truth be told. She would not deny him, not when her own body was responding so unmistakeably. Already his breath was hot upon her neck, and his hands seeking out the familiar places he visited in his lonely dreams and found on his return. Dragging himself away from her for but a moment, his eyes met hers and he was lost. Reflected in the clear pools he saw the mirror-like translucence that he always wanted to immerse himself in. They dragged him down and drowned him in their bottomless depths.

Sweeping her off her feet, he carried her up the stairs, his strength honed by the daily work of hefting and carrying, heaving and loading. She was but a feather in his arms and he soon had her on the bed in their room. Her body had filled out in all the most appealing places, although she was still slim and lithe, her movements flexible and complementing his own vigour and muscularity. Drowning, dissolving, melting until everything was spent.

George greeted her next morning by pulling her close as the first light of dawn crept over the rooftops. Just as she started to respond to his caresses, becoming roused from her sleep, baby Henry started to whimper and demand to be fed. As she made to pull away, George tried to restrain her and hold her tight, but Henry was not in a mood to wait and she knew that soon he would be giving vent to full volume shrieks that would brook no hesitation in responding to his demands. Regretfully she pulled away as George reluctantly released his hold on her. Picking the child up from the small wooden crib at the side of the bed, she returned to sit back and cradle him close. The baby's cries had also woken Annie and soon her footsteps could be heard as she tapped down the wooden treads of the stairs and into the kitchen to light the stove, one of the jobs she was well used to doing for Laura, if her hands were full with looking after Henry. This time her hands were full with George as well, but he had to be content to look on as the babe fastened on eagerly to her breast and began to suckle greedily.

"He's growing strong George," she smiled at him over the head of the child at her breast.

"Thank God – an' thank 'ee as well. Tha've given me a bonny son," George beamed back at her, pulling himself closer to revel in the union of mother and child.

"Go downstairs. I'll be down directly. I baked a pie yesterday that you can take with you today."

Reluctantly George raised himself from the bed, the covers crumpled and bearing witness to their time together. His footsteps clattered down the stairs and soon she could hear him and Annie talking together. She had started to stoke up the fire from the embers of the previous night using some screws of paper and other things that would burn to coax it into life, then adding small pieces of coal to get a good heat going. Without being there Laura knew the sounds of her house and she knew that the sound of water in the sink would accompany George splashing his face to greet the day. A small mirror hung over the sink, and she could imagine him looking in it and appraising his appearance and preparing to shave. A few moments later the sound of a razor being stropped accompanied by the kettle being swung over the fire indicated he would soon be pulling faces in the mirror as drew the blade across his chin, much to the amusement of Annie who always laughed at the grimaces he made that went along with this routine task.

Once they had eaten and daylight had come fully to break the gloom of the small kitchen, he would be off again on his usual route, transporting the black cargo that fuelled the homes and factories of the towns and cities of Leeds and Castleford, York and Selby, Goole and Hull. Industries were springing up everywhere and towns were spreading as workers were drawn to the towns to gain work which was poorly paid but regular. In response tenements and courts of back to back houses were being hastily constructed to home them. Whole families might be employed in factory work, the youngest children, some under ten years old, bringing home a weekly wage to add to the family's income. By the time any girls had reached their teens they would be employed in the mills or the factories, and as soon as mothers had come to the end of their child bearing years, they would be there also. Sons would bring in better wages than daughters or women so there was a great reliance on the money they brought home to add to the family's income. And this was especially so if the father was to be injured, rendering him incapable of work, or worse still if he died. Then reliance on the male wage earners became even more important.

Laura knew why George wanted sons, sons equalled security, and that was what she hoped she could give him. She was hoping that Annie could start soon in domestic service, not wanting her to undertake factory work if possible. She would start making enquiries about homes needing a young scullery maid or similar. Although George was bringing in a steady income, they were far from financially secure and with one less mouth to feed, that would ease the situation a little. Her thoughts turned to Eliza. Perhaps her sister might know of someone requiring a girl. She determined to write to her soon.

27

As she put pen to paper, her thoughts returned to her childhood, when she and Eliza would practise their handwriting at the table in the parlour, usually copying out a few verses from the bible, while their mother would sit at her sewing. Their father would be in the overstuffed chair nearest the fire and one or other of her brothers would be deep in discussion with him about matters of the day, read from the newspaper that he held in his hand. Her mother would offer no opinions, and indeed, she would not have been expected to voice any thoughts of her own on such matters.

Mama was a pale bird-like creature with huge dark eyes, which at one time may have been a source of attraction for my father. She, of course, came from good merchant stock, and was therefore deemed worthy of my father to be acquired as an alliance with others of his perceived station. She gave him eleven children in sixteen years. I never saw him give her a comforting arm or a kind word. She was simply there as a partner in the most basic of terms, consideration for her deeper emotional needs were quite absent. She had his guardianship – what more would she require?

In her letter to Eliza, she inquired after her health, and that of Charles and the children and informed her of the continued good health of baby Henry. A few more pleasantries were added and then she came to the reason for her letter. Although she would have preferred if Annie could have set her sights higher, George fully expected that his daughter would go into service, laundry work, dressmaking or else into factory work. She was able to read and write reasonably well but with no great aptitude for either, she would not be suitable for any other occupation, of which there were very few available to women anyway. Also Laura hoped that a fresh start in a new place would benefit Annie, rather than having the locations of so many tragedies nearby. It did not occur to her that perhaps the child might need the contact with her family; after all Laura had had to make her own way in life and she saw no reason why it would not be quite possible for Annie to do the same.

Within the week she received a reply from Eliza which commented upon the timeliness of the letter. Eliza had discovered she was once again with child. Charles' business affairs seemed to be doing well and he was making plans to move his family into a larger house. He felt they were in a position to employ another servant or two, and therefore they would be happy to take on Annie in the position of scullery maid, under the watchful eye of the cook/housekeeper whom they already employed. In time she might progress to housemaid, or even nursemaid if they were to be blessed with more children in the coming years. With George coming into Leeds on business on occasions, they would ensure that she could have her half days off whenever possible to coincide. And Charles had also enquired whether George and he might meet up soon to discuss some business propositions of mutual benefit.

Laura was delighted with the response from her sister about a position for Annie. She was also heartened to hear that Charles wanted to continue his acquaintance with George. If they could build on their businesses in tandem, Laura felt sure that this would be a steadying influence on George, giving him direction and encouraging him to further his own interests and give them greater security as a family.

She thought about how to broach the subject with George when he next came home. Deciding to bend the truth somewhat, she sat him down one evening a few days later and told him that a letter had come from Eliza enquiring after their health and informing her that Charles would be pleased to meet up with George the next time he was in Leeds as he had a business proposition for him. George was obviously impressed that he had been so favourably mentioned by Charles and said that Laura should write back soon when he had details of his next trip there. Then she told him about Eliza's news and that they were planning to move up in the world with a bigger house, and that they were in need of more servants.

"In fact, she asked about Annie and what your plans were for her employment, being now of an age to cease her schooling. If you are agreeable, she has said that she would be happy to have her as scullery maid under training from her own cook/housekeeper. What do you think George?" she asked.

"Well, I 'adna thought t' lose 'er so soon. But ye're reet, she'll need a job soon. Better wi' som'un we know than a stranger," he considered. And adding sadly, almost to himself, "Last link wi' Sarah."

Standing behind him, she put her arms round his shoulders and leant in close. "I know, it is hard on you. But you have Henry and me now. It would be a fresh start for Annie, away from the places which must hold such sad memories for her."

"S'pose so. She'll miss 'er da though," he added.

"Eliza has said you may meet up with her when you are in Leeds on Annie's days off. If you let them know your dates, then they will hope to allow this to happen. And of course, then you will be meeting Charles to discuss business too," she added, playing to his sense of vanity at being sought out by a man such as Charles.

And so it all seemed to be planned out. They sat Annie down the next morning and told her of the offer of a position in Eliza's household. At first she was visibly upset at the thought of leaving the only decent home she had known in the last few years, but then Laura explained that if she were to stay in York, it would only cause her more sadness, being reminded of the tragedies she had been party to. And when her father was able to reassure her that he would be visiting Charles and Eliza's home when they would be able to meet if she had her days off then, she brightened somewhat.

"Ah'll miss t' baby," she said, sniffing back her tears which threatened to turn into a flood.

Laura quickly added the news that her step-aunt (for that is what she would be) was going to have another child soon, as there would be a baby in the new household before long. What she didn't say, but knew very well, was that the chances of Annie being allowed above stairs and mixing with the family would be very unlikely. But no need to dishearten the child. She would cope like so many others before her.

George stood and wrapped his arms around his daughter, allowing her the comfort of shedding her tears into his rough woollen jacket. "Nah, nah lass. Tha'll be fine. Dry yer tears." Always gentle to his girls, mused Laura.

Papa was always distant and apart in my memories. He did not play with us – he barely even talked to us. My mother, like all women of her time, knew her place. She was his possession, her ideas and suggestions bore no credence with him, he was lord and master in his own home and woe betide any of us who dared to question him. The boys he treated firmly. They knew the end of his belt was a threat not to take lightly. The girls he merely assigned to the care of Mama and the housekeeper.

It was the first bright day for weeks and it seemed like spring was truly on its way this mid-April morning. Annie was standing in the kitchen with her small bundle beside her, her layers of clothing adding to the waif-like appearance of her face under her little straw bonnet. Laura had adapted one of hers and added a blue ribbon to tie it with and some tiny fabric flowers scattered along the band at one side. Her father was preparing to leave, collecting a tin which held some food for the trip – a mutton pie that Laura had baked yesterday, some bread and cheese, a couple of apples, a jug of beer, some cocoa powder and a little bag of sweets that Laura had tucked into a corner – Annie's favourite, barley sugar twists.

Giving baby Henry a gentle kiss on his forehead so as not to wake him, George then pulled Laura close and embraced her before taking Annie's hand and bidding them both farewell.

"Ah'll be back in't few days, an' ah'll 'ave news t' tell 'ee of 'ow young Annie 'ere 'as joined yer sister's household. Yer Ma would be reet proud, lass," he added, smiling at his daughter, which caused Annie's lip to tremble as she felt even more unhappy at leaving the only place she had known and the few close family she had left

In an attempt to lighten the atmosphere, Laura remarked upon the beautiful sunshine and how lovely it would look upon the water when they left the town and headed out into the countryside. What an adventure.

"Be sure to write and tell me how you are getting on," she encouraged her as she gave her step-daughter a hug to send her on her way. The last she saw of them both was as they turned the corner and headed along Lord Mayor's Walk, the trees just beginning to show a haze of fresh green as the sunlight caught the new buds. A wave from George and they were out of sight.

28

H aving delivered Annie to Eliza's home in Leeds, and after spending a congenial evening with Charles discussing his new business plans over a few beers, George bade them all farewell and climbed back upon his boat, preparing for loading up and an early start the next morning. Already aboard was John Hope, his partner and mate, preparing to bed down for the night in the cramped cabin space. They would be headed down the River Aire to Castleford, where they would unload and reload before the next set of deliveries would take him onto the Calder headed for Wakefield. These were waterways George knew like the back of his hand and ones he had travelled countless times with his father and brothers from a young lad, no older than Annie was now. It was a community split between those families who lived their whole lives upon the river, gave birth there, grew up, courted, married and had their own families and eventually died there, their only forays on to land for baptisms, marriages and burials, and precious few in between, although the waterway inns and alehouses were the exception, and it was there that stories were exchanged, friendships made and arguments started or settled, depending on the belligerence of the combatants; the others were those like George who plied their trade upon the waterways, travelling back and forth but always with a foot on land. Their families would grow up there and use the rivers and canals as their highways, upon which all manner of goods would be transported. Having a base in some town sited along one of these gave them a place to call home, but there was always the need to be back on the water soon enough. It could be thought that these men would have some affinity with the water they sailed, but in truth they looked upon it as a way to a means. It offered no place to play or take your ease. It was rightly respected as one of the greatest cause of death. Very few, if any, could swim.

At first light they were already loading up the boat with coal and preparing to head off through the five locks that would bring them past Astley and Allerton Bywater to arrive at Castleford. There they unloaded the delivery of coal at the Aire and Calder Chemical Works. A voice calling his name echoed across the river and looking in the direction it hailed from, he saw the waving arm of his brother Robert as his boat was drawing up level with them. Unable to stop for any length of time for fear of congesting the busy waterway, there was just time for them to discover where each was headed and plan to meet up in a couple of days at Bottom Boat, a popular overnight stop. George was heading back up to Astley to load up with another consignment of coal bound for Wakefield, so it made sense to meet up there. A final wave of his arm, and Robert was caught up in the traffic heading south.

With a full load of coal, they were soon heading back downriver and taking the left fork to join the River Calder. Travelling through the dusk, they reached Bottom Boat and there moored up, preparing to spend the evening in company of the men they knew and frequently ran into as they all plied the waterways of this part of the West Riding. The local inn, the Ferryboat, was a popular place with the watermen and indeed he was not surprised when seated at a bench was John Hope's cousin Henry, whose boat was moored nearby.

Stories and laughter resounded from the inn as the door opened and closed, beams of golden light flooding the tow path and staith nearby. As the night wore on a few of its customers left with their arms around each other's shoulders as they walked none too steadily along the trackways to their boats or homes in the village, a short distance away.

Having spent that night on the boat while John slept on his cousin's boat, George rose the next morning as the mist was still rising from the river at first light. Already drifting on the still air were the voices of families rousing themselves and the clatter of crockery and the wisps of smoke rising from small stoves as kettles were set to boil for an early morning brew. George did the same and soon had his hands wrapped around a mug of steaming tea, while his breath wreathed about him in the chilly April morning air. This being Sunday, a few folk roused themselves and set off into the village to attend morning service at the local Methodist Chapel in the main street of the village nearby, but George was content to light his pipe and enjoy a few moments of peace and quiet. His thoughts turned to Laura and his baby son at home in York, knowing that before the coming week was out, he would be back there again, enjoying the comfort of his own fireside in the arms of his wife. Surely now, he thought, things were taking a turn in the right direction. He was now owner of two boats and could afford to employ a captain for both. He had a decent home and a new baby son, and hopefully more to come, a wife who fulfilled far more than his material needs, a brother-in-law who was already setting his sights on expanding his business with the possibility of using George's transport to convey the goods required and as a result, there might even be a share of the profits for him in any future successful ventures. Watching the smoke curl upwards from the end of his clay pipe, he allowed himself a smile. Throwing the tea dregs overboard, he went into the small cabin area and busied himself with various tasks he had been putting off and now required his attention. For a start, he needed to wash some socks and soon they were pegged on a line he had strung from the bows to the roof of the cabin. The full load was covered with tarpaulins which rose in a curve, fastened to a spine which rang the length of the boat. This left a narrow ledge along which he could pick his way the length of the gunwales. By the time he had stoked up the stove again, he had a pan on it and bacon and eggs sizzling, making his mouth water.

Later some of his waterman acquaintances hailed him and an hour or two were spent exchanging gossip and stories. As the afternoon wore on, he walked up to the Ferry Boat Inn with a few of them, and as he stood in the doorway he saw his brother Robert approaching from further down the staith. Together they walked into the inn and spent the next couple of hours over a few pints, as George updated his brother on his turn of fortune in being acquainted with Charles and the possibilities that might arise from it. In fact, it occurred to George, though he did not feel it appropriate to say it yet, that he might be able to put some business Robert's way in the fullness of time.

The sun which had shone brightly all day, bringing the first feel of real spring warmth to herald the coming season, was starting to lower behind the trees which edged the riverside, and the lights were being lit in the inn. Partaking of the good food on offer from the landlord's wife, they tucked in and soon had full bellies as well as contented smiles.

The door opened and Robert looking over George's shoulder, shouted out a greeting to Michael Calvert, a local farm labourer they both knew. He worked on the farm close by, living in a tied cottage near it and often met up with them if he saw their vessels moored near the inn. With him was Tom, his son, and pulling up a spare stool each, they were soon all enjoying another pint of ale, while lighting up their pipes adding to the warm fug reeking of ale and tobacco that wrapped around them comfortingly as they sat into the evening.

A while later, Michael suggested they go back to the cottage where he lived as he was sure his wife would be able to rustle up a bite to eat before they went their separate ways. Henry declined the offer and headed back to his boat. The cool air of the evening hit them as they walked from the inn, reminding them that spring was not fully here, and that it had been merely toying with them. The water and the air above it was still chill, causing them to pull up their collars for the short walk to the cottage, set back from the pathway with the dark shapes of the farm, adjoining barn and farm buildings barely discernible, looming in the distance.

Robert had not been there long when a knock at the door heralded the arrival of his wife Maggie. She made it clear that she was here to collect her missing husband, and her with two children asking for their father aboard their boat. As Robert pushed his chair back and stood up, walking away from the rough wooden table around which they sat, the men's looks that they exchanged said it all – who wore the trousers in that marriage? Once Robert was out of earshot, a roar of laughter echoed round the walls of the cosy kitchen. As time went on and it grew late, Michael offered that anyone who wished could stay overnight by the fire and initially George was sorely tempted to lay his head on a pallet in the enveloping warmth of the room. But John reluctantly turned down the offer and made to depart. George then thought better of the offer and said he would walk back with him.

Bidding Michael farewell, the pair made their way out of the farmyard and back along the river to their boats. John suggested they look in on Henry for a nightcap and soon was walking up the plank onto his cousin's boat. His cousin was asleep and had to be roused, reluctantly pulling himself up and deciding to join them as no more rest would be possible with them in the cramped cabin. Although a good few pints had been swilled throughout that day, it was with steady steps that George trod the plank and boarded the vessel, crouching down to squeeze into the small locker which doubled as the cabin. The atmosphere soon become warm and stuffy what with the closeness of bodies and the haze of tobacco smoke, even though they were sitting in shirt sleeves and waistcoats, their coats and caps long shed.

"Ah'm gangin' up top," decided George. "It's too warm in 'ere. Ah need some air t' breathe." And with that he went on deck and sat on the hatch atop the locker, smoking his pipe and enjoying the clear air. Laying back, he stared up at the inky black sky dotted with twinkling stars and picked out the larger groups and constellations, the unblinking points of light marking the distant planets and the moon waxing gibbous, on its way to being full. The light it shed was broken as it shone through the still bare branches of the trees along the banks, making fragmented patterns on the water as it flowed past the various dark shapes of the craft moored along its length. The distant hoot of an owl, the rustle of a creature in the plants that came down to meet the water's edge, the bark of a courting fox returned by another in the far distance, the lap of the current against the wooden hulls, the creak of ropes straining to hold the vessels in place against the pull of the river's flow towards the distant destination of the sea; all these sounds lulled George into a half slumber, although he knew he ought to make the effort to return to his own craft. The river intoned its own lullaby, insidiously wrapping him in the arms of Morpheus. If he heard the sinister whispers, who knows, but he was soon oblivious to anything and everything.

Perhaps the fox or the owl or even an otter may have seen or heard. But no-one else did. The merest splash after he had turned over in his slumbers, unbalancing and tipping off the edge of the locker roof, his forehead smacking onto the sharp edge of the boat and causing him to be roughly jerked into semi-consciousness with the sharp pain of it as he briefly sensed a flash of light before the terrible shock of the cold water hit him. Involuntarily he drew in a deep breath as a reflex action, and in so doing so found that he could get no air. As he was dragged down and out into the current, he floundered briefly in an attempt to gain the relief of life-giving air, but only found himself being pulled down further. His final gasps brought a choking blackness as consciousness left him and he knew no more.

29

FROM: <u>WEST YORKSHIRE, ENGLAND. COUNTY CORONER NOTEBOOKS, 1856 – 1909</u>

ENTRY FOR: <u>GEORGE SHIPTON</u> DIED: <u>27 APRIL 1874 AT WAKEFIELD</u>

Inquest held at the house of Thomas Turner, Ferry Boat Inn, Stanley, Wrenthorp on Tuesday the 28th day of April 1874, on view of the body of <u>George Shipton dec'ed</u>

<u>Evidence from: Robert Shipton</u> of York, Canal and River boatman sworn says,

Dec'ed was my elder brother. He was 37 years old & a Coal dealer & Vessel Owner. He was married & lived at York. Last Sunday afternoon about 3 o'clock I saw him standing at the end of this house. I had left him at Castleford last Friday as he was going with his vessel to Astley & I came with mine to Bottom Boat. Last Sunday we met up and we walked about. He seemed to be perfectly sober & in good health and spirits. At 7 o'clock in the evening we came to this house where he & John Hope, one of his captains & partners, had 2 or 3 pints of beer between them. All 3 of us left this house about 10 o'clock and went to Michael Calvert's (a farm labourer) where we remained about an hour when my wife came for me & I left dec'ed & Hope with Calvert & his family. I expected that dec'ed and Hope were about to stay there that night. Dec'ed could swim a little. He was not subject to any giddiness or fits. About 9 o'clock yesterday morning Henry Hope brought me dec'ed's coat & cap & I went up to Astley. On returning & there being no sign of dec'd turning up I & John Hope & James Hope began to drag the river Calder & in about ten minutes we found dec'ed's body in the middle of the river & alongside of Henry Hope's vessel. The bridge of dec'ed's nose was grazed and froth issued from his nostrils.

Robert Shipton (signature)

<u>John Hope</u> of York, Canal & River boatman, sworn says,

Last Sunday afternoon about 1 o'clock I left Astley with dec'ed & came to Bottom Boat. After walking about we got tea at this house & then went out until about ½ past 6 o'clock. After leaving here a little before 10 o'clock we went to Michael Calvert's where I thought dec'ed intended to sleep. I left about ½ past 11 o'clock at night to go to sleep with my cousin Henry Hope & then dec'ed said he would go with me. Dec'ed & I then went on board my cousin's vessel. Deceased walked steadily over the plank. He pulled off his coat & cap & sat on the locker smoking a pipe. I went down into the cabin & he followed. He said it was too warm down & that he would lie on the cabin deck & he went up. After a while Henry asked him to come into the cabin but dec'ed said he would rather not. He seemed to be all right & cheerful but somewhat talkative from drinking. I heard nothing more of him. About a quarter to 5 o'clock I got up yesterday morning & saw his coat & cap still lying in the Cabin.

George Hope (signature)

<u>Henry Hope</u> of York, Canal & River boatman, sworn says,

About 10 o'clock last Sunday night dec'ed & others left me at this house. I left him about a quarter of an hour after that & went on board my vessel. I was in bed when dec'ed & my cousin John came on board. Dec'ed went into the Cabin & smoked & then went on deck. He sat on the hatches. After a while I went up to him & tried to persuade him to stay in the Cabin. The night was fine. His body was taken to his brother's boat yesterday. His watch was standing at a quarter past 12 o'clock & had only run out a very little of the chain.

Henry Hope (signature)

<u>Verdict:</u> *Found drowned probably accident.*

*****

After the inquest, a group of the watermen returned to Robert's boat to pay their respects to one of their own who had succumbed to the ever-present danger that was a way of life with them. John was left to take care of George's boat. It was with great sadness that Robert cast off his moorings as men stood on the banks or on the vessels, respectfully removing their caps and holding them in their hands, while Robert steered the boat out into the channel and headed back along the Aire.

I have news ...

I have news.

I HAVE NEWS

But the sound didn't carry across the dew-damp roof tops or through the foetid narrow water lanes, over the old embankments topped with the mediaeval walls or through the stone gateways that marked the entrances to the city in times gone by, over the square tower of the minster, the gargoyles at its corners glowing gold in early morning sunshine or through the back yards of the terraced houses where lines of washing hung limp and damp awaiting the first stirrings of the morning breeze. No sound roused Laura from her sleep, the sleep that mothers gratefully fall into between the demands of their babes. The sleep that was deep and dreamless. The sleep that allowed no intrusions from outside bar the whimperings that would immediately cut a swathe through the dark curtains that gave the gift of total oblivion, taking away all the worries and cares of the day. As the first few mewling cries began, the darkness would become fainter and conscious thought would impose itself as the whole world shifted and awareness of the here and now became dominant, demanding full awareness of the needs of the infant. And so she turned and almost with automatic motion, scooped the wriggling infant from the crib and snuggled him to her full breast, aching with its plenteous supply of nourishment.

But soon another ache was also there, deep in her core – the ache of absence, the ache of loss and missing another whose being you have become dependent on, as much as food and drink itself. But she pushed away those thoughts. She must not become lessened by this, she must be strong and focus on her needs for the future, the life she had begun to shape and build for her, for them.

30

May 1874
York

S tanding at yet another graveside – and so soon after the last time. Here he was, laid to rest near his father, his wife, his child. Kneeling to place a few early daffodils upon the hump of freshly turned soil, while cradling Henry against her hip as she twisted to keep her balance, she denied herself the indulgence of tears. They mended nothing. Struggling to stand upright again, she pulled her black cape around her and retied the black crêpe ribbon of her bonnet against the sharp wind that whipped between the gravestones and monuments of those more wealthy than she.

Frances and her husband insisted that they accompany her to pay a call on Mr Marr, the solicitor in New Street. The imposing three storey red brick building stood at the corner of Davygate and upon entering and stating their business, they were ushered up to the first floor office of Mr Marr. Her first impression of him was that he looked like a weasel, and a short sighted one at that. Obsequious in his attitude and simpering in his voice, his eyes were nevertheless sharp and piercing behind the pince-nez that perched on his beak-like nose, missing nothing. Standing and leaning forward to offer his hand first to Frances's husband, then to Frances and finally her, he indicated the seats arranged in front of the large desk at which he sat. Laura irreverently thought to herself that he must have cushions upon his chair to raise him up otherwise he would have been hardly able to see over it.

"May I extend my most heartfelt sympathies to you

madam at this sad time. And to you both," he continued, nodding to Frances and her husband. All three of them nodded in response, accepting his condolences.

"Now, I believe that you wish to discuss the will of your late husband," this was a statement more than a question and he started to shuffle some papers around the desk, threatening to disturb the stacks perched precariously at each end, leaving only the minimum of space in the centre for him to lay the slim folder which he opened and peered at. After a few moments in which he appeared to have scanned the document before him, he sat back and folded his fingers together under his chin, leaving the forefinger of his right hand free to lay against his thin pursed lips.

"Your husband had only recently consulted me. Only a mere couple of weeks ago I believe." Again he studied each of their faces looking for some response, but getting none. "One might say, very perspicacious of him." At the puzzled looks of Frances and her husband, he illuminated his statement by adding, "Forward looking in the circumstances, hmm?" And here he was greeted with their mutual murmured agreement.

"He had only come to me to begin to lay out his wishes, and indeed I intimated that he should arrange another meeting to outline his will with me and add any bequests made from his estate. That being the case, since he was deceased before the will was actually drawn up, it means that he died intestate. It is therefore very clear and straightforward – the whole estate will pass to his relict, you madam," and here he nodded at Laura. "By law you will be the sole beneficiary and as such, I urge you to allow me to deal on your behalf with any outstanding creditors or debtors."

Frances and her husband turned to look at each other, simultaneously drawing in breath.

"Are ye sure?" interjected Frances. "Not e'en for 'is daughter? Or – 'is tother family?" she added somewhat peevishly.

"No madam. The entire estate will pass to his wife, his widow I should say. We only have to await probate, which should not prove complicated. Now may I be of any further assistance at this time?"

Laura was far more in control of herself and quickly spoke before the others could add any further opinions. "Thank you Mr Marr. I shall call upon you in a day or so, if I may, and discuss what we need to do next." And with that she stood, causing the others to do the same. Leaning across the desk, she took his limp hand once more in hers and turned to head for the door. At this, the weasel scuttled around the desk and leapt at the handle, turning it and drawing the door open to allow them all the leave.

"Good day, good day," he rapped out as he ushered them through, beckoning to a junior clerk to escort them downstairs and out into the street below.

Only when they reached the cobbles did Frances explode with all the pent up emotion she had been keeping in check. "Well! It looks like tha've done well out o' it!"

Her husband hurriedly laid a hand on her arm to try to calm her but she was in no mood for it. It was clear that she had to restrain herself from adding, "An' what about us!" Her husband, as usual, said very little, Frances having more than enough to say for both of them. As they started to walk back down Davygate, Laura allowed her to simmer and seethe as she fulminated against the injustice of it all.

When she eventually ran out of steam, Laura was able to speak at last. "I will make sure that the children are well provided for, have no fear on that account. I will let you know if I require your further help. Thank you both for supporting me today." And with that, she turned and headed for home, leaving them both at a loss for words.

When she reached her own door and closed it behind her, only then did she allow herself to give in to her anguish. He hadn't done as she had asked. As usual he only thought about the present, not the future. If only he hadn't died so soon. What position did that leave her and Henry, and Annie, in now she wondered. She would need to consult Mr Marr again to discover what the estate would be worth and also ascertain what debtors and creditors there might be. But first she allowed herself to crumple into a chair at the kitchen table and bury her head in her hands as sobs of frustration broke from her. Once again she foresaw that her life was ruled by men and with trepidation, she realised that she might once more be without the means to be self-supporting. Again her security, like that of so many other women, was bound to that of their husband.

A further visit to Mr Marr, alone this time, clarified the position as regards those who might have any call upon his estate. But there was also the matter of what to do with the boats and his business. At first she thought she was quite capable of taking it over and running it herself, but the solicitor assured her that perhaps that was not wise. After all, it was a man's world – coal and boats.

And she would not have any standing with the business men whom she would have to deal with. Robert, George's brother, offered to take over some of the deliveries that had been contracted and acting on her behalf, hired men to run George's boats and fulfil the orders in the short term.

As Mr Marr had said, it was a relatively straightforward matter to have probate granted and by mid-May she received word from him to call at his office at her convenience. This time she took baby Henry with her, now just over three months old. Making sure he had been well fed and changed, she bundled him up and headed down Lord Mayor's Walk into town, lifting her head towards the sun and drawing in the warm air which bathed the city. Feeling stifled in her black bombazine dress and short over-cape, her face shadowed by the bonnet covered and tied with black crepe, she headed through Goodramgate, busy with traders and purchasers going about their daily business. Once again she wondered at how the world could go on around her, seemingly untouched by the depth of despair she felt in her soul, unaware of her circumstances. But then again, her very dress and manner would mark her out as recently widowed and in full mourning, as befitted a newly bereaved widow. A voice hailed her by her married name and at first she could not ascertain the owner, however as it repeated the call, she spotted an arm waving in the crowds. She slowed and waited for the owner to draw near. She did not recognise the figure who was approaching. He was of average height and with almost white hair which sprang up untidily as he had hastily pulled his hat off to greet her.

"Missus Shipton, ah was reet sorry t' hear about tha 'usband. 'e were a good man an' a decent waterman, very fair in his dealings."

"Thank you," she replied, looking somewhat puzzled. "Were you a friend of his?"

"Oh sorry Missus Shipton, ah should 'ave introduced me'sen. Ah'm William Hoxton. Ah've sailed wi' George, yer man, many a time. We've met along t' rivers an' canals since 'e were just a nipper wi' his father on t' boats."

Laura guessed the man would be about sixty. "Thank you," she replied again, repositioning Henry who was squirming in his sleep, oblivious to all around him having a full belly.

"An' this'll be the babby – Henry, int'it? Like 'is grandpa," he added, walking in closer to peer into the bundle she held. "'e's a grand lad."

"Thank you, Mr Hoxton for your kind words. I have an appointment so I am sorry, I must take my leave," and with that she turned to continue to head down the crowded street as he touched his forehead and stood back to allow her to continue on her way.

Her only thoughts as she walked away was that he seemed a cut above some of the rough watermen and seemed a gentle soul.

Arriving at the solicitor's office, she was once more shown upstairs to his office by a clerk. Inviting her to take a seat, he returned to perch behind his desk, still piled with papers and files, and leant forward to wait while she settled herself and the baby comfortably.

"Madam, I now have notice of probate having been granted to you. The next step is to ascertain what assets your husband possessed in order that we may draw up some accounts and settle the estate. From what you told me before, his effects have been estimated as under £1000 – that takes into account the boats that he owned, etc. but what is more pressing is that we have to also draw in any debts that he was owed and also any outstanding payments he had to make. Is there a gentleman family member that might undertake this for you?"

"I think I could quite adequately manage to do this myself," she replied, feeling irked that he assumed this was something beyond her abilities.

He was visibly taken aback by her retort and looked distinctly uncomfortable as he laced his bony fingers together under his pointed little chin. Clearing his throat, uncertain how to proceed, he paused, then continued, "Perhaps you misunderstand me, Madam. What I mean to convey is that in the business circles in which your late husband undertook his trade, it might be more – er, feasible, for a man to make these enquiries."

Laura drew in her breath, about to further press her capabilities, but then realised that perhaps he might have a point. Men would not be so willing to discuss these affairs with her. But she still intended to keep a track of George's dealings. How else was she to make plans for her, and her son's, future?

"I quite understand Mr Marr." She felt she was diminishing herself in her own eyes, but realised that it was the way things were done and that she must bow to convention if she wanted to be able to move forward.

"Indeed, indeed," the solicitor continued, visibly relieved that she was, after all, taking his advice, which she was paying for by the minute as they spoke. "Now, the next step will be to draft a notice to go into the Yorkshire Gazette, informing all debtors and creditors to your late husband's account to come forward and make themselves known so that we can start to balance the books, as it were. I will do that shortly but first I would like you to avail yourself of a gentleman's help in these matters. When you have done so, please inform me of his contact details so I can keep him abreast of developments."

Laura's mind was spinning as she thought about who she could approach to do this. But she assured him that she would be in touch shortly and with that the solicitor stood, indicating that the meeting was over. Scuttling round the desk, he opened the door for her and bade her good-day.

31

The brightness of the spring sunshine temporarily dazzled her as she stepped out of the doorway and into the street. The shaft of sunlight had managed to insinuate itself between the misshapen and uneven rooftops that lined the streets, which still followed the mediaeval layout from centuries before. Needing time to think away from the bustling throngs, reluctant to move along as they basked in the warmth of the sun, she shouldered her way through St Sampson Square and headed back up Goodramgate. Alleyways lined each side between the haphazardly arranged shop fronts and doorways opened on both sides, inviting customers to enter and sample the wares on offer. As she reached about half way along the thoroughfare, a narrow alleyway opened up on her left and ran between two buildings, the contrast of depth of shadow making it look almost black by comparison to the street.

Without thinking, she turned and entered it, and within a few steps could see the bright spot where it opened out into a patch of green, brightly viridescent, in the strong sunshine. In this little haven of peace within the busy city streets stood the ancient church of Holy Trinity. Its very concealment had perhaps been its saviour as it still had the mediaeval stained glass, miraculously overlooked in the Reformation, when so many other religious buildings had theirs smashed and put out in a fit of religious fervour. Around it stretched a patch of green and beyond that the walls behind which sat the Minster School and in the further distance, the towering facade of the Minster itself, glowing gold in the afternoon sunshine. Some of the graves that were here dated back many centuries, their stones already leaning precariously while other occupants lay in unmarked isolation, their markers lost to time. The contrast was so marked. The sounds of the street and all the hubbub were muted and faded into the background, while the sweet song of a blackbird trilling in an ancient blossoming hawthorn tree gave the place an otherworldliness, beckoning in the burdened visitor.

The baby stirred in her arms as the sounds of the bird permeated his slumbers and blinking his eyes he tried to stretch, unsure whether he wanted to be asleep or awake. Laura walked over to one of the flat gravestones and perching on the edge, unwrapped his shawl and allowed him to stretch his arms and legs in the warmth of the sun. Few people were around and Laura was glad of the time to clear her mind and start to think about the repercussions of what the solicitor had said. She had not been able to get George to allow her access to much of his business dealings in the short time they had been together. And with the arrival of baby Henry so soon after their marriage, little opportunity had arisen thereafter.

This is not the way it should have been. It was all too soon. I had plans that would have secured our future. I would have been able to undertake the role of a sleeping business partner. How I laugh at that term – correct in more than one way! He needed guiding, as all men do, whether they realise it or not. Even my father ...

My father was a man of resourcefulness. He made his own way in the world. He was dependent on no other, his own effort and ambition steering him to his goal in life – to be a man of means. Later I knew how he achieved this. But when I was small I only knew he ran a business in town. He was prosperous enough to ensure both his sons and daughters had an education. The boys were expected to follow him in his business pursuits. The girls were expected to marry as be-fitted their place in society. And then there was me …

As she thought about who to approach to aid in bringing George's affairs together, she discounted Frances' husband – he was an ineffectual man, under the thumb of a shrew of a woman. And not a waterman. She also considered asking Charles, her sister Eliza's husband but apart from the fact he was in Leeds, and he was sure to be burdened with the new business venture he was trying to launch, he was also not a waterman. So the only other obvious option was George's brother Robert. She doubted he was the most educated of men, like George himself, but at least he knew the watermen, the business of coal and he had the respect of the men who travelled upon the waterways. And he had been with George almost at the time of his death so he might feel he had a duty to provide for the widow and orphaned children. And so she determined to contact him as soon as possible and outline what was required by the solicitor. Decision made, she drew in a long breath, letting it out slowly and closing her eyes.

A shadow crossing in front of the bright canvas painted behind her eyelids caused her to snap them open, but then she found she was squinting almost into the sun itself as it silhouetted a figure standing before her.

"Pardon me madam, are you alright?" a voice enquired of her.

Moving her head to try to blot out the sun in order to gain some impression of who stood before her, she made out the dark robes of one of the church officials. Realising she was temporarily blinded, he moved swiftly to the side of her so that she could look at him more obliquely.

"Oh, yes, quite alright, thank you. I was merely enjoying a little peace and ease in this tranquil place."

"Indeed, it has that effect on many," he smiled at her and she could see he was quite a young man, perhaps newly assigned to the parish. As she made to wrap up Henry who by now was curiously turning to try to see where this new voice came from, the man continued, "I am the curate here. I hope you do not think it forward of me to mention it, but I see you are in full mourning. May I enquire how long ago it is since you lost, I am assuming, your husband?"

"You are correct in that assumption. It is less than a month." With that she made to stand and found that she was unbalanced as she was still holding Henry awkwardly while rising from the low stone.

The curate shot out a hand to steady her. "Are you quite alright? Would you like to come inside and sit for a while in the shade and compose yourself?"

Mistaking her unsteadiness for being overcome with grief, he led her up the little pathway towards the arched porch with its open door beyond. He showed her into the dark interior and settled her into one of the old Georgian box pews near the door where she might feel a cooling current of air. Standing beside her, she was able to meet his eyes more easily and saw that they were staring at her quite fixedly. Ah yes, the eyes.

He had never experienced anything quite like it. He felt his head swimming and his feet seemed to release their contact with the floor. He felt held by something he could not describe, something spiritual, but not of the spirit of the place where they were, not of the spirit he served, an altogether more mesmeric and darker force than he had ever encountered. He could have stood here forever, he thought, yet why, what power did it have over him? The edges of his vision were becoming hazy and blurred. He felt that he was looking down a tunnel through which he wanted to travel. It both tempted him and repelled him, teasing and tugging, dragging and caressing simultaneously.

The slamming of a door shattered the moment as another clergyman entered into the main part of the church from a vestry room. The spell was broken and in that split second he felt the pain of a severance, like something he had never known before.

"Please feel free – to sit here – as long as you wish," he gasped, while putting his hand up to his forehead, to wipe away the beads of sweat that had broken out upon it, even though the skin itself was ice cold. With that he turned and hurried over to the other cleric, seeking comfort in the closeness of a familiar figure.

32

K ate was settling back into University life and getting to grips with her studies. She was really enjoying the tutorials, especially the ones where they made links to local historical places. Just before the end of the Christmas term the tutor took them to Holy Trinity Church just off Goodramgate, in the centre of the oldest part of York. With the Christmas Market in full swing in the nearby square and stalls spilling out into nearby streets, it was curiously quiet and peaceful when they came through the narrow alley and into the churchyard. The tutor told them they had walked through an eighteenth-century archway which had been added on to buildings that served as artisans' workshops in the fourteenth century.

Kate was captivated by the scene in front of her. The frost still lay on the grass in the sheltered corners of the grassed graveyard where the low sun's weak rays had not reached. The church itself dated back to the 12th century, according to the tutor, and had been added to and enlarged over the centuries. However, regular worship was suspended in the late 19th century and restoration work had to be carried out throughout the next fifty years. The church had played a very central part to the lives of the parishioners and many of life's important events would have taken place here – baptisms, marriages and of course, burials. He also drew their attention to a blue plaque placed on the wall of the alley they had just walked through which was unveiled to mark the occasion when Anne Lister and her partner Ann Walker took Holy Communion together at the church at

Easter 1834. So there was plenty of stimuli for them to explore in one of their chosen modules. The small group dissipated and spread out around the churchyard, some entering the church and others taking pictures with their phones of the various architectural features. Kate drew apart and quietly sat on the cold stone of a grave further away from the group, wanting to savour the atmosphere and get a feel for the place.

Pulling her hood up over her head and holding it tightly around her ears to keep out the chill, she closed her eyes and tried to imagine what joys and tragedies must have taken place here. The muffled sounds of other students' voices receded and she found herself almost in a trance. A blackbird was singing in the distance and she could feel the warmth of the sun on her shoulders. She felt a tightness around her body and a stiffness unlike the usual freedom found in her baggy jacket and oversized jumpers. Without opening her eyes, she looked down and could see the black folds of a full skirt and felt the tightness of buttoned leather boots instead of her Adidas trainers. There was movement in her arms and she heard the whimper of a baby as it stirred and wakened. Happy thoughts. But then anger, frustration and a sense of helplessness.

"Are you alright?"

Kate jumped, startled by the voice breaking through her reverie. As the images faded, she felt a loss, annoyed at feeling them slip away from her, annoyed at being interrupted. But then she had a sense of disquiet and realised that she felt faint and thought she might be sick.

"You're white as a sheet. No wonder sitting out here in the cold," remonstrated the tutor. "Come inside with the rest. It's not that much warmer but at least it's out of the wind."

Kate looked about her, fully expecting to see the blackbird perched in the blossoming hawthorn tree but instead only saw the stark bare branches and felt the gloom of the day replace the warmth of the spring sunshine. Looking down at her jeans and trainers, she was momentarily puzzled.

"Come on," urged the tutor, and standing up Kate followed him through the doorway of the little church and into the dark interior.

33

Yorkshire Gazette 30 May 1874

GEORGE SHIPTON DECEASED

NOTICE IS HEBEY GIVEN ,that all persons having CLAIMS against the Estate of GEORGE SHIPTON, late of No 4 Wheatley's Row, Lord Mayors Walk, in the City of York, Vessel Owner and Coal Dealer, Deceased, are requested to forward the Particulars thereof to us, the undersigned, in order that the same may be examined, and if found correct, discharged. And all Persons INDEBTED to the said Estate are requested to pay to us forthwith the amount of their respective Debts.

Dated this 28th Day of May, 1874

MARR & SON, Solicitors to the Administrix, 1 New Street, York

Having secured Robert's support in contacting those who might have debts outstanding which would have been due to George and his business, it soon became clear to Laura that her husband had been less than careful about extending credit to those he dealt with. It was as if there was an unwritten code; the watermen looked after their own and when someone needed more time to settle a debt, so be it. It worked both ways. And it also appeared that he had been somewhat over-confident in borrowing money and also running up debts of his own. As she knew, he had obtained the latest boat by paying in instalments so the balance of that had to be settled from the estate. A few people came forward after the notice had appeared in the newspaper, and Robert managed to spread the word on his travels, but it was obvious that George had not kept any proper records and Laura had to try to find what she could among his papers scrunched into the drawer of the dresser in the kitchen.

Over the next few weeks she realised that her position was coming difficult. The ready money was becoming low and she was beginning to feel that she was yet again, less than secure financially. The winding up of George's affairs seemed to be dragging on, not least the difficulties being that his debtors and creditors were spread far and wide along the waterways of the north of England and if they were as disorganised as George had been about his finances, it was no wonder that Mr Marr could not bring her affairs to a close. Contacting Robert, she asked him to call by when he was next in York, in the hope of ascertaining if he could put some pressure on the outstanding creditors to help her obtain some few pounds to add to her dwindling account.

He arrived one late summer morning, just as she was trying to placate young Henry who was teething. Giving him a crust to chew on, she sat down with Robert at the kitchen table, having offered him a strong brew of tea which he readily accepted. Two years younger than George, he looked very like him in many ways, and Laura found herself missing her husband's company all the more. Robert had just returned from a trip to Castleford and was heading off to Leeds in a couple of days. After talking to Robert, it was evident that he was trying his best to spread the word and contact all those with debts and encouraging them to pay up – no doubt his bulk and stature helped send the message home. However, George's creditors were also demanding what they were owed, and although there were not too many of these, the new boat was in the most perilous position.

As baby Henry started to wail again, she hoisted him up onto her knee and tried to soothe his cries. Robert's own son was just over four years old and he could commiserate with her. However, as the cries grew in intensity and Henry squirmed and arched his back, Laura had to stand and start to walk around the kitchen with him, jigging him upon her hip in an effort to staunch his cries. Unable to hear themselves speak, Robert took his leave, grateful to get away from the noise, leaving Laura feeling both stressed and weary, not just with the baby's fractious wails but also when she tried to envisage how they would manage in the future.

The next morning, after a disturbed night's sleep for both of them, Laura awoke to the rattle of the door. Creeping past Henry who was now mercifully asleep, his face blotched from all the tears during the night, she opened the door a crack and accepted the letter handed to her from the post boy. In the dim light of the hallway she squinted at the handwriting. It was addressed to her directly and was of cream coloured paper folded up and stamped. No clue to the sender was upon it so she walked thoughtfully into the kitchen and after stirring up the embers in the stove and setting the kettle upon it to boil, she regarded it again more closely, still unsure as to who had sent it. Letters usually brought news, and all the news she had had in the last years had been far from good. Pushing it away from her into the centre of the table, she rose and quietly looked in on the baby, now peacefully asleep as if the previous night hours hadn't passed with fractious cries. Resolving to purchase something to soothe his pains that day, she pulled her shawl around her and returned to the kitchen, once more to stare at the missive lying gaunt and stark in the centre of the worn table, taunting her with its hidden message.

Filling the teapot and pouring out a cup of tea filled another few minutes, putting off the deed of revealing its contents. But soon there was nothing else for it. Pulling it to her and looking properly at it, she recognised the sender after all.

Unfolding the paper and flattening the creases, she stared at the careful, if somewhat spidery handwriting, before finally focussing on the words themselves.

Dear Sister, I hope this finds you and baby Henry well. Annie is settling into our household although I think that Mrs Grimes keeps her busy so that she has no time to dwell on her recent sorrows. Charles' time is very taken up with his business ventures and to be honest, I hardly see him from one day to the next at the moment, as he is often away meeting prospective backers for his ventures. The children are well and growing quickly. Frederick will be starting schooling soon and Charles wants to send him away to school but I could not bear to see him sent away so soon and have entreated him to allow him to be schooled with Becky at a school nearby. However, in time it will no doubt come to pass. I am keeping well and with God's good grace, our baby should be here by the end of the year.

The purpose of this letter is to ask if you would be able to come to Leeds as I have something I need to speak with you about. Charles does not know I have contacted you and if you were able to come down on the train early on Thursday we would have time to talk before you could get the afternoon train back to York. Do bring baby Henry as I should love to see him.

Please reply soonest,

Your loving sister Eliza.

Laura sat back, laying the letter at arm's length and exhaling while she wondered what Eliza needed to speak about – and without Charles knowing. This was unlike Eliza as she was never one to brook convention or authority and would never normally go behind her husband's back, of that she was sure. Although her curiosity was piqued, she also felt unbalanced and unsettled about what this could be.

It was later that afternoon before she was able to put pen to paper, having given in to all manner of worries and possibilities. Henry thankfully seemed to be all smiles after the tears of the previous night, but his cheeks were still puffy and little red blotches showed where he had been rubbing at his tears throughout the previous night. Giving him a wooden spoon to play with, which immediately went into his mouth and gave him something to chew on, she was grateful to sit down for a few minutes. She had rinsed out and washed his nappies, soiled even more so because of his upset stomach and having boiled them and hung them out upon the line in the back yard, she swept her hair back from her face with a sigh and organised her thoughts as she stared at the sheet of paper before her. Pen poised she thought back over the empty gulf of years between them.

Dear Eliza! I bless the day I met her in Leeds. She was only a year older than me and therefore less aware of so much of the atmosphere around me. And she was married when she was quite young so was soon out of the house. But obviously some of the comments about me must have attached themselves to her. I knew that she had known – something, but perhaps wanted to believe the best of me, yet still she was wary. I can understand why ...

Having kept her reply short and to the point, she said if she got the 8.55am train on Thursday morning, she would be in Leeds by 10am. She would take a cab as she would have the baby with her and would be at Eliza's home within half an hour after that. Having folded up the letter, she put on her bonnet and cape, still in deepest mourning black, and set off to catch the evening post. On the way back she called in at the chemist and procured some Godfrey's Cordial, which she was assured would soothe Henry, giving them both some rest that night.

34

H enry was mesmerised by his first trip in a railway carriage. Initially all the noise and bustle as passengers crowded the platform at the station in York made him fractious but after they were inside he became lulled by the rhythmic motion and sound of the wheels rattling along the track. Alighting in Leeds and taking a cab, she was soon at Eliza's address. Mrs Grimes answered the door and they were shown into the parlour where Eliza was waiting for them. After asking for tea and refreshments Eliza dismissed the housekeeper then came forward to admire young Henry, who by now was sound asleep. Laying him gently on an overstuffed chair, Laura was embraced by her sister, now beginning to show her pregnancy.

"I have been terribly sick with this baby, Laura, else I would have made the trip to York to see you. I am so glad that you came down."

"Of course," Laura replied. "I quite understand. I have been fortunate in that my last pregnancy, my only I should say … was quite uneventful." If Eliza showed a flicker of puzzlement, it quickly passed as she indicated that they should both sit next to a small side table on which some unfolded letters lay.

"I am not sure how to begin, Laura," Eliza whispered hesitantly, and Laura merely inclined her head and looked at her, waiting for her to compose herself. Picking up one of the letters from the table, she spread it open, the thick paper crackling as she did so. Laura could see it was edged in black. Silence opened out and lay between them for some few moments.

"I received this letter from Mama nearly two years ago now. She wrote it to tell me that Papa had died suddenly from apoplexy. I was very ill at the time. I lost a child, born too early Laura, and I could not travel, even if I had wanted to."

Laura leaned forward to take Eliza's hand to offer some comfort for her loss, the child – not their father.

Eliza continued, "I know you and our father did not get on well …" and here she paused to look across at Laura, "so I have not felt the need to speak to you about this, given the circumstances of your departure from our home and family."

Laura could see that Eliza was quite discomfited and as the door opened and the housekeeper came in with a tray bearing tea cups and plates, she was grateful of the opportunity to compose herself and consider her next words.

As the door closed, she leaned forward and began to re-arrange the crockery upon the tray, which had been laid on another side table which had an extending leaf for this very purpose. Laura said nothing, but her thoughts returned to those dark days.

I could not remain. Too many disapproving looks. Mama was the only one. She understood. Of course she did! I was the result of her one moment of feeling wanted and cher-ished. But every time she looked at me, she was reminded of that time. It destroyed her. Half wanting me close, half needing me gone from her presence. Of course, I never knew all this at the time. I just knew that I had to be gone from there. I would not be missed. The censorious looks from my

211

elders, my brothers mimicking their father's attitudes and beliefs, seeking his approval and acceptance and becoming replicas of him; how he loved that. My sisters were soon married off to men of good prospects, chosen by my father of course. Mama tried to quell their nerves and fear of marriages as her own had been – cold and unfulfilling. But what else could us women expect. Money and position. The men earned it. The women were married to achieve it as appendages to their husbands.

As if by mutual agreement, the conversation was halted while the pleasantries of tea pouring and offering of cakes was completed. By then Eliza felt able to continue.

"I had not been in contact with the family much since I married and came to Leeds. And there was such a cold feeling in that house that when I did visit in the early days, I was always glad to return here to the home Charles and I had built together. I am very fortunate that Charles is such a kind and loving husband. Although our father was instrumental in bringing about the marriage, I have been blessed." Here she looked across at Laura who could only smile and say how pleased she was that they were so happy.

Eliza continued, picking up another letter from the table, "I received a letter last week from Mama, the first she has written to me in over two years. She told me she had sold up the house in Hull." Here Laura recollected the time she had stood outside the address when she was at her lowest and watched as strangers had arrived and entered the home where she had grown up. Yes, she had realised then that they were no longer living there but had no way of finding them, if she even wanted to – and of that she was unsure, having left under such circumstances. Would she have even been welcome? And that is why she had turned and walked away, her next bed a pallet in the workhouse. That seemed so long ago but it had been barely two years earlier.

"Matthew and his wife have set up a small hotel in Hornsea and offered Mama the chance to move in with them. She always loved the seaside. Do you remember, we went there a few times on the train when we were young. Little Joseph was just a baby ...." But here she abruptly stopped and looked disturbed and tried to deflect attention away from her words. "More tea?" she added, her voice clearly tremulous, as was the hand that tried to hold the milk jug.

"Tell me more about Mama, how is she?" asked Laura.

Grateful for the question, Eliza continued to fill in some information about her – she was enjoying the sea air which was contributing to some improvement in her health. Matthew and his wife had not been blessed with children so they were glad to be able to have her with them. There were distractions in the form of the guests who stayed with them. Apart from the transient summer trade, there were two regulars who had rooms on the top floor as permanent guests. Both were spinsters and provided some company for her when there were less seasonal boarders. The other family members were scattered around the East Riding, in fact Martha and her husband, the doctor, were still in Hull, as was Ann and her husband.

Laura felt herself shiver at the recollection of the glances and recriminations that she had suffered from her older siblings. There were many dark times, cruel words, harsh deeds and painful memories. She was not sure that she wished to remember those times. But Eliza continued, "Mama has asked me about you. I was not sure how you would like me to respond. After all, your departure was …" but here she let the sentence fall away as she wrung her hands and looked at the floor. "She says she would like to see you, if you could find it in your heart to visit." Lifting her eyes to Laura's, she was met with the translucent stare that conveyed no emotion or hint of meaning.

Laura was at a loss for words. She needed to make sense of the emotions that were tumbling around inside her. Standing, ostensibly to check on Henry as he stirred in his sleep, she gave herself a few more moments to evaluate her feelings. As she tried to tuck his arm into the folds of the shawl, having flung it out in his sleep, Henry started to stir and soon his whimpers filled the silence. Picking him up she walked over to her chair and sat him on her knee. "Here is your Aunt Eliza," she said to break the awkwardness of the moment. Eliza leant forward and cooed at him, holding his hand and tickling him under his chin. Wiping away his dribbles, Laura chattered about what he could do and how he had started teething, and the sisters spent the next quarter of an hour discussing baby tips and remedies. Laura knew she would need to give Eliza an answer for her mother and eventually she said that would consider the request, and that if Eliza could tell her that, she would be grateful. As for when she could not say, after all there were many loose ends to be tied up after George's death. She did not say a lot, but gave Eliza to understand that she had been left in a precarious position financially. In the end she decided that if Eliza was to give her the address of her mother's residence in Hornsea, she would try to write to her at some point in the future, but she could not say when.

"Now sister, there is one more thing I would ask of you today. May I see Annie? I know she would love to see her baby brother and I could not leave without seeing her myself. I know Mrs Grimes will think it quite irregular."

"Of course," Eliza agreed. "I will ask her to fetch Annie and send her to you here in the parlour. I will let you have some time with her."

As predicted, Mrs Grimes thought it most improper that the scullery maid should be entertained in the parlour, no matter who the visitor was, but with a sniff she led the girl into the room and shut the door behind Eliza and herself as they departed.

It was obvious that the housekeeper had not apprised Annie of the reason for her summons to see the mistress in the parlour, as the girl's pale face and saucer eyes showed she was fearing a reprimand. However, one look at who was waiting there for her removed all apprehension and she ran towards Laura and hugged her tightly. Laura could hear her sobs and allowed her to rest there till she felt she could gain her self-control before standing back and wiping her nose on her apron. Then she spied baby Henry and without asking, swept him into her arms and danced around the room with him, causing him to giggle and laugh with glee. It was a heart-warming sight and Laura almost weakened at the thought of allowing Annie to return with them, but common sense prevailed when she knew the girl had to have employment and anyway, she was in no position to have another mouth to feed.

If Annie thought she was being fetched home, she soon realised from their conversation that Laura was here only to visit the mistress and enquire after Annie's welfare. Grudgingly Annie admitted that they were treating her well but, "Ee that Mrs Grimes makes uz fettle reet hard! Ah'm up afowa t'birds an' ah just fall into ma bed a' neet!" Laura laughed but nevertheless had sympathy for the lass. What a lot she had had to suffer in the last year or so. Steady employment in a secure position, learning domestic duties and with someone she knew and could trust was the best solution.

"We must be going soon, Annie. We are going back on the train this afternoon. Your father left his affairs in quite a mess so I'm afraid that we have not been able to settle things as quickly as I'd hoped. Your uncle Robert is helping with the watermen and calling in their debts to your father, but I am not confident that we are yet secure. Now I know that you will have chores to do so I must not delay you from them or else Mrs Grimes will be after us both! Here, ..." and leaning across to the tea table, she bundled up two scones that remained uneaten and popped them into the pocket of Annie's skirt under her apron. Putting her finger to her lips, she swore her to secrecy. Giving Henry a final hug, Annie took her leave of Laura. Henry obviously missed the attention and started grizzling, bringing Eliza back to the parlour as Annie disappeared through the kitchen doorway, dropping her a bob on the way.

"She is doing alright," Eliza assured her. "Mrs Grimes says she has a sensible head on her shoulders and is a willing lass. Not that she would let Annie hear her giving that amount of praise!" she added with a wry smile. "Her bark is worse than her bite!" she added with a whisper and a smile.

By now Henry was in full cry so Laura sat down to put

him to her breast while she and Eliza passed the time with idle chatter. By the time he was sated, Eliza had asked Mrs Grimes to hail a cab and they took their leave of each other, Laura folding a piece of paper with her mother's address into the pocket of her skirt.

35

J anuary came around all too soon and Kate and Jen waved goodbye to Sue from the train as it took them back to their studies in York. As they settled back into their seats, they chattered about what they had done at Christmas and Jen regaled Kate with what she and her brothers had done at New Year while their parents had gone to visit relatives. She shared a few images from her phone and swiped over a few less flattering ones.

"You know you could have come over," chided Jen.

"I know," replied Kate, "But I didn't want to leave Gran, and anyway I had come down with a stinker of a cold. I wouldn't have been very good company."

"So what did you do to fill in the time? I was getting bored – couldn't wait to get back to York," Jen sighed.

"Gran's been doing our family history research. She has already got quite far back." And so Kate began to tell Jen about the generations Sue had found. After a few minutes she could tell that Jen wasn't quite so enamoured with her family history as she was.

"I suppose someone else's family isn't as interesting as your own. It's a bit like sitting through someone else's holiday photos. OK. That's enough. Promise I won't bore you with it any more. Let's grab a coffee when we change trains. This train is freezing and my fingers are numb!"

"Sorry. Didn't mean to sound disinterested," began Jen,

but Kate held up a hand to stop her and they turned their attention to gathering up their stuff to get ready to get out at the next station.

Having changed at Newark, they struggled with all their bags onto the train heading to York and started to discuss the coming term's modules. As Jen was doing a PE course they didn't overlap much on campus but back at the flat they would talk about their day and what they'd been doing.

Meanwhile, Sue was eagerly awaiting the delivery of the two records she had sent for before Christmas – her grandmother, Eliza's birth and death certificates. In the interim she had managed to find the marriage of her other grandparents, Robert William Miles and Annie Beatrice Barford, on the FreeBMD site in 1919. Their son David, her father, had been born in 1922, the second of their three children.

As the first week of January drew to a close, she woke to the clatter of the letterbox and on the mat found the familiar brown envelope. Pulling her fluffy dressing gown tightly around her, she shuffled through to the kitchen in her slippers and switched on the kettle. Taking a knife from the drawer, she slit open the envelope and lay the contents on the worktop as the kettle boiled.

The first piece of paper was the Death record for her grandmother. It showed she had died on the second of January 1947, aged 45. The cause of death showed as heart failure and pneumonia (4 days). Her husband Henry had registered the death two days later and was still residing at the same address and when they had married almost twenty years earlier. A quick check of the dates and Sue worked out that her grandmother had died about fourteen months after the tragic death of her son George when on a training exercise in 1944, as she had learned from the newspaper clipping.

"I wouldn't be surprised if she died of a broken heart," she mused out loud.

Turning to the next piece of paper, she scanned Eliza's birth record. She was born on 5 Aug 1901 but – again, there was no record of a father. Two blank columns.

"This is becoming a bit of a habit!" said Sue aloud. Five generations of girls born to unmarried mothers, or in Sue's case, born to a woman already pregnant at their marriage. But who were the fathers? Would she ever be able to find out?

Returning to the birth record, she noted that Eliza's mother's name was Kate Eliza Hoxton and that she was living in Caistor Road in York at the time of the birth.

"What a lot of Kates and Elizas. This is getting confusing!" she exclaimed, thinking that she needed to colour code the generations in some way to keep her records straight. "So now I need to start looking at the censuses ..." she added.

Standing up she readjusted her dressing gown and made a dash upstairs to the bedroom to throw on some warm clothes and resume her search.

By the time she had grabbed some muesli and made a slice of wholemeal toast smeared with honey, she was itching to fire up the laptop and start her search. Taking a second mug of hot coffee through to the dining table, she opened her file and found her notebook and pens, also switching on the printer on top of the bureau in the corner.

Logging into Ancestry, she found the Census and Electoral Rolls search page and chose the 1911 England and Wales Census Collection option from the right hand column. Filling in the name Eliza Kate Hoxton into the search boxes and year of birth 1901 brought up no results. Removing the middle name Kate, she hit search again and up came 11 results from around the country. Narrowing her birth date round to a year either side of 1901 narrowed it down to four results, but none were in either Lincolnshire or Yorkshire. Sue was baffled and sat back while she thought what to do next.

"OK", she said aloud, "Let's try searching for your mother," and typed in Kate Hoxton instead, removing the date of birth. Still nothing relevant. Then it dawned on her that grandmother had the surname Davis, not Hoxton, so it was probable that her mother had married after Eliza's birth. Entering Eliza Davis and the year of birth either side of 1901 brought up twelve results. Scanning down them she found the one she had been looking for. They were still in York. But clicking on the link brought up the image and squinting at it she could see that the head of the household was a Herbert John Davis aged 41, a gardener working for the Parks Dept, born in York.

Beneath his name was that of Kate Eliza Davis, wife, aged 34. They had been married eight years and in the columns for children it was recorded that she had had two children, one living and one who died. She was also born in York. But beneath her were the names of two sons aged 16 and 12. Kate would have only been 18 when the oldest boy was born – but then of course, they had only been married for eight years. Then Sue recalled that baby Eliza had no father entered on her birth record.

Momentarily confused, she looked again at the columns and scanning down saw Eliza Kate Davis recorded as stepdaughter. Sue noted that Eliza now had the name of the man Kate had married. Was she his, or had he married her mother and given the child his name? Anyway, she was aged nine and a scholar, born in York. The two sons of the father were named James Arthur, a labourer, and Amos Henry, a scholar. At the bottom of the page was the added information about their home – address 9 Granby Road, York and the house had five rooms.

Sue sat back to digest the wealth of information she had now gleaned from just one image on the screen of her laptop. Wow! Doreen was right. You could learn so much from the censuses. So now she could hazard a guess at a marriage date for Herbert Davis and Kate of about 1902 or 1903. Scurrying to open a new tab for FreeBMD, she entered Kate's maiden name and searched from 1902-1903. Sure enough up came a set of names for December quarter 1902. Scanning down the names there were two males and two females and yes, one was Herbert John Davis. Now she had a rough date for their marriage and Kate's year of birth, which would be about 1877. She would find the exact quarter in FreeBMD. Yet another bunch of certificates to send for!

Noting the volume and page numbers in her notebook, she returned to the open tab for Ancestry and sent the image of the 1911 census to the printer. As it chuntered away printing out the image, she saw that by clicking on suggested links in the right-hand column of the search page which she had opened for the 1911 census, she could go back to the 1901 census and possibly beyond. With her hand trembling with anticipation, she clicked on the link for the 1901 census for Kate Hoxton.

Instead of a single image of one household, she now had to look through a group of households but her eye quickly fixed on the name Hoxton. She could see Kate Eliza Hoxton among a group other names in a household in Caistor Road, York. The head of the household was a widow named Mary Simpson, aged 53 and a laundress. There were three names beneath hers. Annie C Burton, 26, a dressmaker, Kate E. Hoxton, 24, a dressmaker and Doris E Williams, 23, a laundress. They were all single women and all boarding with Mary, the widow whose house they were in.

Printing off the image of the 1901 census showing Kate boarding in York and working as a dressmaker, Sue returned to see if she could track Kate back to the next census, the one for 1891. The first thing that surprised her was that it was in Hull. She was in the home of Charles and Eliza Atkinson, both in their fifties. He was listed as a shipbuilder born in Leeds while Eliza was shown as born in Hull. With them was their son Frederick Charles, aged 20, an engineer. Kate Eliza Hoxton was shown as niece to Charles and Eliza, aged 14. Below that were listed three servants – a widow named Doris Grimes (housekeeper) aged 56 and two housemaids – Mary Hall, aged 20 and Isobel Peel, aged 18.

Sue started to add names and dates to the now spreading family tree, but then realised that she didn't know which of the two adults Kate Eliza was related to, in whose house she was on census night. She sat back to stretch and free the crick in her neck, before deciding that she needed to take a break and headed to the kitchen to make another cup of coffee.

T he months were dragging on and summer had already surrendered warm evenings to cold nights. A chill had come into the air and the leaves were already turning, blowing into coloured drifts along the roadways and into all the corners. She was fearing that she and baby Henry would soon be out on the streets or at least looking for somewhere smaller and cheaper to rent. She had started to take in sewing and dressmaking to earn a few shillings, bringing her previous skills back into use. But every day was a struggle to make ends meet and the looming figure of the rent collector at the door each Friday brought both trepidation and relief. The entry in his little book beside her name and the tick that showed the rent had been paid and nothing owing brought a reprieve for another week.

A few weeks later there came a knock at the door and when she opened it, she looked at a vaguely familiar face but could not place it immediately. Seeing her lack of recognition, the white haired man in front of her pulled off his cap and introduced himself.

" 'Tis William Hoxton, missus. Ah met 'ee in't town a few months back when tha were hurryin' off t' an 'ppointment."

It took her a few seconds to recall the occasion, but then she remembered that he had said that he had known George well, and for many years. Apologising for her lack of recognition, she showed him into the small front room where he stood somewhat uncomfortably, unsure how to proceed, screwing his cap in his hands.

"What can I do for you, Mr Hoxton?" she asked.

"Well, 'tis like this. Ah 'ave me own boats an' I spoke to yer brother-in-law Robert a few days back an' 'e told me 'bout how tha were trying to get yer late 'usband's money matters and so on in order. Ah saw notice in't paper too so thought ah could mebbe be of some assistance."

"I'm not sure in what way you mean, Mr Hoxton. Did you owe him money?"

"Naw, naw 'tis not in that way. Ah'm thinking to get me'sen 'nuther boat an' ah thought ah might be able t' buy yon one that George was in t'process of payin' up."

"I see. So – if I am picking you up correctly, you are offering to buy the boat and pay off the remaining payments due on it? So I would then be reimbursed the monies my husband had already paid? Is that correct?"

"Yes'm. That's it. An' – if it's not too for'ard of me, ah wud also be in t' position t' take on some of 'is business contracts."

"Mr Hoxton, you seem to be in a very strong position, money-wise, if you don't mind me saying so."

"Ah'm doin' aw reet, if ah say so me'sen. Ah spoke to Robert 'bout it an' 'e felt that t' were a good arrangement an' would benefit us both, so t' speak."

"Can you let me think about your proposition, Mr Hoxton? And of course, I will also have to speak to Mr Marr, the solicitor. He may wish to speak with you also. Can you tell me where I can contact you?"

"Well, when ah'm not out on t'rivers ah'm at home wi' me son William just up Goodramgate, not far from where ah met 'ee. College Street, off Minster Yard."

"Well, thank you Mr Hoxton. I appreciate you coming to see me. You must think me very rude, may I offer you some refreshment?"

"Naw, ye're aw reet. But thank 'ee all t'same," and with that he made to head toward the door.

After he had left, Laura sat down at the kitchen table to think about what Hoxton had said. She soon began to realise that the proposition he had made her was in fact quite advantageous as it removed both the need to sell the boat and the burden of paying off what was owing on it from the estate.

The days were shortening and the nights were descending earlier and earlier, bringing cold weather and chilly winds which stripped the last of the leaves from the trees, tossing them down streets and into gutters, piled into sodden heaps in corners of walls and blanketing the saturated grass area that bordered Lord Mayor's Walk. Hanging on firmly to her bonnet, Laura turned the corner into the Row and let herself through her front door. Putting Henry down on the rug in the kitchen, she threw off her damp coverings and raked the embers to get some heat to warm them both. Henry was almost crawling now and by shuffling around he could soon reach the side of the stove. Pulling the guard back around it, she removed his coat and mittens, dismayed to find that he had lost one en-route from their visit to the solicitors in Davygate. Tutting her annoyance, she put the kettle on and while she waited for it to boil, re-visited the conversation she had had with Mr Marr that afternoon.

In the intervening weeks the solicitor had spoken to Mr Hoxton and was appraised of his offer. Having con-sidered the options, Mr Marr advised Laura that it was a sensible way to proceed and would give her some se-curity in the short term, which she certainly needed. Having consulted both Hoxton and the owner of the boat that George had been in the process of purchasing, the solicitor had been able to draw up an agreement transferring the remaining payments due to Hoxton, while drawing up an agreement that Hoxton would pay Laura the equivalent amount that George had already put up. Her visit to Mr Marr today had been to put her signature to the agreement, in the presence of Hoxton, who also was required to sign his part, with two wit-nesses, arranged by the solicitor. There were now only a few loose ends requiring tying up before she hoped that the estate would be finally settled. The solicitor would be putting another notice in the next edition of the York-shire Gazette, requesting any further and final demands upon George's estate be forthcoming forthwith as by the first of January, all remaining assets would be distrib-uted and debts paid off.

It left Laura feeling both relieved and uneasy. She was in some measure more secure, at least in the short term, but doubts began to creep in again about her long term future, and that of Henry. Should she resume contact with her mother? The thought chilled her and she pulled her chair closer to the stove, tugging her shawl from off the chair back and pulling it round her. A rush of emotions flooded her as she recalled the many painful times that had eventually caused her to abandon her home and family. No support had come from her mother, but then that was hardly surprising as she was so cowed by their father and totally under his authority. Her siblings were cold and distant after it had happened. What no-one understood was that it was totally beyond her control, although she suspected that her mother knew and understood more than she was willing or able to say. What had happened in the past was firmly locked away in this household, as if a door had been slammed shut and bolted tight. But although the family never talked about it, she began to discover threads that began to help her understand ...

I heard them talking. Muttered gossiping in the basement corridor. I used to crouch in the dark, eavesdropping. I would have been punished had I been found out, but I was a wraith-like child, almost invisible and often overlooked. When I realised I was the object of the conversation, I listened more keenly. But the disjointed phrases and snatches of dialogue meant little at first. ... not like the others ... he can't look at her ... she was crying again ... she ran away, leastways that what I heard ... with child soon after ... not his ...

Henry's chatter brought her back to the present with a start, and she leant forward and pulled him close, thinking how it must have been for her mother. How did she brave the reception she would have got from their father? But he made her pay, every single day. She was sure of it. In that house, you knew whose side you had to be on, and her older siblings chose theirs with grim certainty. And then one by one they made their lives elsewhere, leaving just Laura and this yawning chasm of emptiness and lack of any affection. These were not happy memories and it cut her to recall them, so often burying them deep so that she did not have to become imprisoned by their hurt and submerged in the despair they caused.

So what kind of person would her mother be now? Would she be willing to forgive? To explain? To excuse? To understand? Would she share the secrets that she had locked away which would help Laura make sense of it all? Or would she still maintain the barrier between them, the cold hard wall of silence that blanked out all that had gone before but yet overshadowed everything that had happened afterwards? With a shiver, Laura pushed the thoughts away and consigned them to a place that she was not yet ready to visit, the here and now more pressing and immediate. By the time that she had a steaming cup of tea in her hand, she was already looking to the future and formulating ways to move forward and build a future for herself and George's child.

GEORGE SHIPTON DECEASED

Pursuant to the Statute 22nd and 23rd Victoria, Chapter 35, instituted "An Act to further amend the loss of Property and relieve Trustees"

NOTICE IS HEREBY GIVEN, that all demands upon or affecting the Estate of GEORGE SHIPTON, late of Wheatley's Row, Lord Mayor's Walk in the City of York, Vessel Owner and Coal Dealer, Deceased (who died on the 27th day of April last, and to whose Estate and Effects Letters of Administration were granted by the York District Registry of her Majesty's Court of Probate, on the 13th day of May last, unto LAURA EMILY SHIPTON of Wheatley's Row aforesaid, widow, the relict of the said Intestate) are hereby required to send the particulars of such claims and demands addressed to the said Administrix, at the Office of Messsrs MARR and SON, New Street, in the City of York, her Solicitors, on or before the First Day of January next and at the expiration of such time the said Administrix will proceed to distribute the assets of the said Intestate among the persons entitled thereto, having regard only to the claims and demands of which the said Administrix shall then have had Notice, and such Administrix will not be liable for the assets, or any part thereof, so distributed by her to any person or persons of whose claim or demands she shall not then have had Notice. And all Persons indebted to the said Estate are hereby required to pay the amount of their respective debts to me forthwith.

Dated the seventeenth Day of November 1874

MARR and SON, Solicitors to the Administrix, 1 New Street, York

Yorkshire Gazette 21 November 1874

37

A knock at the door a few weeks later brought Mr Hoxton to her house. Showing him in, she quickly shut the door against the chill wind carrying flurries of snow over the rooftops and along the narrow terraced streets.

"Please sit down, Mr Hoxton. You will have some tea? I've just made a pot."

"Thank ee, Missus. Reet kind, 'tis bitter out and by the looks of 't, only goin' t' get worse."

He loosened the knitted scarf he had wound twice round his neck and pulling off the woollen gloves, he laid both on the table in front of him in the kitchen where they sat.

"I hope you do not mind me receiving you in here, Mr Hoxton, only with just the two of us here it makes no sense to set a fire in the parlour."

"Not at all. T' be 'onest ah'm 'appier here, thank 'ee."

Laura waited for him to elaborate on the reason for his visit, but he merely shuffled his feet and looked about him. Henry had toddled over to grab the side of the chair in which he sat, so he seemed glad to have the distraction of talking to the child, which he did with the practised ease of a father.

Taking her cue from this, Laura asked, "You have children Mr Hoxton? I believe you mentioned you had a son, William?"

"Indeed, we were blessed wi' three girls an' a boy. There was 'nother babby we lost newborn but t' were a long time ago. The girls are married now wi' bairns of their own." At this he smiled in satisfaction. "An' me son William lives wi' me. 'E works as a clerk wi' t' railway," he added with pride.

Laura smiled at him, warming to his obvious sense of pride but wondering if he might feel some sense of sadness that the boy had not joined his father on the waterways. "And your wife, Mr Hoxton? Forgive me, I believe you said you were widowed. Was that some time ago?"

His face fell, and he took a deep breath before replying, "Aye, she's been gone these five years since. She were a good woman, an' she did well by t' family, bringin' 'em up on her own when ah was away on t' rivers an' canals."

"You must miss her Mr Hoxton. Being without a partner is indeed a hard task, is it not?"

"Indeed, indeed. An' 'ow are tha doin' if you don't mind me askin'?"

"Well, as you are aware, my husband died very unexpectedly and left his affairs in a far from organised manner. It has been a very difficult time, trying to keep a roof over our heads, while trying to sort out his estate. Mr Marr has been most helpful. And indeed, I am very much indebted to you, Mr Hoxton. You were like my knight in shining armour, come to rescue us from the darkness that threatened to drown us," and at this she looked straight into his eyes and smiled.

The room was silent as William felt himself held by the

look she fixed upon him. The eyes were so compelling, yet also disconcerting. They seemed to have no bottom to them, as if they were clear and deep and went on for ever. The darker rings around the almost colourless irises framed the black pupils that held his gaze and all around him seemed to become fainter and blurred. In an instant he knew everything, and nothing about her. She seemed timeless, as if she belonged in a different place far from this cosy room in a city street.

It was Henry's squeals that broke the trance-like atmosphere, as the child grabbed at William's jacket and demanded attention from this interesting visitor. The moment passed and they both turned their attention to the child, passing the next few minutes in talking to him and getting him to utter his repertoire of newly learned words.

"Would you like more tea, Mr Hoxton?" she asked, pushing a plate of biscuits towards him as well.

As he nodded in thanks, sliding his cup towards her over the table's well-worn surface, he cleared his throat and seemed to recollect the purpose of his visit. "Ah'm reet glad t' see tha lookin' so well. But ah don't see mes'en as a knight in shinin' armour somehow!" he added with a chuckle. "Tha asked me to come t' see ye. What can ah do for ee Missus?"

"Well," Laura began, "you will think me perhaps a bit presumptuous but I would like to be your partner – your business partner," she added hastily. "I need to have some income to live on and as a woman on my own with a child to raise, doing sewing and laundry is hardly going to allow us to live in much comfort, I think you would agree. George was always happy to share his business dealings with me, indeed I was going to take over his paperwork, accounts and such-like once the baby was born and less dependent on me. At least that was the plan, but his untimely death put paid to all our plans …" and here she turned away and retrieved a handkerchief from her pocket which she pressed to her cheek. Allowing a few moments to pass, while William shuffled in his chair unsure whether to comfort her or not, she eventually turned back to continue. "So, Mr Hoxton, I am making you a proposition. Will you allow me to become your – shall we say – silent partner? Now that the estate is finally settled, I am in a position to invest a small amount into your business, and if you, we, can renew the contracts that George had, then you can increase your business, and with the extra boat and extra business, then I may be able to have a little money to be able to put away for me and my child's future. How does that sound to you, Mr Hoxton?"

William sat back in his chair, and scratched at the sparse strands of white hair at the top of his head. His eyes strayed to look once more at hers, but he found himself both drawn in and repelled at the same time. "Well, it's certainly summat t' think about. Ah'll give it sum thought and ah'll come and see 'ee next week after ah get back from next trip."

"That would be ideal, thank you. I appreciate that you would wish some time to think about it." And as he stood to take his leave, she leaned forward and laid her hand upon his arm. For a moment neither of them moved, and then Henry shouted, "Ta ta!" and broke the spell.

38

William returned as he said he would, about a week later. As he walked up from the river, having moored his boat at the staith as usual, he pulled his collar further up around his ears and stuffed his hands in his pockets. His breath was wreathed around him in misty clouds as he took the slight hill up into the city. Still early, there were only a few folk about as the low sun crept over the rooftops in the east, and those that were about were focussed on the business in hand and not in a mood to stop and chat. The merest of nods or a short "How-do?" acknowledged an acquaintance.

He had had time to think out on the waterways and was somewhat at a loss to understand why he had even thought of considering her offer. After all, he was a man just past sixty, a widower, father and grandfather. He had a few working years in him yet but he had hoped to take those at his own pace, being master of his own decisions, choosing what jobs to take on and slowing down in due course when, and if, the time came. His family were grown; there was no-one who depended on him now. Yes, his home and his bed were lonely places nowadays, cold and cheerless to return to after days, or even weeks, away. His son was working and often would join some mates for a drink after work, so the house was regularly empty on his return. But he was his own master and yes, the last few years without Betty had been lonely but he had grown accustomed to making his own routines and choices, with no-one to consider but himself. Did he want to be tied into the whims and demands of someone else at this time in his life? And a woman at that. And yet, here he was, his footsteps clattering on the frosted cobbles this early February morning, veering off from the direction of his own home and instead leaving the Minster on his left and heading on through the Monk Bar and onto Lord Mayor's Walk.

The trees which lined the walk were bare and still, not a breath of wind disturbed a stubborn leaf that had clung on throughout the storms and squalls of winter. It was as if his feet had a mind of their own. As he turned towards the Row, he suddenly became aware that he didn't know what he was going to say to her. His steps slowed as he approached her door, noticing the glimmer of light that escaped through a chink in the curtains at the front window and another that lit an upstairs room. A door opened and closed a few houses up the street, and he was almost bowled over as a young man broke into a run as he passed him, no doubt late for work. As William turned to remonstrate with him, he shrugged as he realised the lad was already almost at the corner and would soon be out of sight, leaving a swirl of misty breath behind as his only apology.

Turning back to Laura's door, he hesitated again. He had nothing planned to say and his resolve seemed to be leaving him. But doing nothing wouldn't achieve anything, so reluctantly he raised his hand and knocked lightly on the door. At first he thought that he had not been heard, but as he raised his hand to knock again, he heard movement behind the door and the lock being turned. As the door swung inward, a weak light flooded out and she was almost silhouetted, framed by the door frame.

"Mr Hoxton. You are an early bird. But come in, it is far too cold to be standing on the doorstep."

As he stepped into the small narrow hallway, he was

aware that she was only freshly out of bed, her hair still unpinned but in a thick plait that lay over one shoulder. She was still in her nightclothes, he assumed, but over them she had a thick robe and a shawl over that in an attempt to keep warm. Henry was crying in the background, no doubt hungry for his breakfast.

"Ah'm reet sorry, missus. Ah shouldn't have come so early. Ah've just docked an' thought ah'd ..." but here he appeared to run out words. What had he come to say, to do? His mind was a blank.

"I was already up with Henry, as you can see. Well, come through to the kitchen. We all need warming up, isn't that right Henry?" and with that she headed into the kitchen, Henry toddling after her, whining for his breakfast.

Once Henry had been pacified with some bread and warm milk, the two of them sat with their hands wrapped round their steaming mugs of tea. Again, William was at a loss to know what to say, and an awkward silence began to stretch between them after the various pleasantries about his health and the weather were completed.

At last Laura took the initiative. "Mr Hoxton, I assume you have thought about my proposition? And I assume that is why you are here at this early hour?"

Shuffling his feet under the table, William cleared his throat, grateful for a topic to open the conversation. "Yes missus, ah have, an' ..." but here he hesitated. Had he made a decision? What was it – for the life of him he couldn't fathom it out. Giving his head a shake to clear his thoughts, he found his mouth opening and the words just tumbled out. "Ah would be reet glad t' accept yer proposal an' join forces – in business o' course, ah mean." He felt the heat rise into his cheeks – when was the last time a bonny lass had made him blush?

"I'm delighted to hear that Mr Hoxton. I think we will make a good team as business partners. My brains and your experience – no disrespect meant to your previous successes."

"None taken, missus," he hastily replied, allowing himself a small smile, as she reached out and shook his hand. It was small and warm in his large calloused one, but he felt that it was slightly rough from the household chores that she carried out daily. It was a hand that was not afraid of hard work. He felt a warmth spread up from it into his core, even though the moment was fleeting. He looked up at her and smiled again, caught by the shine of her eyes behind the stray strands of her hair, not yet pinned back from being tossed about in bed.

"Thank you Mr Hoxton. Shall we make it official? I am sure Mr Marr would be happy to draw up the relevant paperwork for I would not wish the arrangement to put any demands upon either of us. You will understand that I must have security for myself and my son, and I do not wish to find myself in the straits I found myself in when I became a widow all those months ago."

"Of course, of course," agreed William, nodding and leaning back on his chair.

"More tea?" she asked, as Henry toddled round the table to stand by William's chair, holding up his arms to be picked up.

◆ ◆ ◆

If Mr Marr was surprised, he did not say so and soon the paperwork was drawn up and duly signed in his presence by both parties. Over the next few weeks William continued to ply his trade, carrying coal, timber or whatever up and down the waterways of the East Riding. He was, as George had been, a frequent sight in Goole, Castleford, Selby or Leeds. Men greeted him as an old friend and frequent companion in wayside inns. The winter was a harsh one, and there were times when the ice at the edges of the canals and slow-flowing waterways held up business and delayed deliveries, but as the days started to lengthen and the trees began to burst into bud, William had to agree that his partnership with Laura had been a good move – of his, or was it hers? No matter, he now had three boats running and crewed by trusted men. He had regained some of the clients that George had served, thanks to Laura's correspondence with them, stressing George's good name and her hope that they would value that and continue to feel that they could do business with his widow through her new business partner and well-respected boat owner and coal dealer. And he found that he looked forward to getting back to York at the end of his trips and updating Laura with all the news and gossip from the waterways. Henry also looked forward to his return, running towards him, arms outstretched, demanding to picked up and carried. And William found that he enjoyed this long lost warmth and sense of homecoming that he had been missing these past years of widowerhood. Their lives settled into a new routine. William would return and walk through Monk Bar, his spirits lifting and his heart lightening as he neared the house where he knew there would be a warm meal and a welcome. He would bring little items for Henry – a small figure he had whittled from wood while waiting to get through a series of locks, finishing it off with some details while in his cabin of a night, moored near a waterside inn where he had earlier enjoyed a drink with workmates.

And Laura would look forward to the knock on the door, the comfort of his tread as his footsteps thudded along the wooden hallway into the warmth of the kitchen. He always greeted her the same way, "Well, missus, that's another trip done. How's ee an' t' babby?"

On one of these evenings, as his familiar knock came at the door, she greeted him, impatient for him to sit down at the table so that she could impart some news.

"Mr Hoxton, I have some good news for us. You recall my sister Eliza who I told you about, who lives in Leeds? George had been in discussions with her husband Charles about entering into a contract with him to supply the materials for his new building projects. I hope you do not mind but, as your business partner, I felt I could write to Charles and ask if he might consider your – our new business as one which might be able to undertake the contracts that he had discussed previously with George. I got a letter yesterday from him, to us both, to say that unfortunately he had had to find new contractors to transport the materials he had immediate need of, but his interests were still expanding and he had been commissioned to undertake another project, which required transport of more raw building materials, which we would be perfectly able to undertake. What do you think William?" she asked, her eyes shining with excitement.

He was somewhat at a loss for words, and it wasn't lost

on him that this was the first time she had addressed him as 'William'. After some further discussion, he had to agree that having contacts was definitely a good way to go in business and that if that meant using the good will of family members, all the better. After all, business was business. She suggested that she would reply to him by letter tomorrow, if William was in agreement. Or would he prefer to do so, she asked knowingly, as the male member of this partnership? She had no doubt that he would acquiesce to her doing so, as she was far more literate than he. And so it was agreed.

A few days later, the reply from Charles came. He indicated that he was interested in the proposal and intimated that he would be pleased to discuss the matter with William in person. Laura had it ready to show William the next time he was back in York, which was a few days later.

Sitting around the table, she lay the letter from Charles in front of him. He squinted at it and after hesitantly struggling to read the first few sentences by holding it almost touching his nose, she offered to read it to him as she realised his eyesight was not up to it. When she finished, they talked about it what this would mean to the business and what they should do next.

"Well, obviously Charles will want to discuss all this with you in person and, of course, meet you. You will have your own knowledge and understanding about the details of the trade which I, of course, am totally unaware of," she said, playing to his male pride. "Shall I write and let him know when you will be next be able to go to Leeds?"

William thought this over for a few minutes. Everything seemed to be moving so quickly. A good thing perhaps to have ambitions and aspirations in the world of trade. This was the age of industry and the self-made man; opportunities were there for those who were willing and able to take them, provided they put in the effort. 'Nothing comes from nothing' as his old father had said. Aye, and where there's muck there's brass, he thought ruefully, thinking of the filth that lay over him – coal and brick dust, sawdust and clay. Hands ingrained with years of it and a back bent with the manhandling of cargoes and sacks, steering boats and winding lock gates, all of the sweat and grind. But with it came profit, and then expansion as there were opportunities to add to and expand into another, then another, boat; to employ one, then two then four more men to manage the routes and cargoes, providing them and their families with a living, and adding to his own. Opportunities had to be grabbed with both hands when they appeared. This he understood, although there were times when he felt that all his life had been one long grind and he looked forward to the time when he could spend some time by his own fire, taking his ease, maybe even having a doze while the hours passed and others worked for him. Perhaps with Laura this might be possible. With her as a partner, at his side ... Suddenly the thought crept over him. He wanted more. He wanted someone to comfort and care for him in his older years.

His attention was brought back to the present as Laura repeated her last question, "William – when will you go to Leeds again? So that I can let Charles know?"

"Tha'll need t' be there too. After all, t'is 'ee who's family. An' a partner in t' business. 'Tis only reet. We'll go t'gither. Tha can come on t' boat wi' me."

A chill came over her. "No, no I cannot. We will go by train. We can meet up with you there. I shall write and ask Eliza when would be convenient. I could even spend a day or two with her and see the new baby. And of course, Annie will be happy to see us. That's settled then."

Later that evening, when she had laid Henry to sleep in his cot and William had gone to his own home in Good-ramgate after staying for a meal of ham, potatoes and cabbage, she sat by the table and composed her letter to Eliza by the soft light of the oil lamp. Things were working out well, she thought to herself. How good of Charles to offer this chance to them both. Yes, things were definitely looking up and at last she could look ahead with some sense of optimism, rather than dread.

Having finished the letter, she folded it and sat back, her gaze in the half distance as her thoughts turned to arranging the train and taking Henry there, planning what she would need to take with them and so on. Yes, the train, not the boat, she thought with a shudder. Not the river – no, never.

I went to the river, I was drawn there. The park was left far behind and I carried on walking until the shimmer of sunlight reflected on water acted like semaphore signals, drawing me closer and closer. That's the first time I heard it.

Henry's cries brought her back to the present with a jolt. Her hands were clammy and sweat trickled down between her breasts. Standing up, she felt the trembling in her legs and for a moment had to steady herself by holding on to the table, before calling out, "I'm coming darling. Mama's coming."

39

February 2018
York

K ate was getting engrossed in her coursework and the corner of her bedroom in the flat was getting piled up with books. She had always been an avaricious reader and was blessed with being able to scan-read and retain what she read, almost like a photographic memory. But she was getting sore eyes with straining to read the handouts from the tutor, some showing copies of old manuscripts with faded script.

"I need a break!" she called through to the other room as she stood and grabbed her padded jacket, gloves, scarf and beanie hat. "I'm going for a walk. The rain's stopped at last. Back soon!"

"OK. See you. Don't be too late. Remember we need to tidy up a bit as the guys are coming over later," Jen replied, her voice muffled from under her duvet as she was lying in bed with her phone on and bluetooth earbuds in.

There had been heavy rain for the last week and intermittent sleet and snow. At last there seemed to be a break in the weather but the wind was still chill and the whole city seemed to be holding its breath, waiting to see if the stormy weather really had abated.

Wrapped up, Kate didn't mind the cold. She soon got a good pace going and her breath wreathed around her as she headed through the old part of the city, the minster behind her and the roads sloping down towards the river.

The recent rain and snow had swollen the river and now it was lapping at the banks and threatening to flood cellars and pathways at the edge of the river. Kate stopped for a breather and leaned over the parapet of the Ouse Bridge looking downstream at the water as it swirled and rushed through the arches below her, the occasional bit of flotsam being tossed and spun as it was carried along. She felt herself drawn towards the steps that led down to the staith below. Other people were also looking at the swollen river and taking pictures with their phones or else posing for selfies to send into the cloud and impress friends and relatives. Like them, Kate felt the fascination of watching the water and stood with her back pressed against the corner of the building at the top of the steps. The chatter of the passing throng receded and she found her gaze held by the water.

"At last ... "

She felt sure she had heard some whispered words, but didn't turn to look around to identify the source. She must have imagined them, she decided.

"You have come at last. I wondered when you would ..."

This time she was sure that she had heard the words more clearly. Looking round she was aware that no-one else was near her, nor looking in her direction. Shaking her head, she looked to her right at the lapping waters on the staith below. Her feet seemed to have a mind of their own and were leading her step by step down the worn treads.

Suddenly a hand grabbed her shoulder and she was stopped in her tracks.

"You don't want to go any further, lass. You don't want wet feet and that current's stronger than you think!"

She turned and looked over her shoulder at the owner of the restraining hand. A man stood behind her, his anorak pulled up around his neck, a worn knitted scarf tied under his chin and a woollen hat with a bedraggled pom pom upon his head. His accent she now recognised as belonging to a native Yorkshireman.

She gave him a weak smile and shaking her head, realised that she was unaware that she had already gone down two or three of the steps.

"Of course. Sorry. Yes, I wasn't thinking. You're right," she stumbled over her words. She headed back up onto the bridge pavement and stood a moment longer as she watched him head off across the bridge and disappear into the general mêlée of people.

"What on earth was I thinking?" she said to herself. She rubbed her forehead with her gloved hand and tried to focus. The cold air and general hubbub of voices with the background sound of the surging river swirling beneath soon filled her ears beneath her beanie. She headed back over the bridge, looking down at the Slug and Lettuce pub on the corner and beyond it the Kings Arms pub where the waters were already lapping at the doorstep.

40

T he arrival early one Monday morning of the envelope containing the birth certificate for Kate
Eliza and her marriage certificate in 1902 to Herbert,
had Sue once more dying to sit at her dining room table
and spread out the growing family tree, eager to add the
new information. But infuriatingly she had to wait till
that evening as she was meeting a friend for coffee first
thing that morning and she had her furniture upcycling
class at the community centre after that, so wouldn't be
back home till the evening.

That afternoon as she fired the staple gun to fix the
webbing on the chair she was renovating, her thoughts
returned to the anticipation of what new information
was contained in the envelope waiting back at home
for her. By the time the class had finished and she had
packed up her stuff and manhandled the half-finished
chair into the folded-down back seat of her old car,
steady sleet was driving across the rapidly emptying car
park as everyone headed homeward to warm homes and
welcoming cuppas. Sue was no different and with relief
she pulled up into the driveway, cursing that she had
better get a new windscreen wiper as the right hand one
was making a woeful attempt to clear the view of the
roads she had negotiated in the rapidly darkening late
afternoon.

Leaving her stuff in the car until the sleet relented or
until tomorrow, whichever was the sooner, she locked
the car and dashed to her front door, almost falling
into the cosy hallway as she pushed the door closed

behind her and leant against it getting her breath. By the time she had shrugged off her wet coat and shaken out the scarf she had tied around her hair, she was already headed for the kitchen, her eye on the kettle and thoughts of a steaming cup of coffee already buoying her spirits. Running a hand through the damp strands of her mauve hair, she gave it a shake and snapped on the kettle, watching it light up with the comforting red light.

As it boiled she went through to the living room and turned on lights to illuminate the gloomy room and pulled the curtains against the slapping sleet that bombarded the windows. Walking through to the dining room she looked excitedly at the brown envelope, sitting propped up against her pencil tub crafted out of a misshapen pottery jar she had made at an evening class many years ago.

"Just coming," she said aloud, as if her ancestors were waiting for her. She laughed at the thought and turned back towards the kitchen where the click of the kettle confirmed that a hot coffee would soon be in her hands.

Digging in the tin for a flapjack, which she thought she thoroughly deserved, she carried it and her steaming coffee mug to the dining room where she sat it down on the crocheted coaster by her laptop. She allowed herself a moment of anticipation, before tearing open the envelope and spreading the now-familiar red and green papers in front of her.

First she studied the birth record for Kate Eliza. The date of birth given was 11 Feb 1876 in York. Her father was shown as William Hoxton and her mother as Laura Emily (late Shipton, late Cowper, formerly Harrison).

Sue sat back with a gasp. This was the first instance of the name Laura coming up in the family tree – and yet that was the middle name that her daughter Debbie had given to her baby daughter, Sue's granddaughter – Kate Laura Innes. Coincidence? Or … ? The hairs prickled at the back of Sue's neck as she exhaled, aware that she had been holding her breath while staring at the paper laid out in front of her. With shaking hands, she lifted her mug and took a few deep slugs of coffee to steady her.

Returning to the birth record she noted that William was shown as a waterman and they were living in Wheatley's Row, York. The birth was registered on 15 Feb 1876.

Sue sat back, smugly pleased that she could now add a father and mother for Kate Eliza as well as a date of birth, although she was perplexed by the number of surnames given for Laura. She noted this down as a question to ask Doreen, the tutor, at the next genealogy class. She also made a note to look up Wheatley's Row in York to see where it was located.

She then turned her attention to the next piece of paper; Kate Eliza's marriage record to Herbert. It was dated 18 October 1902 and took place at the Register Office in York by licence. Herbert was aged 32, a widower and a labourer. His father was shown as Albert Henry Davis (dec), also a labourer. Kate Eliza Hoxton was aged 26, single and a dressmaker. Her father was William Hoxton (dec), a waterman. What drew Sue's attention was that both parties gave their address as Lowther Street, in York. Sue wondered if this was unusual for the times. Were they living together or just near each other, as no house numbers were given? Might that have been why they married by licence rather than in a church?

She recollected Doreen having said something about marriages by licence and that often couples chose to marry this way if they were in a hurry or if there was something they wished to hide, avoiding three weeks of banns being called in church and drawing the attention of neighbours and the congregation. Turning to her folder and unfolding the growing family tree she checked the dates, and sure enough Eliza Kate, Kate's daughter, had been born over a year before, so she had an illegitimate child at the time of her marriage to Herbert – which probably explained a lot. She wondered why Herbert was happy to marry a woman with a child.

Sue slotted the papers into clear plastic pockets and added them to her growing file of documents. Returning to her laptop she opened up Google maps and typed in Wheatley's Row, York. The window opened at a street in Redcar, near Middlesbrough – obviously not the one she was looking for – but there was no option for one in York. She had more luck with Lowther Street and as she zoomed out the map, she let out a little gasp of surprise as she saw that it was located very near the university campus where Kate was studying, and even closer to the flat that she and Jen were sharing.

"What a coincidence!" she mused out aloud.

41

1875 York

The last days of May gave way to joyous June. Children discarded the layers that had constricted them for the last few months and ran with gay abandon through the grass, barefooted if they could avoid their mothers' admonishments. Everyone seemed to have a smile upon their face. Market traders' cries were cheerful and jocular. Gentlemen doffed their hats to pretty young ladies, matronly ladies unearthed their lace gloves and put away their kid leather ones, bonnets were adorned with flowers and new ribbons and trimmings were purchased to brighten up tired outfits in the hope that they would do another summer. There was a sense of a lightening of spirits and cares abandoned, at least in the short term. But of course, there were still those who slouched in alleyways, no boots upon their feet, no clothes worthy of a flower or a bright ribbon, no place to call home. And there were those who came out as the light faded and made their living in the shadows, along the ginnels and in the single-roomed dwellings where people forgot their cares for an hour or two, drinking and sharing any other pleasures that were on offer.

On one such bright warm morning Laura bundled up a few items in a bag and taking Henry's hand, shut the door behind them and headed to the railway station. By the time they reached Monk Bar Henry had already tired of trying to walk and so she hefted him up upon one hip while she held onto the bag with the other hand. Cutting down Minster Yard the bright sun reflected off the mellow stone of the cathedral, causing the shadows to appear even deeper and darker in contrast. The bell ringers were practising and Henry was momentarily startled by the volume of noise. As they headed down Museum Street and made for the Lendal Bridge, the noise decreased and his whimpers became more subdued as he caught sight of the different craft on the river. "Boat! Boat!" he shouted, pointing his chubby finger towards them. But Laura kept her head down and did not look up until the red brick façade of the railway station reared up ahead of them. Already the sound of trains and steam could be heard and Henry's attention was diverted in that direction as a train whistle sounded.

"Choo choo!" announced Laura and he repeated it over and over as they entered the building and found their platform. He was still repeating it as they settled into their seats in the second class carriage, squeezed in next to an oversized woman and her scrawny husband. But soon the motion of the train had lulled Henry to sleep, and Laura could look forward to seeing Eliza and Charles again. And Annie.

Charles had insisted that they take a handsome cab from the station to their home at their new address in Leeds. As they pulled up outside the well-appointed house, set in a street of similarly proportioned houses, Laura quickly realised that Charles' business must be thriving and that they had definitely begun to take steps up the social ladder.

Mrs Grimes was still there, running the household with her iron grip, but a different maid opened the door to them and showed them into the parlour where a few minutes later, Eliza bustled in and embraced her sister, before remarking at how much Henry had grown and how healthy he looked. Putting him down, Laura was happy to give her sister a kiss on her cheek and greet her with genuine pleasure. Oh, how she missed proper family life, she thought, but then considered how little of that she had ever known.

Charles had arranged to meet William at the wharf and see the boats and so on, giving them time to talk business, as Eliza said, before bringing him to the house that evening where they would all dine together. Laura suspected William might feel somewhat overawed by the house and her family but nevertheless looked forward to seeing how Charles and he had hit it off. So with the afternoon ahead of them Eliza suggested they collected the children and go for a stroll in the local park. Becky, now eight, took charge of Henry, fussing over him and happily chasing after him through the grass, while Frederick, now nearly five played with a bat and ball with another boy they met there. Eliza's new baby was in her perambulator which Eliza proudly pushed along the gravel paths by the bright flower beds. Finding a bench near the bandstand they were glad to sit and talk, while keeping an eye on the children. As the band arrived and started to tune up, Eliza told the children to come and sit on the rug they had brought and shared out some apples to eat. By now Henry was exhausted and Laura laid him down on the rug, shading him with her open parasol while he fell deeply asleep, oblivious to the music and everything else.

The only time Laura felt uncomfortable was when Eliza mentioned their mother. Had Laura written to her? Because her mother had been in touch again, asking if Eliza had passed on her address to her sister. Laura made excuses about so much to do after George's death, looking after Henry, going into partnership with William and so on, but in the end she knew that Eliza just recognised these as excuses. As the band began a stirring rendition of 'Rule Britannia', their conversation became impossible, especially as the crashing cymbals woke Henry and his cries were added to the general cacophony.

By the time they had walked back Charles and William were already in the library enjoying a smoke. At the sound of the family's return, Charles came out into the hallway to greet Laura, William following him. The children were bundled off upstairs to the nursery with Mrs Grimes and the maid, while the adults retired to the parlour. Henry seemed happy to be in the company of his cousins and Laura was glad of the respite for a while.

Laura watched William and tried to gauge how he and Charles were getting on. Charles was such an amiable and genuine person that he seemed to have put William completely at his ease. Thankfully, thought Laura, William had managed to get cleaned up before meeting him and coming back to the house. In fact, she noted, he sported a smart white shirt, complete with stiff collar, which was obviously something he found uncomfortable but she felt both gratitude and a fondness for him that he had made the effort. She had no opportunity to be alone with William to ask how the meeting and discussions had gone. Over dinner it would not be a topic of conversation which the ladies would need to be party to. And after the meal, the men withdrew to the library for a drink and a smoke and the ladies were once more left to more feminine chitchat.

William eventually took his leave as eleven struck on the clock in the hall. Charles shook his hand with great enthusiasm and as William stood in the doorway, he said he would come for Laura at noon the following day, after he had ensured the boat was loaded.

"But we are returning to York by train!" she said, as her

emotions got the better of her.

"There is a problem wi' t' track. Just 'eard as we left t' docks. T' embankment 'as collapsed and they don't think it'll be cleared for two or three days. Tha can come back on't boat wi' me."

Laura's heart sank and she reached out to steady herself on the newel post at the bottom of the staircase.

She spent a restless night, tossing and turning and it was not because the bed was unfamiliar nor that Henry woke her up whimpering in the night before returning to a deep and settled sleep beside her. She felt fear and trepidation for what lay ahead of her. She could not do this. In the darkness all manner of shapes swam in the gloom before her and she could not shake the sense of utter dread. As the pale light of day crept through the curtains, and shapes took on a more familiar appearance, she tried to reconcile her fears with common sense. Telling herself that she would be in the company of William, he would be with her all the time and would let nothing befall her, she would not be alone. There are times when you have to face your fears, she told herself. You cannot live your life like this. With what reason?

By the time full daylight had flooded her room, a gentle knock at the door brought the maid with a jug of hot water so she might wash. And also the invitation to join the family in the dining room for breakfast when she was ready. Going through the daily routine of washing her face, combing out and pinning up her hair, then giving Henry a wash and a change before getting them both dressed and packed calmed her nerves and helped her decide to face her fears, not hide away from them.

Henry was delighted to be fussed over again by his cousins and soon he was contentedly chewing on a crust, while being entertained by Frederick playing peek a boo behind the chair back.

"It has been lovely having you here with us Laura. Please feel that you may come again at any time. You will be very welcome."

"Thank you Eliza. That means a great deal to me."

"And Charles has asked me to pass on his best wishes. He left early this morning – more business, I'm afraid," she added apologetically. "But," she continued, "he did say to me last night that he felt that Mr Hoxton was a very steady chap and known along the wharves as a reliable man, and has been well thought of for many years. He wanted me to tell you that he felt he would be a good man to take over George's business and that he would be happy to deal with him. No doubt he has already, or will soon, let Mr Hoxton know that he will be happy to put some business his way in the future."

Laura bridled at the phrase 'take over George's business' but decided not to rise to the remark. After all, she doubted Eliza could see where a woman might make her mark in such a business.

"And before you go, I know you will want to see Annie." Leaning across to a bell pull on the wall, she tugged at it and soon the maid arrived. "Please ask Mrs Grimes to send Annie to the parlour, Jane."

The maid left with a bob, her eyes large in surprise as

she muttered, "Yes'm," and closed the door.

Laura stood and scooping up Henry, followed Eliza into the hall. After opening the door for her, Eliza returned to the children and left Laura with Henry. Soon light footsteps were heard and Annie appeared at the door, her linen apron over her dark dress. Her eyes lit up when she saw them both and she was beside them in a few steps, her arms flung around Laura.

"Annie! How well you look! I'm sure you have grown two inches since I saw you last."

Annie pulled away and hugged Henry, who thoroughly enjoyed the attention, bouncing up and down and giggling as Annie tickled him under his chin. They spent about a quarter of an hour together, Laura making sure that Annie was happy. It seemed the family were good to her, although Mrs Grimes was still the bane of her life, according to Annie. She had met another servant girl from one of the houses down the street and they would meet up on their day off and spend time together. Laura was glad that she had company. Laura told her a little about the business plans that she and William were in the process of bringing about. And of course, Henry was the centre of attention.

When it came time to take their leave, Henry burst into tears and had a tantrum when Annie went out of the door and headed back to the kitchen. Trying to quieten him, Laura jiggled him on her hip and tried to distract him. The cries brought Eliza into the hall as they gathered together their bags ready to be collected by the cab which would take them to meet William at the wharf.

After saying their goodbyes, Laura and Henry sat back in the cab and as the sound of the hooves and the rocking motion began to soothe Henry to sleep, he murmured, "Choo choo."

"No, boat boat," Laura whispered back, with a sinking feeling in her stomach.

42

March 2018
Lincoln

Having shown the birth certificate of Kate Eliza Hoxton to Doreen, the tutor, at the next genealogy class, Sue had been advised to try to hunt down the previous marriages for Laura Emily, Kate's mother. She certainly had married quite a few times in the few years up until she was twenty-six years old. Unusual but not impossible. Her tutor thought that it might be quite a nice little project for Sue, to put together a timeline of events, reminding her to use deaths and marriages online as a way to plot Laura's life through the years. She also reminded the class that evening of the online resource of archived newspapers, and Sue noted that down on her pad, wondering if she might be able to find any of her ancestors mentioned in them.

On her return home that evening, Sue pulled up outside the cottage and noted the first few spikes of the bulbs poking through the earth. A welcome sight as she thought longingly of the spring days to come. And that Kate would be home for Easter in a few weeks.

Settling down in front of her laptop with the obligatory coffee, she decided to look for Kate Eliza whom she had last recorded on the 1891 census as living in Hull with her aunt and uncle. But which one was her bloodline? And where were her parents? Locating the image she had found before on Ancestry, she located the 1881 census link on the right hand side of the page and sat back as it loaded.

As the image of the densely packed page of information

filled her screen, Sue zoomed in looking for the Hoxtons. Sure enough she found them about half way down the page living at Lowther Street in York. But there were four names listed. Head of the household was William Hoxton, aged 65 and a waterman. Under his name was that of Laura E Hoxton, wife, aged 38, born in Hull. Below her was a stepson named Henry Shipton, aged 7, scholar. For a moment she was puzzled but then the name Shipton rang a bell and a quick flip though her file found the birth record where Kate Eliza's mother's previous married names had included Shipton.

"So an earlier marriage as we thought," Sue muttered to herself.

Kate Eliza, aged 5, was listed under her half-brother as daughter of William Hoxton.

"Quite a difference in ages", noted Sue aloud again, as she saw there were twenty-seven years between Laura and William.

Returning to the typed transcript version of the census, Sue clicked on Laura's name and looked to the right hand pane to see where she was on the 1871 census. Sue was perplexed when Laura Hoxton did not at first appear, but then she realised Laura might have been married to one of the other men whose names had been listed for her on her daughter's birth record. Sue expected that Shipton would be the most obvious one. But Laura Shipton wasn't there. Nor was Laura Cowper. She realised this was not going to be an easy search.

43

1875
on the River Ouse

As the last rays of the sun fell behind the trees that bordered the bank, William pulled the boat over to the side and made it fast fore and aft with mooring ropes and iron pegs driven into the soft side of the bank. They were near no town or village. It might have been thought idyllic; green fields stretching as far as the eye could see, cows grazing in lush meadows that ran down to the water, barley swaying in the gentle breeze, still blue-green with the feathery whiskers catching the light and emitting the softest whispers as they brushed together and apart. A lark rose up in the distance launching its mellifluous song into the evening air. A flash of colour from the opposite bank as a kingfisher darted from its overhanging perch and took flight at the new arrivals. Already the insects of the evening were gathering in clouds over the shadier reaches of the water and soon the last few swallows would be darting and cruising low over the water for their last meal of the day before the bats took over their patrol.

But for Laura it was far from idyllic. Every mile had been torture, her ears straining for the voices she dreaded hearing. But all had been silent. The families and crews of passing boats had greeted them with waves, shouted phrases and cheery farewells. Perhaps with so much traffic upon the water, all would be well. And she was not alone. William made occasional conversation as the miles slipped by and Henry was fascinated with the passing tableaus, pointing at the boats as they passed and joining in the waves of greeting. But he soon became drowsy with the warmth of the low sun and the motion of the boat, and had eventually dozed off in Laura's arms. Taking him below into the compact cabin, she laid him on a rug and piled a couple of cushions beside him, rolling up her coat behind his back to wedge him securely against them. With a slight murmur, he wriggled onto his side with his thumb in his mouth and was soon sound asleep, the only movement the steady rise and fall of his ribs as he snuffled against his fist, moisture dribbling onto his chin.

William came down to join them and after making some tea on the small stove and cutting some rough bread and cheese, which had been stowed in a cupboard above their heads, they once more fell silent. Laura was both annoyed and distressed that they had not been able to reach anywhere where they could have joined a train headed for York. She did not want to be on the water a minute longer than absolutely necessary. But now here they were – night falling and no escape in sight.

Eventually William cleared his throat and announced that he would sleep on deck. It was a warm night and it was something he had done many a time on evenings such as this. Taking his pipe and tobacco pouch, and another blanket from a cupboard, he bade her goodnight and stepped up out of the cabin and onto the deck.

Having tidied away the dishes and remnants of their simple meal, Laura folded up the small table and prepared to make up the bed, such as it was. A simple board with a long thin bolster upon which they had been sitting now served as bed and mattress. Piling the few remaining cushions at one end, she propped herself up against them and took stock of the situation.

What harm could befall them? William was on deck,

right outside the hatch. The night was still and the moon had risen, making shimmering patterns on the surface of the water as it lapped gently against the hull. Any untoward sound or movement would be instantly noticeable. Attempting to rationalise her thoughts, she closed her eyes and drew a few deep breaths. The night would pass all the quicker if she could allow herself to sleep. Midsummer nights were short and soon the first shades of daylight would appear to chase away the shadows. As an owl hooted in a nearby tree, preparing to set off on a night's hunting, she pulled herself together and made ready for bed and hoped for a dreamless sleep.

The cabin was stifling, the latent heat from the stove, the warm evening and the closed hatch all contributing to the stuffy airless atmosphere. Undoing her blouse, she slipped it off and folded it on a small shelf nearby. Unfastening and letting her skirt fall free and rolling down her stockings, she added them to the neat pile. Removing her corset, she felt the air upon her clammy skin as her white cotton chemise loosened and hung freely around her. It reached beneath her knees and left her arms half bare. Grateful for the freedom, she stretched up and arched her back, aware that she almost reached the ceiling and walls as she did so. Unpinning her hair, she dropped the pins into a nearby saucer and then reaching into her bag she felt the solid handle of her brush. Pulling it out she proceeded to brush out her long hair until it was tangle-free and laying smoothly over her pale shoulders. Within a few more minutes she had plaited it into a single braid which she secured it with a ribbon tied in a bow – a routine she followed every night, and in so doing it soothed her into a state of calm, ready for sleep.

With a final check to see that the baby was safe and

secure, and relieved that he was sleeping soundly, she stretched out on the makeshift bed and pulled a thin cover over her up to her chest and folded her arms over each other on her stomach. For some minutes her senses remained alert and she heard William moving about on deck. The strike of a lucifer, a cough and a light thump as he sat back against the side. Eventually she succumbed to the slight rocking and gentle lapping of the water against the hull.

A light mist started to form above the water and began to swirl and snake through the rushes and around the vessel moored by the bank. It both shrouded and combined with the moisture beneath. It veiled the snaking fingers that crept up and over the edge of the boat, the moist form that flowed over the boards and examined each crack and cranny, the sinuous flow that found the gap beneath the cabin door, the silent trickle that explored the shapes and forms below. It revelled in the new textures it discovered and its attention grew more intense as it tentatively explored the sleeping form that lay cocooned in a pile of cushions in the corner. But much as it found this intriguing and of interest, it had a more urgent focus for its explorations. Reluctantly withdrawing from the small recumbent form, it curved back around and crept up the side of the wooden board, overhung with the edge of a thin blanket. It had found the object of its quest.

The first touch of warmth confirmed the contact of the liquid form with living flesh. As it hesitated, keeping contact, it could sense the pulse of another liquid keeping up a rhythm of its own.

Laura stirred as she felt a coolness upon her ankle. It barely caused her to react, but she instinctively drew her foot towards her and beneath the blanket. When she was still again, the probing form resumed its quest, cautiously creeping upward beneath the covering and feeling more warmth as it followed her calf upward. It hooked a liquid finger under the hem of her thin chemise and quivered in excitement as the flesh highway continued to stretch onward and upward. It felt the downy hairs upon the skin stiffen and bend, the tiny bumps caused by the contractions of the muscles at their base extending in a sensory plain across the surface. She shivered ever so slightly, but not unpleasantly. A deep breath left her partly open lips.

Where now, it asked itself. What would give me – her – more pleasure? Tracing the broadening expanse of thigh and hip, it curved around the prominence of bone and fell into the soft hollow behind it. A new sensation, soft, warm, welcoming with reciprocating moisture. She moved again and shifted so that the fingers were able to explore more fully. But wait, there was more. Reluctantly abandoning the familiar dampness, it resumed its journey up the sleeping form. By now its whole presence was off the floor and upon the recumbent woman.

She shifted again, now moving to lie on her back, her arms flung back on either side of her head, her breathing deeper, her lips slightly parted. By now, shrouded beneath the blanket, it could cover her lower limbs. It continued to traverse the hills and valleys of the fleshly form and found the twin mounds that it circled and played with, finding smaller peaks that grew and became firm under its touch. The thick rope of hair that lay over one shoulder, pale and smooth, gave it another texture to explore. But it soon found more pleasure in the warmth and pulsing flesh that it now totally enveloped. Reaching out other fingers, it returned to explore the dips and hollows, all the while enjoying the reaction it witnessed in the woman. It cleaved closer and more firmly, tightening and sealing itself against her totally, and began to match the movements that she had started to make. Her eyelids fluttered, her breathing grew faster and small sounds came from deep within her. Entering the moistest cave, it found a sanctuary, a familiar place where it could both rest and play. Here it felt at home. This was the prize, the object of this assault. It blended its own moisture with that which bade it welcome. Together they mingled, moved and danced to a familiar rhythm that grew more frantic, like a storm building or a torrent pouring. This was exciting. This was tumultuous. This was – release!

She shuddered and brushed a hand across her face, also wreathed in moisture of its own. Her eyelids fluttered and partially opened, and in them it could see its own shape and colour, as if she was one of its own.

But it needed to return. This was just a brief moment, but a triumph. It had succeeded. It trickled back, reluctantly leaving the troughs and hollows where it had rested and pooled in pleasure. It left her with a whisper as it brushed past her ear.

'Fljót vættr'

Remember my name.

I have succeeded.

We are one

The first pale light began to colour the horizon as dawn began its inexorable journey to herald a new day. The mist still lay over the water but it withdrew a little more each minute until its filmy fingers had withdrawn back through the reed banks, leaving the merest hint of a gauzy veil over the surface. And then it was gone, as if it had never been.

William stirred and groaned at the stiffness in his old joints, the dampness of the morning creeping into them and making him aware of the years advancing. Time was a night spent on deck would have been easy and he could have stretched and stood without so much as a groan, bending to the task in hand with suppleness and strength. Ah well, such was life. The cabin door still remained firmly shut so thoughts of a welcoming hot mug of tea were quickly dispelled. At least he had his pipe beside him. As he filled it with tobacco from the pouch he had stuffed in his pocket the night before, he looked along the deck to where the light from the morning sun dispelled the shadows. On one side there was a trail of water that led from the cabin door to the lip of the edge, and then disappeared. The canvas covering stretched taught over the high spine of the hold was still damp with tiny drops of dew so no doubt it was leftover moisture from the night. As he looked, it had already begun to evaporate and by the time he had lit his pipe and had a few deep puffs upon it, there was barely a trace to be seen.

Laura stirred, momentarily unaware of where she was. Pulling the thin blanket up to her chin, she shivered involuntarily as she felt herself wreathed in dampness. Even her hair lay damp upon her shoulder and her chemise was gaping open. Moving her legs, she felt that it had ridden up and lay tangled under her hips, her abdomen and thighs exposed and uncovered. Although the cabin felt airless and oppressive, she could not imagine how she had sweated so profusely. Stretching out her limbs as far as she could in the cramped space against the boat's side, scraps of memories came back to her. She found herself reliving pleasant sensations and tensed her muscles, enjoying them again. Then reality began to intrude upon this half-asleep, half-awake state and she saw a form in front of her. She felt coolness and saw shimmering but no solidity. She felt coldness spreading across her body, like streams searching for a way to the sea. She felt both elation and fearfulness at the same instant. She felt simultaneously violated but also complicit in what had occurred. And she instinctively knew who the night-time visitor had been. It had succeeded at last. It took this opportunity when her guard was down. And a word kept fluttering just out of reach, her mind tried to grasp it but it drifted that bit further into the distant mists of oblivion.

"*Fljót vættr* ..." She jumped as the word broke through the mist, then dissolved into the void.

A whimper brought her fully to consciousness as Henry stirred and found himself wedged against a pile of cushions and her rolled up coat. Pushing back the blanket, she stood up, her chemise sticking damply to the form of her body, causing her to shiver involuntarily. Hearing the baby, William tapped lightly on the cabin door and she hastily grabbed her coat from behind the baby, shaking out the folds.

"A moment please, Mr Hoxton," she hurriedly called out, pulling her damp arms through the sleeves with difficulty and fastening the buttons with fingers still shaking.

If he noticed her appearance when she opened the locker

door to admit him, he made no sign. Moving over to the stove, he stated that they both needed a brew to start the day, which she heartily agreed with as she picked up Henry and wiped his tear-stained cheeks.

44

After untying the mooring ropes, they joined the growing crowd of boats heading north, while a steady stream passed them going in the opposite direction. The sun rose higher in the sky and Laura was glad to get dressed and stand on deck in the growing warmth of the day.

By the time the three square towers of Selby Abbey could be seen just rising above the horizon, Laura was relieved to hear the sound of a train whistle in the distance and shading her eyes, she could see the plume of smoke as it came nearer. Shortly afterwards, William was able to moor the boat at the jetties in Selby and she and Henry were able to alight in preparation for the short walk to the railway station. Thanking William for taking care of them, and asking him to come to see them in York as soon as he returned, she bade him farewell.

Once more Henry got excited at the prospect of another train journey, bouncing up and down in her arms and shouting "Choo choo!" to the amusement of the other passengers waiting upon the platform. And as before, he soon fell asleep, rocked by the motion of the train and the rhythmic refrain of the wheels eating up the miles as they headed to York, home – and sanctuary.

It was not until she had closed her own front door and set Henry down upon the floor to run up the hall into the kitchen, and sat down on a chair beside the table that she permitted herself to finally revisit the events of the last twenty four hours. It had finally found her – and overcome her.

The next few days passed quickly as she got back into the routine of caring for Henry, of housework and shopping, cooking and cleaning. But the nights were the time she had to face up to the memories of what had happened. Lying in the darkness, hardly fully dark through the midsummer nights, she tried to blot out the fragments of that other night. Curiosity about the who and what wrestled with the feelings of being powerless and not fully conscious of what had truly happened. At times, when she had almost succumbed to sleep, when her mind was at its most open and receptive, she felt a sense of being embraced and caressed in a way that had her surrendering to what she lacked, and then she would be pulled back with a start that caused her whole body to jerk awake and she would find herself trembling and her heart thudding in her breast.

William arrived late one afternoon less than a week later and she was glad to have the company of another to take her mind away from where it kept wandering. They sat and chatted about how William had got on with Charles and what they had discussed. As before, Charles had been most amiable and welcoming, and Laura became more aware of William's quiet ability to talk business and manage his affairs. He would not have been so successful up till now if that had not been the case, and in him she saw a spark of something she had not seen before. He may have been a working man but he was savvy in the ways that business was conducted and she saw in him a deeper understanding and perception which gratified her. Looks might be deceiving, she mused. Here was a solid, reliable man who was dependable and on whom she could trust. He may be a man of few words and with them he sounded like any other Yorkshire working man, but there was an intelligence and gentleness that she found reassuring and companiable. He had originally been shy and reticent with her, at times almost diffident and withdrawn, but as the weeks and months had passed and they got to know each other better, they both were seeing something deeper in each other.

After an evening meal together, and with Henry put to bed, she encouraged him to stay a while and if he wished, enjoy his pipe by the fireside while she sat opposite nearer the lamp and finished some mending. He seemed pleased to do so, after all he too was going back to an empty house she discovered, as his son had been offered a position in Doncaster and had left the previous week. They both seemed genuinely disappointed when the mantel clock struck eleven and he said he'd better be going as he had an early start tomorrow.

"Thank 'ee missus for t'meal. It were reet nice," he announced on the doorstep.

"William, I think perhaps we know each other well enough now that you might call me Laura, don't you?"

William reddened in the light from the lamp in the hallway, and shuffled his feet, looking somewhat abashed.

"If tha wish, missus – er, Laura," and with that he unscrewed the hat he had been mistreating in his hands, and settled it atop his thinning grey hair. "Goodnight mi ... , Laura. Ah'll see 'ee when I get back. Say cheerio t' Henry for me." And with that he turned and headed down to the corner where he was lost from view. With a small smile, Laura closed the door and again faced the prospect of her bed and the realm where dwelt other uninvited guests.

◆ ◆ ◆

As the weeks passed, Laura began to realise that a change had come over her. Counting the days upon the calendar pinned to the back of the kitchen door, she had a sense of trepidation as the cold wash of awareness came over her. Checking the days again, she felt her legs fail her and she slumped onto a chair, holding on to the table for support. She knew what this meant, but how could it be? Once more she was not alone ...

She went over and over the events nearly a month ago, not wanting to relive them, but trying to extract shreds of memory that were fast fading. Was it possible? And how? Why had she not resisted, put up some opposition? And yet there were also threads of pleasure and gratification that laced through the misty memories, causing her shame and humiliation. And now? What would the outcome be? What would 'it' be? Any thoughts of seeking backstreet help, she soon dismissed – not really sure why. There was a tugging at her core that made her want to nurture and cherish what was growing inside her, not extinguish that spark which wanted to remain close by and grow and blossom within her. Her sense of protection overcame any other thoughts. But with that realisation, came other considerations. Again, her plans were shattered. Life once more had interfered and set her on yet another path, in another direction.

She knew what she had to do ... and she knew it had to be soon.

William arrived late one afternoon a few days later. Answering the door, she welcomed him in and he made his way into the kitchen, now a familiar routine as she put the kettle on to boil and they sat down companionably at the table as Henry chattered and wanted William's attention. William had made him a small wooden train engine, roughly shaped from wood he had worked on the long evenings moored up by canal sides and river banks. He had attached four wheels and added a funnel shaped block upon the top.

"Choo choo!" yelled Henry, jumping up and down in delight. Within minutes he was alternately crawling across the floor playing with his new toy and then sitting chewing at it as the dribbles ran down his chin. They both laughed and Laura was struck for a moment at how homely the scene must appear.

The evening crept in and it was taken as read by both parties that William would join them for their evening meal. Once Henry had been washed and changed, Laura put him down, still clutching his toy engine which he refused to part with. Returning to the kitchen William had already stacked the plates and cutlery by the sink, a man used to looking after himself, she mused. Sitting back down at the table, he went into the breast pocket of his working jacket and withdrew some folded papers wrapped in oilcloth.

"Charles gave me these. Ah've signed ma part, as tha can see. An' t' others are receipts as usual." William unwrapped the sheets and handed them to Laura.

Looking over them, she nodded and smiled. "That is great news, William. I am so pleased that things have worked out so well with Charles." And taking the papers, she folded them and walking over to the dresser, slid out a drawer and extracted a slim leather pouch into which she inserted the papers alongside other documents. William stood again and took his bowl and cup over to the sink, rattling them as he attempted to make a tidier and more stable stack.

"Leave those for now William. Let's go into the front room. I am sure you would enjoy the opportunity for a softer seat and a pipeful of tobacco?" and with that, she swept past him and led the way into the front room, turning up the oil lamp and filling the room with a gentle glow. William gratefully eased himself into one of the chairs that sat each side of the fireplace, unlit as it was still warm enough being July. She watched as he went through the routine of filling and lighting his pipe and she did not find the aroma of the tobacco smoke unpleasant, in fact it seemed both familiar and comforting.

They talked about inconsequential things. She finished hemming a little shirt for Henry and darned a hole in one of her woollen stockings.

As she stretched the fabric over the wooden mushroom, William looked over and said, "Ah fine remember nights like this wi' Betty, 'er sittin' at 'er mendin' an' me wi' me pipe." And with that he looked down and let out a slow breath as he recalled her head bent over her work in the light of their own living room.

"How long has she been gone, William?" Laura ventured to ask.

"Nearly five years now. She were taken so quick. There were nowt anyone could do. She'd been complainin' of pains in her stomach for a while but she wouldn't go t' doctor. Said it were jus' old age an' t' stop me mitherin'. But it didn't get better an' ah come back one time an' found her in her bed in such agony. An' then she were gone." William looked down at a spot between his feet and his shoulders slouched as his head dropped. Laura said nothing for a few moments, then she heard him give a deep sniff and pull a crumpled handkerchief from his trouser pocket with which he proceeded to wipe his face.

She rose and walked over to put a hand upon his shoulder. "I am sorry to have brought back such unhappy memories William. Let me offer you something a little stronger than tea this time," and walking over to a small cupboard she took out a small bottle of brandy and two small glasses. Filling both, she handed him one and sat back opposite as he took a sip and sat back in the chair, setting the glass on a small table at the side.

"Thank ee, Laura. Ah'm reet sorry for makin' a fool of me'sen."

"Not at all William, it shows me how much you cared about her and how much you miss the comfort of the times you had together, am I right?"

"Indeed. She were a grand woman an' ma t' the bairns. We were t'gether jus' ower thirty year. An' now bairns are grown an' there's jus' me rattlin' round in t'house. Ah well, ..." and here he let out another sigh.

"William, I too have had my share of loss. Did you know that I was married twice?" At this he looked up and she continued, "My first husband was badly injured in a terrible accident at the docks in Goole. He clung to life for nearly two weeks in the infirmary but in the end he died. Not long afterwards I lost the baby I was carrying." At this, she looked down at her hands, gripping them tightly in her lap and paused, gathering her composure.

"Ah did'n know that. Tha've 'ad it 'ard, without a doubt. 'ow long ago were that?"

"That was barely three years ago William. We had only been together for a very short time. And then I met George and … well, you know the rest." Pausing again she allowed herself a small sob as she recalled the emptiness and distress she had felt when her future had crumpled around her a second time.

This time it was William who ventured to lean across and put a rough work-worn hand over her two smaller ones as they lay in her lap. With the other he passed her the glass that lay on the table by her side. "Drink this – ye'll feel better for 't," he said. Looking up at him she smiled wanly and accepted the glass, taking a deep swallow and feeling the burning liquid course down her inside, spreading its warmth and comfort as it reached her core.

"We are both set adrift upon the tide of life, are we not William?" she murmured. His only response was a nod and a grunt of agreement. They sat in silence for some time, each lost in their own thoughts. As the chime of the small mantel clock broke the silence, Laura drained her glass and made to refill both hers and William's.

"Ah should be on me way, t'is getting late," and with that he made to rise and drain what was left in his glass.

"No, please – stay a little longer. We both have no-one

waiting for us. Here – a refill, and we can toast our future ventures." Tipping up the bottle, she watched as the amber liquid refilled the small glass and then looked straight at him as he looked up from his chair.

He found himself unwilling to rise, to return to the dark cold place he called home. The comfort and company, not to say the warming contentment of the spirit in his glass all made him relax back again into the delve of the cushion that was still warm and moulded into his form. He found his gaze held by her eyes, and realised that he had never really looked closely at them. Holding her gaze, he studied the pale coloured centres, edged in darker grey. The pupils were large and dark in the dim soft light of the room and there was a hypnotic effect to the liquidity of their paleness. He felt himself held and drawn in deeper. It felt as if he was in a familiar place and yet, its very novelty made him want to explore further.

Standing beside him, he could feel her closeness and the cloth of her black skirt brushing his arm. The thought crossed his mind that she would look so much more handsome in bright colours and he longed to be able to give her something to wear rather than the mourning colours that society and convention demanded. Looking up into her face again, the light caught the glistening tears welling in the corners of her eyes, growing and threatening to overspill onto her cheeks. Taking her hand in his, he stood and took the bottle from her other hand and set it down, then grasped that hand too. Standing he was barely a head taller than her, solid and broad. The movement brought with it a waft of tobacco smoke and the faintest trace of coal dust. He brushed away a tear that had escaped and started to course down her pale cheek. She could feel the slight roughness and warmth of his hands. Allowing herself a small sob, she closed her eyes and another tear fell upon the back of his hand.

As she lifted her head to look up at him, her very closeness drew him in and he put his arms around her shoulders and pulled her close against his chest. She sobbed more deeply and allowed her head to lay against his body, while he extended his arms around to meet at her back, stroking and comforting her. He allowed her to stay like that for some minutes until her sobbing subsided. He found he did not want to release her, nor did he attempt to, the familiarity of a smaller slighter body cleaving to his was both a pleasant memory and a new sensation. It was she who moved apart, but only slightly as she met his gaze and whispered, "Don't leave me tonight. Please stay." Without thinking he drew her closer and brushed her parted lips with his own.

45

1875 York

L ying in the soft grey light of approaching dawn, she felt the solidity and warmth of the body lying next to her. The steady rhythmic breathing was a testament to the fulfilment of the moment's invitation. It was more union than passion. But with it they had crossed the divide. She slipped back into a sleep intensified by the warm spirit that flowed through her as much as by the accomplishment.

Henry's cries brought her back to consciousness and this time she awoke to find herself alone, the only remnant of his company, the dented pillow and crumpled sheet. Rising and wrapping her robe around her, she collected Henry and carried him upon her hip downstairs and into the kitchen where she was surprised to find William in his shirt sleeves and waistcoat drinking tea at the table.

"There's a brew ready for 'ee," he announced, not meeting her eye.

"Thank you William," she responded, glad of the distraction of Henry's cries so as not to have to meet his eyes. Putting the child down, she pulled her robe tighter and tied the cord, sweeping back her hair which lay tangled across her shoulders and quickly attempting to tidy it into a swirled bun at the nape of her neck.

"Ah'll be off then," he stated, rising and putting the empty cup by the previous night's dishes. "Ah've 'nother trip t'day to Wakefield. Ah'll be back by end of t' week."

"I hope – I hope you will feel that you can come back and stay here again with us," she said, surprised at her coyness and timidity.

He didn't reply but picked up his jacket from where it lay over the back of the chair where he had left it the previous evening, and collecting his pipe and hat, he made for the hall and started towards the door.

"Ta ta!" called Henry after him, waving his pudgy hand in his direction, before returning to chew upon the slice of bread he had been given.

Having followed him down the hall, Laura stood and watched as he made to undo the latch, then hesitated, before turning back and giving her a brief kiss upon her cheek. A moment later he was gone, leaving the faintest scent of tobacco smoke and musky sweat behind him.

Laura stood with her back against the closed door and wrapped her arms around her, mulling over the events of the last few hours. Then with a nod, she straightened up and returned to the kitchen to begin another day.

Over the next few weeks William became an infrequent visitor but always left before dark. If the neighbours wanted to talk, they had little substantial to go on, not that that would have stopped them. But as the weeks passed, Laura knew the time would have to come to tell him her news. She needed some time to think about how and when, and decided that as it was a bright warm day, she would walk down and meet William as he moored the boat at the staith. Henry needed to stretch his legs and being out in public, there would be less chance of an explosion of temper or unpleasantness, at least she hoped so. She did not feel she knew William well enough to predict his reaction, but she was sure it would be one of surprise and possibly something worse. Perhaps telling him on neutral territory would make it somewhat easier. Nevertheless she did not enjoy the thought of being near the river, but the knowledge that there would be plenty of people around was the only way she could quell the unease she felt as they walked hand in hand down the hill, towards the bridge that would take them across the river. Henry chattered and pointed at the bright wares in the shop windows and the dogs that ran past, learning new words and getting ever steadier on his feet. But eventually he tired and she had to heft him onto her hip for the remainder of the journey.

As they neared the bridge, Henry perked up at the sight of the boats, pointing and shouted, "Boat, boat!" at the top of his voice. Looking over the rows of boats moored together and the sea of men climbing over and around them, it took her a few minutes to locate William. He was at the far end and she flinched involuntarily at the thought of walking along the cobbled path of the staith before she could draw level with his boat.

The sun was glinting on the water, causing her to have to shield her eyes with her hand as she tried to watch him as he worked. But the brightness and the scintillation of the flashes of light started to make her feel dazzled and confused. And then she heard it …

Welcome again.
You have not been to see me. I missed our … time … together.
Have you come to join with me again?

283

Shaking her head to clear the unbidden summons, she put Henry down and clapped her hands over her ears. Forcing herself to look away from the sparkle and glint of the river, she looked down the staith again, picking out William as he busied himself on deck. Having unloaded his cargo earlier in the day, the canvas covering lay loose and concave over the spine of the hold and the boat sat high in the water. Grasping Henry tightly by the hand she forced herself to focus on the scene in front of them – boats, men, noise, movement.

At first he did not see them, but as Henry spotted him he shouted out, causing William to look up as he heard the young voice over the noise and bustle of men shouting and boats being tied up and moored in tight order for the day. Laura gave a hesitant wave and William bent back down, completing coiling up a rope before he straightened and stepped off the edge of the boat onto the staith. She waited on the bridge until he came up and drew level with them.

Henry was all excitement and leaned over to William, holding out his arms, shouting "Up, up!" as he demanded to be carried. William's face broke into a smile as he reached out and swooped the child into his arms, throwing him up and catching him a few times, much to Henry's enjoyment.

"May we go for a walk William? Henry needs to work off some energy as you can see or he'll never go down to sleep this evening! Perhaps a walk through St George's Field?"

This was an area of green with a walk that ran parallel to the riverside. Passing the Prison housed in the ancient

Clifford's Tower, bold and brave, its circular form atop a mound so that in the past any enemy could be seen approaching, they continued down Tower Street and turned into the relative peace and calm of the wooded grassy area of St George's Field. At one side sat the buildings of the public baths but they carried further on to find a seat where they could sit and watch Henry as he stretched his legs, chasing a small ball that Laura had brought with her.

They passed a pleasant few minutes chatting about inconsequential things and then William updated her on his latest trip and business dealings. Pulling out a leather pouch he unfolded it to hand her some receipts and papers which she would sort away with the others she kept relating to their business dealings. As she put them into the bag she carried, she turned to look into the distance and took a deep breath, preparing herself to broach the subject that she had been dreading. Now that the moment was here, she found she couldn't think how to start and the seconds stretched into minutes as she struggled to begin. Eventually, Henry came toddling back demanding William threw the ball for him again, and the tension was broken.

"William, I have something to tell you. I am with child." There, it was done. The words had been uttered and could not be taken back. Nothing would be the same from this moment on. William did not respond in any way, and at first she was not sure if he had actually heard her. He lifted his head from looking down at Henry and stared into the middle distance, still not saying a word or making any indication of his feelings.

Eventually she broke the silence. "Did you hear me William?"

"Ah heard," he replied in a monotone. "Are tha sure?"

"Of course. I – I waited until there was no doubt before telling you. I know the signs after all."

"Ah'm old enough t' be yer father," he murmured.

"You're not too old to be a father!" she responded, more forcefully than she had intended.

Only then did he turn to look at her. Could he see the panic in her face? The uncertainty and fear? He looked at her for a long time before he eventually spoke. "What would ye 'ave me do, Laura?"

"I rather think that is up to you, don't you think William?" she replied quietly, looking down at her hands clenched in her lap, the knuckles white and the skin stretched taut.

Another interminable silence stretched between them. People walked by, couples, families, men out for a constitutional before evening fell. But she noticed none of them. Only Henry seemed to register the tension between them and toddled over, grabbing at her skirt and demanding to be lifted up onto her knee. As she settled him, glad of the few moments of distraction, she played over in her mind her options, which were few.

Eventually William cleared his throat, and rising to his feet, stood looking down at her. "Will tha marry me, lass?" was all he said. Suddenly the absurdity of it struck her as she feared that he might go down on one knee in the middle of the park. However he remained looking down at her, waiting to gauge her response.

"I will, William," she answered, almost in a whisper. "I appreciate that this is not how you would have planned your latter years. I hope you will not regret it. But you must know that this is not love between us, William. Yes, I do have a genuine fondness for you. And it will be more of ... a partnership, shall we say. It strengthens both our positions, and that of our business ventures. But I will be a good wife and undertake my wifely duties as is required of me. You will not go without comfort or companionship."

William had stood looking at his feet throughout this long response and now seemed unsure of what he should do next.

"Please, sit down William. You are giving me a stiff neck looking up at you," she added, with what she hoped was a little humour to ease the tension of the moment.

He resumed his place beside her, glad to sit down and take stock of what the future would bring, but still saying nothing.

"And be assured, if that is what is going through your mind, the child is yours." She felt a shiver of deceit run down her spine. But what choice had she?

"Ah did'n doubt it. Ah would'n have asked 'ee if ah 'ad," he responded gruffly. "Have 'ee an idea of a date to wed? After all, we don't want t' babby born a ... " and here he hesitated, not wanting to say the word.

"Indeed," she replied quickly. "And I am still in my widow's weeds," she added, looking down at her black skirt and high buttoned jacket, tied with black ribbon, her bonnet also with its black ties, although thankfully convention now decreed she could remove the crepe, the period of a year having elapsed. "I feel that it would be more – appropriate in the circumstance, to organise a register office wedding, don't you think?"

William merely grunted in response, the enormity of the situation becoming ever more clear to him. He wondered how his family would feel about it. After all, he was already a grandfather to three children by his oldest daughter, Harriet.

The sun was starting to fall behind the trees and a cool breeze had arisen. Henry was getting fractious as he had tired of his game and now that no-one was paying him any attention.

"Shall we go back?" she asked, as she stood and lifted Henry onto her hip. William stood beside her and reached forward taking Henry off her and hefted him effortlessly onto his shoulders, a new sensation for Henry which, once he had got over the shock of being so far above the world, delighted him as he chuckled and hung on to William's head. And so they walked back the way they had come and then headed up through the town with the towers of the Minster coming into sight, a familiar signpost wherever you found yourself in the city.

46

As Laura and William walked together to the Register Office a week or so later to arrange a date for their marriage and complete the formalities, William found himself going back and forth over in his mind the events of the last few days, not to mention that night nearly two months ago. He could have just walked away, he mused, but then he realised that he was bound by business ties so breaking free and leaving her to fend for herself would have been even more complicated and time-consuming, not to say to both of their detriment – and morally wrong. No matter what he thought, he was an honourable man and would not shirk his responsibilities, even though events had taken an unexpected turn. And it was his child. He could not deny that the events had taken place, and neither of them had been party to them against their will. And a part of him thrilled to the thought of the companionship and warmth of a woman again about the place, to come home to and to warm his bed after days away. With that thought, he also began to think that they should get a bigger place to live. He would leave the place he had on Goodramgate, and she could give up renting her place, so that between them they could afford a larger property – for there would be two children in due course. Maybe more, he surprised himself at the thought.

◆ ◆ ◆

The license was issued and the date was set for seven days later – the twenty eighth of September. By that time Laura would be well over three months pregnant, but thankfully not yet showing. With no family or close friends in the city, Laura was saved much of the censure which might have come her way. George's family were naturally taken aback and Frances, his sister, had had plenty to say on the matter – most of it along the lines of 'hardly cold in his grave, still in her period of mourning', etc. But Laura knew Frances would never have been in favour of any replacement for her brother. However, even she could not have doubted that Laura's choices were few. A widow on her own with a child had few options for future security. It was the timing that seemed to rancour most with her, and the age of Laura's future husband.

Even the registrar had raised his eyebrows when William had given details of the two parties intending to wed and had given their ages. But it was not so unusual for widows to marry quite soon to give their fatherless children, and themselves, security. But only Laura and William knew the reason for haste.

Laura had gathered pen and paper towards her one evening and constructed a letter to her sister Eliza in Leeds. As expected, her reply was both one of surprise but also congratulations. After all, she and Charles had met William and seen in him a solid and reliable man. But she was surprised at the difference in their ages. If Eliza had wished for a more suitable future partner for Laura, she did not say it, but if truth be told, she had hoped that just for once Laura might have a partner who was more of her own class and background. In her reply, Eliza once more asked if Laura had written to their mother. And, she begged, surely she should now.

Autumn had well and truly settled on the city and the leaves were by now either displaying the full range of autumn colour or had already been stripped from the trees and were lying in drifts along the paths and streets. It was late morning and the low sun flickered through the exposed branches as William and Laura walked together down past the Minster and turned into the fine street with its Georgian buildings where the Register Office was situated. It was to be a quiet affair, with only two of William's acquaintances as witnesses and no one to support Laura. The marriage was conducted simply and was soon complete, as William slipped a gold band on the finger from which Laura had previously removed the one that George had placed upon it not even eighteenth months earlier. She had the pleasure of wearing William's gift to her – a new outfit, now no longer attired in black but in a deep blue silk, with a bonnet adorned with matching ribbons. But there were no other fripperies as she had to maintain her decorum as a widow, even though she was celebrating her marriage day.

A marriage by licence also ensured a large degree of privacy which a church marriage would not have afforded. No banns were required and as both parties were resident in the city of York, no further proof of their right to marry was required other than proof that they were both widowed. William gave his age as sixty, while Laura dissembled slightly as she bit her lip and gave her age as thirty three, a year older than she actually was. Even so, there was a huge disparity in their ages which no-one attending could deny. But necessity was the reason – not, of course, that they gave any indication of this to the officials or their few guests.

After they had duly signed the register, and all the official matters were concluded, Laura at last allowed herself to relax and breath a small sigh of relief. They crossed the road to a small inn and had a simple wedding lunch there and lingered for an hour or so more to celebrate with a few drinks with William's acquaintances. One was a boatman and coal merchant whom he had worked alongside for many years, and the other a childhood friend of his who was a carpet dealer. After bidding them goodbye and thanking them for their support, William gave Laura his arm and they walked back together to the house that would become their marital home. He had found a house for rent just off Lowther Street, not far from where she had been living before, but it was in a neat terrace and had more rooms as well as a cellar. It would serve them well and she had spent the previous week packing up and preparing for the move, then settling herself and Henry into their new home a few days earlier. William had added a few items from his own home – a couple of pictures for the walls, a rug or two, a sideboard and various items of crockery, as well as personal items. He also bought a small new single bed for Henry which could go in the extra bedroom, which would in time also hold their expected arrival.

A neighbour had been looking after Henry for the day, and they stopped by and collected him. His little face lit up at the sight of William and he held up his arms shouting "Up, up!", demanding a ride on William's shoulders. Together for the first time as a little family, they walked up to their own front door and William set Henry down as he unlocked it and took Laura's hand as they walked in together. She had left some food prepared and so only had to get the stove going to heat up the kettle while she laid out the cold sliced meat and cake which they could have later. Henry rushed around pulling William by the hand as he wanted to show him his room. A while later William came down with Henry, shaking his head as he entered the kitchen and with a rueful smile upon his face.

"We've been practisin' callin' me Dada but 'e 'asn't gotten th' 'ang o' it yet," he said shaking his head in mock frustration.

Laura felt a small pang of loss for Henry's real father, so quickly taken from them before the child was even two months old; the father he never knew. But she didn't doubt that William would be a solid and gentle stepfather to the child, the only father he would ever know.

After Henry had been cosied up in his bed upstairs and the covers tucked well in to stop him rolling over and onto the floor during the night, they sat down by the soft lamplight and enjoyed the cold meal, followed by some slices of fruit cake that Laura had prepared the previous day.

"Let's go and sit by our own fireside William. I have lit the fire in the parlour and it should be warm and cosy in there."

They sat each side of the fireplace, and neither said much. He reached over and picked up a newspaper that lay on the arm of the chair, opening it and making a great show of reading every column on every page. She matched him by picking up her sewing which she had laid in a bag by her chair the previous evening, and continued to run small neat stitches along the hem of a flannel petticoat for the approaching winter weather. The only sounds were the inexorable ticking of the clock on the mantelpiece and the crackle and spit of the coal as it burned down in the grate, punctuated every so often with the rustling of the paper as William turned a page and shook it out to see it better in the pale lamplight. Their wedding night was on both their minds but now that it was nearly here, they both felt awkward and nervous. After all, as Laura had said, this was not a match made of love, more convenience and practicality. As for William, he knew he had to assume the duties of a married man and he was hopeful that his new wife would assume the role of partner in every sense, although he was not under any misapprehension that he would be the passionate lover she might have wished.

Eventually William reached the last page of the Yorkshire Gazette and folding it beside him on the chair, he stood and walked over to the small cupboard that sat in the corner, pulling out two glasses and a bottle of brandy and proceeded to fill them both. Handing one to her he pulled her up to stand opposite him and raising his glass he said, "Ah think we need a toast. 'ere's to us both."

Taking the glass from him, Laura raised it and clinked it against his, adding, " And many happy years ahead." As she swallowed the burning liquid, she felt glad of its warmth and awaited the slight numbing of her senses which she knew it would soon bring. He put down his glass and leant forward to take hers, putting it alongside his own on the small side table. Bending down, he kissed her very gently and then put his hands around her back, pulling her closer. Closing her eyes, she recalled other kisses, other places and the passion of other times. This was the life that she had been dealt. She had a duty to make it work to the benefit of her and her children. She was no young woman in her first flush of youth. She had the experience and wisdom of her years. The circumstances she had come through brought her here to this time when at last she could find stability and security with a man who would provide for her and her children's future. She must be content with her lot and work with him toward their mutual success, both in business and in their future life together.

Laying her head upon his chest, she allowed herself to surround his stocky body with her arms, and she felt the strength that lay beneath. After pressing further gentle kisses upon her, he emptied the liquid left in his glass and putting the fireguard in front of the fading embers of the fire and dousing the lights, he led her up the slightly creaking stairs and into their bedroom.

47

S ue already missed having Kate home. The house was at once quieter and seemed to have an echo that it didn't have when Kate was here. There was always some music in the background or doors closing, footsteps on the creaky boards upstairs or the clattering of crockery in the kitchen to give that warm familiar feeling of companionship. But Sue was not one to begrudge Kate her life and her studies. Having waved her off yesterday morning, she had headed off to her furniture upcycling class and then collapsed exhausted in front of the telly that evening.

But today she would collect her files and folders, pull out the laptop and resume her search. She had told Kate a bit about what she had found – especially the relevance of Lowther Street, but she sensed a reticence in Kate, as if she was hiding behind a veil and she always seemed to change the subject. Sue put it down to her being tired after the intensity of her studies and blamed the fact that she was probably too conscientious and should be enjoying some of the freedoms of student life more, letting her hair down and enjoying life the company of young people her own age.

It had been a couple of weeks since Sue had last looked at her research and so she took a few minutes to pull out the notes she had made and unfolded the family tree with its added arrows to boxes with new names written in them and notes of dates and places annotated in the margins. She picked up her hastily scribbled To Do list of next steps and looked at the bulleted items.

• *Laura Emily – find her on 1871 census*

• *find out when and where Laura Emily was born and died*

• *find Laura's marriages*

• *Newspapers?*

From the 1881 census she had found out that Laura Emily had been born in Hull and her age was given as 38. A quick bit of arithmetic and Sue pulled up FreeBMD, checked her surname at birth (which was Harrison from the list given on Kate Eliza's birth certificate) and looked for a birth of a Laura Emily Harrison in Hull around 1843 +/- a year. After a few moments she was looking at the Dec quarter for 1843 where she was listed as born in the area of Sculcoates in Hull. Noting the page and volume numbers on her notepad, she added that information under the box on the tree for Laura Harrison, her great great grandmother.

Opening another tab on her laptop and calling up Ancestry she searched for Laura Harrison on the 1871 census. After a few wrong results, she eventually found her as a lodger in a house in a court off Great Union Street in Hull. Above her were listed two names; Annie Briggs, a widow aged 54, a laundress and her son Benjamin, single, aged 22 and a labourer. All of them were born in Hull.

So now Sue could work out that all Laura's marriages had occurred between 1871 and 1881. As the thought came to her, she added the note:

• Laura - any children by these marriages?

Then she ticked off the first bullet point – she knew where Laura was in 1871. Flipping back to the previous page in her notebook she noted the names of the men Laura had married – Cowper, Shipton, then Hoxton.

Back to FreeBMD and she put in the criteria for Laura Harrison and the spouse's surname Cowper. She threw the net wide and covered the widest range of dates from 1871 to 1881. Adding Hull to the district field she clicked the search key and soon the page refreshed. Near the top was the record she was looking for. June quarter 1872 and a list of names of four males and females married in that quarter. Samuel Cowper and Thomas Wilkes were the men, and Laura Emily Harrison and Jane Wells were the women. Noting the volume and page numbers in her notebook, she again realised that her costs were mounting.

She realised that she could narrow down the next marriage by looking for a marriage of Laura Cowper to a man surname Shipton after 1872. Entering the relevant information into a fresh page, she hit search. No results in the time slot. Sitting back in her chair, Sue rubbed her eyes and took a deep breath. Frowning she tried to think through this conundrum and checked the information she had entered. Maybe Laura's next marriage wasn't in Hull, she realised, shaking her head at her stupidity. Removing Hull pulled up far too many names. Deciding to be bold and just enter Yorkshire for the county, she hit the search button again.

This time far fewer options and her eyes quickly spotted a marriage for a Laura Emily Cowper in Leeds in the

March quarter of 1874 and the man was George Shipton.

Leaving Yorkshire as the county to search she re-entered Laura Shipton and spouse's name Hoxton within the same ten year search period and scanning down the results found the marriage she was looking for in the September quarter of 1875 in York. So, Sue thought, the poor woman had been married three times in three years and widowed twice. What on earth could have happened?

48

February 1876
York

T heir life took on a routine and rhythm which was at first new but then became familiar and comforting. The weeks and months passed and with it came a bitter winter, when ice all but blocked the waterways and boats were iced in their moorings and consequently late with their deliveries. William got back to York whenever he could and Henry was always the one to spot him as he stood on a chair by the parlour window, looking down the street for 'Dada'. And with the passing months, Laura's belly swelled and the baby made its presence felt with increased vigour. This child was active and gave her little peace, especially when she lay in her bed, it seemed to come alive and do a dance of its own through the small hours.

Laura knew her time would be getting nearer, having counted the days more accurately in her head than she had admitted to William. Nevertheless she hoped that it might delay its arrival giving her the greatest advantage in convincing him, and maybe herself, that it was truly his. Fortunately as her actual due date approached, she was glad that the child she carried appeared to be small and slight compared to Henry, with whom she had felt both enormous and cumbersome. This child sat less prominently and her added weight seemed to gather around her more than all to the front. Nevertheless, she was grateful that as February approached William had agreed to arrange for the men he employed to take the boats out, as he could now afford to do so with the business doing so well. She persuaded him that he could allow himself some rest from the hardest work, especially with the waters so treacherous and the cold weather causing his bones to ache. He did not need much persuasion, enjoying the comfort of the fireside and Henry's company, not to say the ministrations of his young wife as she rubbed his aching shoulders and back. But every day brought her time nearer and nearer.

As it always happens, after the freeze came the thaw and in the space of but a few days, the river in York had risen and overflowed the staiths, flooding the lowest streets and alleys by the waterside where the meanest hovels existed, and running unimpeded into cellars and waterside inns and warehouses. And to add to it, there came stormy winds and lashing rain as the warmer southerly air met the frozen northern lands. Folk were driven from the Lanes once more and took refuge in the churches and halls made available to them. Thankfully Laura and William's home was well away from the rapacious river as it overran the lower parts of the city, the torrents of water boiling under the bridges which were nearly swamped by the height of the water beneath. Few boats could come up river against such a flow and few ventured to set sail, fearing the current would dash them against the bridge piers or into the banks. It seemed like the river was trying to come into the town and reach them, its rivulets creeping and searching through the streets and alleys in search of something, someone familiar.

The three of them were glad to sit close together by their own fireside, listening to the wind whistling through the gaps in the casement as it rattled behind the thick curtains and hearing the splatter of raindrops as they were thrown against the glass. Henry sat playing with his toys on the rug in front of the fire, the guard across it to prevent stray sparks flying out and him getting too close. He sang little songs to himself and seemed oblivious to the maelstrom outside.

As Laura stood to go through to the kitchen to put on the kettle, she doubled over as the first sharp pain knifed through her core. "Not now, not yet," she murmured to herself. William looked up from his newspaper, his pipe tucked in the corner of his mouth.

"Laura?" he enquired, "Are ye alreet?"

"Yes, it's nothing. I will be fine," she replied, straightening and taking a deep breath before continuing to walk through to the kitchen. But when she reached the table, she laid her weight upon her hands and leant there until the pain had fully subsided. But as the evening progressed, she knew that things were in motion. By the time she had Henry tucked into bed, even William knew what was coming. Suddenly her waters broke and in the space of less than an hour she was holding her baby daughter in her arms. It had all happened so fast. In one great gush, the infant had come swimming out as if she couldn't wait to take her first breath and join this world of people. Not even time to get the doctor or a woman she knew who had attended Henry's birth, both of whom were already out on call on this stormy night.

"But she's come early," said William, as he stroked the still damp hair and gripped the tiny hand in his huge rough fingers.

"Second babes often do," she hastily reassured him. "And although she is small, she is strong and healthy. Just listen to her!" And indeed the babe was exercising its lungs strongly as it demanded security and comfort having been so forcefully expelled from its warm wet world.

"Let me feed her and she will soon calm down."

William left them, taking Henry with him. The child had demanded to see his mother as he had heard her moans and cries and was large-eyed and fearful when William held him in his arms till all was quiet, before the new sounds of the baby's cries had echoed down the stairs. Now having seen his new baby sister, he was unimpressed with her as she made far too much noise and didn't even want to play with him.

Later that evening the midwife appeared to check that all was well, and after being shown up to the room where mother and child lay, she came down sometime later with the soiled sheets for washing and rags for burning, which she stuffed into the stove. Assuring William that both mother and child were well, she took her leave and showed herself out into the stormy night, still battering and bruising the city with its ferocity.

They named the child Kate Eliza, born 11 February 1876. William braved a lull in the continued stormy weather to walk up to the Register Office and register her birth. If the registrar who had married them less than five months before made the connection, he did not show it, merely asking for the relevant details and issuing William with the certificate he folded and tucked into his breast pocket. As he walked back through the town with his collar pulled up around his ears, his eye was caught by a display in a shop window. By the time the rain had started again, he had left the shop clutching a wrapped paper parcel tied up with string containing a small cotton cloth doll for his new little daughter.

By the time he arrived back home, he was drenched and thankfully he had stuffed the package inside his coat.

Shaking the water from his overcoat and hat, he took them through to the kitchen and hung them on the end of the pulley draped above the stove, already swathed in cloths and nappies. Laura was nursing the baby in the corner, sitting in a chair well padded with cushions, while Henry sat in his high chair eating his dinner.

"For goodness sake, sit down and get warmed William," Laura remonstrated with him. "You'll catch your death." As she made to rise and get the teapot down to make a brew, William waved a hand and assured her that he was quite capable of making one for them both. Thankfully she sat back down and manoeuvred the infant against her breast as it grizzled at being detached from the source of food, warmth and comfort. As he walked over to look down at them both, baby Kate opened her eyes wide and looked up at William, her eyes as yet unfocussing but aware of movement and shadow.

"She 'as your eyes, m' dear," William stated, with a smile.

49

A s baby Kate thrived and Laura's time was more and more taken up with the care of two young children, she spent less time focussing on the business or trying to expand and strengthen it. However, William seemed to have found renewed energy and interest and had continued to get new orders and clients on his travels, helped in part by his links with Charles in Leeds. They were becoming financially secure and were able to start to acquire more home comforts. One day a cart pulled up outside their door and the carter said he had a delivery for the woman of the house. It was a new mangle that wrung out the wet linens more effectively and the carter and his mate hefted it through to the back yard, entering from the ginnel that ran behind the row of terraced houses. Another time two comfortable upholstered chairs were delivered and took pride of place in their front parlour. William obviously wanted to provide for his newly acquired family in the best way he could and Laura was gratified by his devotion and concern.

One evening, after the children had gone to sleep, and in the lull before Kate would require another feed, Laura decided to broach the subject which had been concerning her for some time.

"William, I need to ask you something. Have you made a will? Or have you thought about updating it now that you are a father again? I know you will think me presumptuous but, as you know, Henry and I were left in dire circumstances at the lack of urgency that George showed in this instance. I would not presume to dictate to you William, but you should concern yourself with making provision for us all, if anything untoward should befall you."

William puffed on his pipe and thought about her words for a few moments before, nodding. "Ye're reet. Ah need t' update my affairs. Ah would'n wish 'ee all to suffer if owt were t' 'appen."

Laura relaxed a little and sat back into the plump cushion on her new chair. "And you have so many new ventures, everything needs to be well documented and ordered."

"Ye're such a good organiser. Ah know tha've been keepin' t' paperwork in good order. But 'tis true. T' water-ways are a dangerous place an' accidents 'appen. But God willin', ah'll be here wi' ye for many years t' come," he added, smiling and reaching out to give her hand a squeeze.

"Thank you William, I knew you would understand. Will you go soon to see Mr Marr?"

He assured her he would, and the next day strode down to the solicitor's office in Davygate and made an appoint-ment to do just as Laura had suggested.

The months passed and their life took on a pattern that they both came to feel comfortable with. William still went on trips but more often he would employ others to do the longer, more onerous ones, preferring to stay nearer home. But there were still occasions when he was away for a few days at a time and Laura found herself reviewing where she was now and how the future might pan out. The baby was thriving and Henry was now a very active two year old, demanding attention and full of energy. Kate was a very alert infant, always looking around, her bright eyes missing nothing. Another of William's purchases had been a perambulator in which she could walk the infant, while Henry held on to the handle. It was not new, but she was delighted that he had acquired it, even if it was second hand. It made getting about with the two children so much easier.

Late one summer evening, sitting alone in the kitchen having washed and tidied away all the dishes and put Kate's soiled nappies in to the bucket to soak overnight, she found her thoughts turning to her mother, and what Eliza had told her. It had been well over a year since they had had that conversation. Fragments of memories flew in and out of her mind, happier times when the family enjoyed trips to the park or the seaside, times playing games around the fire, toasting bread on forks and making shadows with their hands and fingers by the flickering light of the fire. Her father did not appear in these recollections, chiefly because when he was around the children would have to sit quietly at some peaceful activity such as reading or sewing, or more often they would be banished to their rooms at the top of the house and expressly told that they should behave themselves. Mama never countered his instruction, always acquiescent to his orders, given gruffly and brooking no disagreement. And of course, he ignored her more than the others. She could not recall any times he actually spoke directly to her or acknowledged her presence in particular. And of course, her siblings noticed that, especially the older ones and to keep in favour with their father, would copy and mimic his attitude. And so she became even more ostracised than she had ever been. These thoughts had her almost pushing the notion of her contacting her mother to the back of her mind again, but then she recalled that of course, her father was no more. No longer could he hold sway over her or her mother. And her mother had expressly asked Eliza for news of her youngest – surviving, child.

Collecting paper, pen and ink from the dresser that stood on the opposite wall of the kitchen, she sat down again at the table and found herself looking at the blank sheet of paper, unsure how even to begin to organise her thoughts in order to reach out to her mother after so many, empty, lonely, awful years. Eventually she decided to keep the letter brief and to the point.

Dearest Mama,

I met my sister Eliza some time ago when in Leeds and she told me of your circumstances and your latest place of residence. She also informed me that you have been asking for news of me.

It is very difficult for me to write this letter, given the circumstances that caused us to be parted. Life has been very cruel to me over the years since I was left with no family to call upon. I had to make my own way and Fate did not always deal me a fair hand.

You find me now in a place that I can feel safe, with a man who is caring and considerate and with whom I hope to raise my two children in comfort and security.

I know that much has passed between us and I do not want to relive that and neither, I am sure, do you.

But for the sake of you being my mother and having shown me care when you were able, I am writing this now. If you wish to see me, I will consider whether I can put the painful times behind me and face you again.

I remain, your daughter,

Laura

Sitting back and reading over her words, neatly penned with no crossings out or additions, she wondered whether this was the right thing to do. Once it had been posted, she could not retract the words nor the sentiments. Folding it up before she had a chance to reconsider, she copied the address from the piece of paper Eliza had given her and laid it at the back of the hall stand by the front door, where at some point she could decide its fate, one way or the other. As she did so, Kate's cries assailed her and she went to her, unbuttoning her blouse as she walked, ready to feed and comfort the infant.

"Ah posted that letter for 'ee," William shouted as came in a few days later. "Ah was getting' me baccy so I jus saw it an' took it wi' me to save 'ee a journey."

Her blood ran cold and her stomach lurched. Well, there – the deed was done. No going back. "Thank you William," she replied weakly.

◆ ◆ ◆

She received a reply just over a week later. Every day she had dreaded its arrival but now it lay before her, unopened, challenging her to make a decision. She could throw it away unread and then nothing would change, life would go on and she would not have to face up to any of her deeply buried memories. But the unknown would always niggle at her. She would have no peace that way. Two or three times throughout the day she sat down, holding it at arm's length, her elbows resting on the smooth wooden surface of the kitchen table. And each time she had pushed it away from her, unwilling to take the final step.

But by the evening, as the shadows started to stretch across the street outside, she picked it up and sat down in the parlour in the plumply upholstered chair at the side of the fireplace. No fire burned there as the evening was warm, following a bright summer's day. Both children were sleeping, washed and fed and tucked up cosily, oblivious to the tension twisting their mother's stomach. William was away, not due back till late tomorrow. Some children ran past the window, kicking a ball against the wall and then disappeared around the corner. The rattle of a horse and cart grew nearer, then faded as it turned into the next street. The bang of a door, a few footsteps, the rattle of a dustbin lid, the distant peal of bells from the Minster. This was the tapestry of sounds that made the everyday backdrop to her life. But this evening they seemed louder and more evident as she tried to find the courage to take that final step.

Pushing back a stray lock of hair from her forehead, she sat up straight and taking a deep breath, unfolded the paper which crackled slightly as the creases yielded unwillingly to her touch. The hand that greeted her was at once familiar, but also not – more spidery and shaky than she recalled, but nevertheless recognisable. She flattened out the letter on the table beside her, then held it up so that the lamp light could illuminate it better.

Dearest Laura,

You cannot imagine how pleased I was to receive your letter. I wondered if I would ever hear from you again. Too many years have passed and I understand your reasons for breaking off contact with me, us, your family. Life is very different for me now that your father is no longer with us. I cannot say that being a widow has been entirely hard to bear.

Your older brother Matthew and his wife invited me to join them here in Hornsea and I am a permanent resident in their small hotel. I am well looked after. I do not have to cook my own meals and I have my own accommodation where I can be solitary if I wish. In the summer there are always guests but in the winter the place is much quieter, both of which I enjoy. Do you remember when we used to come down to Hornsea and you all played on the sand? I often think of those times when I go for my walks along Marine Drive and around the Promenade Gardens.

Laura, I have to ask you something which I know you will find difficult. Would you come and see me? There are things I have to tell you. We need to talk. Too many years have passed and there are things left unsaid that you need to know.

Will you come?

Please come alone, if you can.

I look forward to hearing from you soonest,

Your Loving Mama

Laura sat back and leant her head against the cushion, realising how tense her body was and how rigidly she had been sitting while she read the words scrawled upon the paper in front of her. She realised her hands were shaking, and laying the letter down beside her on the table, she covered her face with her hands and shut her eyes as a myriad of memories swirled around her mind. She would not allow herself to give in to tears. Letting down the barriers she had erected would bring all she had built crashing down around her. But her resolve began to weaken when she thought of what she had missed all those years. The closeness of a mother's touch, the kind words and encouraging smiles. These were only very infrequent and covertly given when no-one else could see them. There were answers she needed from questions she had never asked, for fear of hearing what she did not want to know. But her mother desired that time to be now – a time when they could talk, when all the mysteries and secrecy might be uncovered. Was she ready for that? Was the time now?

Having sat in the quiet of the room for a long time, she eventually extinguished the lights as she realised night had fallen. As she climbed the stairs, she stopped outside Henry's room and looked in at the child, hearing the puff of his gentle breathing, deeply asleep with not a care in the world. Gently pulling the door to, she went into her own bedroom where baby Kate lay sleeping in her crib, her arms flung out on either side of her head, her little fists twitching as she dreamed – of what?

As she finally climbed into bed, her hair brushed and plaited, her clothes neatly folded on the chair or hung ready for the next day, she slid under the covers and slipped off to sleep, but her night was disturbed by dreams and fragments of memories which she could not piece together. In the early hours, as the paleness of dawn crept into the room, the baby stirred and started whimpering, demanding attention. Bringing her into bed with her, Laura propped herself up on the bolster and pillows and put the child to her breast. Together they both eventually drifted off, mutually comforting each other.

◆ ◆ ◆

She took quite a few days to process the information in the letter and to ponder the request within it. She didn't want to have to discuss it with William but it became inevitable as it would take a full day to get there and back. And she would have to take the baby with her as she would need feeding and would be fractious if Laura was not around. She struggled to broach the subject and left a few evenings with her thoughts unvoiced, until she realised that she had to face up to this in order to move on with her life, un-weighed down by the inexplicable distance between her mother, herself and her family. She needed answers. Then she could go forward with whatever she had learned, and make a future of memories for her own old age, without the shadows of the past clouding it with dark, unexplored and unresolved enigmas.

In the end, William could not have been more understanding. Without questioning her too deeply, he realised that she needed to do this. And he wanted to help bring this about as best he could. The day eventually arrived and Laura rose early, while the house was still quiet and sat on her own in the kitchen, watching the clouds scud across the sky through the window that faced on to the back yard. A sharp breeze had sprung up and she went outside in her robe to unpeg the few cloths she had left out to dry overnight. Draping them over the pulley to remove the last hint of dampness from them, she then hauled the pulley up over the stove where the warm air would finish the process. As the small wheels squealed with the effort, she heard Kate start to cry and then William's steps above as the floorboards creaked and he rose from their bed and went to comfort her. A few moments later his footsteps accompanied by the gentle creak of each stair tread signalled his imminent arrival downstairs with Kate in his arms. Now over six months old she was always alert and full of energy. Enjoying being bounced in William's arms, she giggled and chuckled, shouting, " 'gain, 'gain!" if he threatened to stop and rest his arms. Soon another voice joined the throng as Henry, hearing all the commotion going on, had wakened and wanted to be part of it all. "Mama, Dada!" he shouted down the stairs. Laura hurried to the bottom of the stairs, urging him to hold on tight to each spindle as he couldn't yet reach the banister. With a sense of achievement he finally arrived at the last step having come down one step at a time, and she laughed at his little face with his tongue sticking out with concentration.

They had a long day ahead of them. They were to catch the train from York to Hull, which would take the best part of two hours, then Laura and Kate would take the connection on to Hornsea, which would take about another three quarters of an hour. William and Henry were going to spend the day together, having a treat by getting hot pies to eat then walking along to West Park and watching a game of cricket or football if there was one being played – well, at least William would enjoy that. Henry would enjoy a kickabout with a ball for a while, but then even he would be tired. William had arranged to meet his cousin who lived in Hull and they would spend the rest of the afternoon and early evening with his cousin's family and grandchildren.

As for Laura and baby Kate, William put them on the train for Hornsea, loading the perambulator into the guard's van for Laura to collect upon her arrival. They had arranged that they would meet up back at the station in Hull and travel back to York together that evening with two, probably very tired, children.

As Hornsea station approached, Laura's heart was in her mouth, she felt she could hardly breathe and as the train gave a final lurch as it reached the end of the track, she found she was frozen to the spot. Other passengers alighted. Families with young children come to enjoy the opportunity of a play on the beach at the end of summer, before school would resume. Older couples come for a day's stroll along the promenade, a breath of sea air and a treat of locally-caught fish and chips. But none had been summoned for her reason. The slamming of carriage doors brought her to, and baby Kate stirred as the motion had ceased and the sudden racket startled her. As she stepped from the carriage, the smell of smoke and the hiss of steam surrounding her, a porter strode over to her and asked if she needed any assistance. Asking him to collect the perambulator from the guard's van, she followed him up the platform in the direction of the main station as he raced ahead and took it from the guard, who had been standing at the van looking out for her. Giving the porter a small coin, she laid Kate down and collecting her thoughts, set off out of the station and into the main streets of the small seaside town. The other passengers had all but dispersed and it was only one older couple taking their time who walked ahead of her. As she passed the Coastguard Station on her left, she headed on down the main road and soon came to the crossroads where looking to her right, she could see the sea and the sand, dotted with people enjoying the sunshine and fresh air. Turning to her right, she headed towards them and joined the excited crowds but then she turned left into one of the small streets that ran parallel to the seafront and which was populated with guesthouses and small hotels.

Her steps slowed as she saw the sign board swinging gently in the sea breeze, proclaiming its name and the added information on a small slider announcing 'No Vacancies'. The white painted porch led into a small vestibule with a black and white tiled floor. Another glass door inside was shut. To one side was a large front window which although it faced the sea, had its view blocked by the opposite buildings of similar type and occupation. As she came closer, she noticed that there was a figure standing at the window, just back enough from it that they were in shadow, but they were looking out into the street. With a lurch, she recognised the shape and form of her mother. As she turned through the gate and up the short path, the inner door swung open and her mother stood there awaiting her arrival.

"Laura. Oh, my dear, it's you," she gasped. "I cannot tell you how happy I am to see you. Thank you, thank you for coming."

Laura merely nodded her head and used the few moments it took to manoeuvre the perambulator into the inner hallway to collect her thoughts. The baby had once more fallen asleep, so she left her to rest, giving her and her mother time to appraise each other and break the ice. Showing her into the room that she had previously vacated, her mother indicated a chair by the side of fireplace and sat opposite her. No fire burned, instead the grate was host to a large and overblown floral display, the contents made of paper and silk and ever so slightly dusty.

For a few moments they looked at each other, neither sure how to proceed. Laura studied her mother's features and tried to match them with those she had last seen over fifteen years previously. The face was still her mother's but there were creases and wrinkles where before there had been none, her hair had threads of silver running through it where it peeped out from beneath her small headpiece made of black straw and net, fancifully collected together and adorned with jet beads. Of course, she realised, her mother would still be in mourning for their father. Although more than three years had passed, her mother was following the Queen's manner of black apparel. The only allowance her mother had made to the end of the obligatory three years mourning for a widow was a pale mauve high-necked blouse beneath her light jacket. Perched on the edge of her seat, she seemed like a little bird perched on a branch, about to take flight. She was obviously nervous and kept fluttering her hands about, unsure where to rest them. She too was studying the face in front of her and saw a more mature countenance than that of the young girl who had left them all so abruptly so many years before. But in that face there were already the suggestions of creases that indicated where the stresses and episodes of the intervening years had made their mark. As yet, she had no full comprehension of what those had been. Even in Eliza's letters giving her news of Laura, there had been little to fill in the gaps. Whether Eliza did not wish to impart these, or whether Laura had never divulged these was a moot point.

In the end it was Laura who broke the silence that stretched out across the space between them. "Mama, you are looking well," was the best she could come up with.

Her mother smiled a little and acknowledged the statement. "As do you, Laura," she replied almost in a whisper. Unsure of another response, she went on to safer ground. "You must be hungry after your journey. I have asked that they serve us a cold cuts lunch, if that suits you? We may have it in here. This is our private sitting room and we will not be disturbed by any of the guests who may come and go, though they are all out at present enjoying the delights of Hornsea," and at this she indicated the outside amusements with a sweep of her hand towards the window.

"That would be quite suitable. Thank you. The baby will probably sleep for a while but I will listen out for her. I would very much like some tea as I am parched with the smoke and stuffiness of the train journey."

"Of course, of course," her mother fussed and leaning over, she tugged at the knob at the side of the fire, the sound of a distant bell ringing indicating that she had summoned the maid.

Over a light spread of cold meats, pickles, cheese and bread, followed by some cake and of course, tea they covered all the pleasantries and made inconsequential chat to fill the time. But inevitably they sat back and pushed their plates to one side.

Laura was prepared to hear the purpose of her mother's request that she wanted to speak to her and had something to impart. Laura thought her mother could not look any more nervous. Her tea cup rattled in its saucer as she laid it on the tea table that sat beside them.

Eventually she leaned forward, wringing her thin bony hands in her lap. The skin was pale and translucent and Laura found herself focussing on the mapwork of thin blue veins that ran the back of them. Over the next half hour or so, all the secrets and unspoken words poured from her. And there were tears, and pleas for forgiveness. And there were recriminations and demands from her daughter as to why her mother had never stood her ground. But in her heart she knew, for after all, her mother was never strongminded nor forceful, and their father would have brooked no disagreement or argument to challenge his attitudes and commands. And of course, the family had to fall in with these or else face his wrath and censure. The line of least resistance was by far the easiest way to go. She understood that, but it didn't make her treatment any easier to comprehend.

Eventually her mother broke down totally, burying her head in her hands, her heavy tears soaking the flimsy lace handkerchief that she dabbed at her cheeks. Laura's resolve splintered and she stood and walked over to her mother, kneeling down beside her and wrapping her arms around the bony shoulders that heaved with the sobs that broke from her thin frame. She found herself rocking her gently, as she might one of her children, and slowly the sobs diminished and her mother's breathing became more measured and regular. But the words she had heard were tumbling around her mind and she could not sort out what she felt, or even discern if she had really understood them. She needed space and time to process what had come tumbling out from her mother's mouth.

The cries of baby Kate from the adjoining hallway brought Laura to the present and she stood and smoothed down her skirts and headed out of the door to soothe the child. Picking her up, she laid the thin blanket back in the perambulator, where the baby had thrown it off. Straightening her little dress and petticoats, she carried her back into the sitting room. Her mother looked up, her face still blotched and her eyes puffy and red. Laura sat in her own chair and sat Kate upon her knee, bouncing her gently to soothe her cries. The novelty of new surroundings soon caught the child's eye and she twisted round trying to take in all the new things she could see over her mother's shoulder. Laura had brought a bottle with her and some soft bread for Kate to chew on. She took the jug of hot water that had been left and poured some into a bowl and laying the milk bottle in it, waited for it to warm slightly.

Her mother was still trying to compose herself and had walked over to the window, smoothing down her crumpled black silk skirt and taking some deep breaths. By the time Laura was ready to give the baby her milk, her mother had composed herself enough to return to sit again opposite them. Baby Kate was hungry and greedily guzzling her milk, her eyes closed and the only sound her sucking at the teat, while her little hands plucked at the hem of her dress in concentration.

"She looks a fine healthy child," her mother ventured.

"Yes, she is. She will be seven months old in two weeks. She is very active and inquisitive already. And strong-willed," she added.

"Just like you were," her mother mused, with a hesitant smile.

Eventually the child had had enough and was more

interested in sitting up and looking at the new person opposite. As she squirmed around and positioned herself to look straight at her grandmother, a cloud covered the sun briefly before another breeze blew it away and a flash of sunlight illuminated the room again, lighting up the child's face.

Laura's mother gasped and was visibly shaken, one hand flying to her mouth while the other clutched at her chest, crumpling the silk jacket and causing the jet buttons to sparkle as they caught the light. A look of utter horror came over her face. Her breath came in short shallow gasps. The only words she could utter were, "Her eyes! Oh no Laura! Not you too!"

As she tried to stand, she staggered, knocking over the tea table and scattering the cups and plates across the deeply patterned rug. The clatter and crash brought the maid scurrying to the door and she gasped as she saw the devastation in front of her. By now, the old woman was on her knees, crumpled at the side of the chair, holding on to it to keep herself from totally collapsing onto the floor. Kate started to cry, startled by the sudden noise and Laura stared as the realisation of what her mother had said came to her fully.

A man appeared, standing momentarily frozen in the doorway, taking in the scene in front of him. He seemed familiar and it took Laura a moment to recognise her eldest brother Matthew. He was stocky and had the arrogant stance that she recognised from her father. As the maid rushed over to aid her mistress, he stood unmoved by the scene in front of him. Looking at his sister coldly, all he said was, "I think you had better leave. I knew this was a bad idea but she would not listen. Goodbye Laura." Then adding as Laura made to rise and go to her mother's side, "We will take care of her. Goodbye."

It was with relief that she closed the front door of her own home behind her, the events of the day taking their toll. William carried Henry in his arms, his little head lolling against the man's shoulder. The child was tired out and had fallen deeply asleep on the train on the way home. The baby slept in her perambulator and was unperturbed by the experience of the day. Unlike Laura, whose legs were like jelly as she slumped down on the chair in the kitchen. As yet she had not given William a full description of the day's events, other than to say her mother had suffered a seizure and that they had had to leave hurriedly. The sound of William's heavy tread climbing the stairs made her smile and she heard him take Henry to his bedroom. He came down a few minutes later saying that he had just laid him on his bed and pulled the covers over him as he was still sound asleep. Laura smiled thankfully at him and watched as he went to raise the embers in the stove and set the kettle upon it to make the inevitable brew.

"William, would you mind if I had a glass of brandy? I am feeling quite faint with all that has happened today." As he went through into the parlour and she heard the clinking of glasses, she called through, "I think we both deserve one, William."

That night as she lay on her side next to William, his arm thrown across her shoulders and the rhythm of his deep breathing the only sound, her thoughts started to unravel all she had been told earlier.

I could not remain. Too many disapproving looks. Mama was the only one. She understood. Of course she did! I was the result of her one moment of feeling wanted and cherished. Her one moment of reciprocated passion and desire. But every time she looked at me, she was reminded of that time. It destroyed her. Never able to look me in the eye. Half wanting me close, half needing me gone from her presence. Of course, I never knew all this at the time. I just knew that I had to be gone from there. I would not be missed. The censorious looks from my elders, my brothers mimicking their father's attitudes and beliefs, seeking his approval and acceptance and becoming replicas of him; how he loved that. My sisters were soon married off to men of good prospects, chosen by my father of course. Mama tried to quell their nerves and fear of marriages as her own had been – cold and unfulfilling. But what else could us women expect. Money and position. The men earned it. The women were married to achieve it as appendages to their husbands. But I did not fit the mould. I was the odd one out. I was – the outsider.

T ime passed and William and Laura and their little family settled into a routine that suited them well. William's business interests expanded and he ran a fleet of four boats, all sailed for him by men he employed and knew well. As time went on, one or two of their sons joined them on board and learned the skills required to steer, load and manhandle the long boats through locks and busy docks, through tunnels and along winding riverways and busy canal highways. Occasionally William would join them on a trip, still hankering after the freedom of life on the water but having to accept that he was not as young as he used to be and his joints were stiffening and aching more as the years passed.

They lived comfortably and had money to spare for the little extras and comforts that enhanced their lives. A piano graced the parlour in their next house, not far from their previous red brick terraced house, but with an extra room downstairs and an extra floor with a small attic room. Henry liked to try to play upon it but truth be told, it was more for show and to display a few family photographs that they had taken, than to provide entertainment. They were able to hire a domestic – a young girl, Mary, and Laura was training her up in the various tasks required of a servant. She helped with the household chores such as cleaning out the grates and laying the fires, doing the laundry and cleaning and dusting. This took much of the load off Laura and she was able to have time to read or visit friends more often. As in the past, Laura also took care of all the paperwork and ledgers required for the business.

William and Laura rubbed along comfortably together. As Laura had said from the outset, it was a practical arrangement, not a love match but one that would provide companionship and comfort as they grew older together. Although Laura was not yet forty, William was now well into his sixties. She noticed how he had started to slow down, how he had to straighten out his stiff joints if he'd been sitting too long, how he had to stop for a breather walking up a steep hill. Yet he was never happier than when he joined one of his boats sailing to Hull, Leeds or wherever.

But although outwardly Laura's life seemed well ordered and running smoothly, only she and William knew how troubled her nights could be. Sometimes weeks would go by without any disturbance, but then she would once again wake in the darkest hour of the night, thrashing about with her eyes staring wildly, yet without seeing. And the words were always the same – repeating in harsh whispers, echoing through her subconscious mind.

Well, look at you.

Who'd have thought it.

Biddable.

Insubstantial.

Malleable.

Acquiescent.

Your mother's child.

And mine ...

Who are you?

Where are you?

I can hear you but I can't see you.

Where are you hiding?

Everywhere ...

I give.

I take away.

Will you come to me?

Come closer ... come closer ...

◆ ◆ ◆

Henry was now at school and he enjoyed learning, proving a quick and able student. He was quite a reserved child, never one to push himself forward but yet he was a popular boy and had many friends. He often asked if he might go on a river trip with William, but Laura always came up with reasons why he could not. She never gave him an acceptable reason in his eyes, and the only time she ever smacked him was when he came home late one afternoon after school, his shoes sodden and his trousers soaked up to the knees. It turned out that he and some friends had gone down to the convergence of the rivers Foss and Ouse by the Blue Bridge and had been playing on an old boat they found, taking it out on the water, only to discover it was leaky and they soon found themselves sinking. Luckily it was only in a shallow part and they were able to scramble ashore none the worse for wear, but due for a thrashing when they got home.

Laura was appalled when she heard what he had been doing. She gave no explanation why she was so angry, and Henry had never seen her so agitated. He was sent to his room and told to stay there and go without his supper. William was away and only Kate and Mary were in the house with his mother. He heard Kate crying downstairs – partly because she had never seen her mother in such a rage and partly at the raised voices which scared her. Later she tiptoed upstairs and sat on the floor outside his room and whispered through the door to him. Then she tried to push a slice of bread she had saved from her meal under the door but of course, it was too thick and fell to pieces.

Later that evening Laura sat with her head in her hands, still shaking from having lost her temper so completely. She could not explain to anyone, nor would she have even spoken to William, had he been home. She shut her eyes and sat in the darkened room trying to calm herself.

My name being called and a red-faced older sister sent to find me. A slap across my bare legs and a reminder never to stray away again. But I was curious.

It happened more than once, but I grew more devious in ways to meet – what? It called itself my friend, and I wanted one of those. It kept asking me to play. To join it in its games. But something always held me back. It became annoyed. It cajoled. It threatened. It grew malevolent. It started to be-

come more demanding.

He was only little. I held his hand and we walked together. He trusted me. He was only three years old. I had no recollection of the moments when it happened. Shouts roused me from my reverie. When I saw what had happened, I was distraught. It should have been me. But I fought against it. In a dark moment something else took charge. And he was gone from my grasp ...

51

K ate was enjoying her studies, especially as the warmer weather and better days allowed for more outdoor tutorials. On this morning in early May the tutorial group had been asked to meet by Clifford's Tower. They made their way in straggling groups of twos or threes past the gathering crowds of tourists queueing for entry at the Jorvik Centre and headed down Castlegate and past the elegant Georgian façade of Fairfax House. Ahead of them rose the grassy mound on which stood the tall stone square tower with its curved turrets at each corner.

The tutor drew them to one side and began to explain about the history of the tower through the various centuries. It had been an original motte and bailey castle constructed by William the Conqueror. It had borne witness to the massacre of the York Jewish community in 1190 who had taken refuge there, committing mass suicide when the tower was set alight. The existing stone tower was built in the 13th century but an explosion destroyed its military use in 1684. By the mid 19th century it was being used as York's prison and today it was open to the public, having undergone much conservation.

The tutor handed out various sheets for them to study, some in old script, and Kate was glad she had spent time studying palaeography. The tutor outlined the assignment he wished them to complete, using various sources and historical reports to look at how first and second-hand accounts could twist and distort the evidence to suit the writer's own ends. By the time he had completed the tutorial it was almost lunchtime, and as the sun was now shining from a clear blue sky, Kate, Sonja and Barney decided to grab a sandwich from a local takeaway and head across the road to the park that ran along the riverside. Spotting a bench in the distance, Barney loped off at an ungainly sprint and flopped down on it before anyone else could claim it. The girls joined him a few moments later, laughing as they sat down on either side of him.

They munched and chatted for the next half hour or so and then Barney stretched his long legs out and announced he was going to have a doze. Kate and Sonja decided to follow the river down as far as they could on the pathway and left their bags with him as they set off together. Walking as far as they could under the trees, they eventually came to a little bridge with blue painted balustrades. They crossed it to the end and discovered that they were at the confluence of two rivers. A smaller one joined the main river, the Ouse, from the left and they merged together at this point before heading south out of York. They stood leaning on the railings looking at the pleasure craft taking groups of tourists up and down the river, just making out the faint sound of the guide speaking on the tannoy to point out items of interest on either bank.

Sonja's mobile buzzed and started to play a jarring tune.

"It's my mum," she said, pulling a face. "I'd better take it." She put the phone to her ear and walked a few paces away from Kate, while the words, "Hi Mum," grew fainter as she turned and walked back over the bridge, her hands gesticulating as she continued her conversation.

Kate turned back to look at the water, the sun now shining brightly on the surface causing her to screw up her eyes and shade them with her hand. Cursing that she had forgotten to bring her sunglasses out of her pack left with Barney, she continued watching a couple of moorhens that were scooting under the bridge and into the vegetation at the side. The flashing of the sun upon the water became almost hypnotic and she found herself captivated and held by the rhythmic flashes as the wake of a boat caused the water to ripple.

I knew you would come to me – one day.

A pity it has been so long. But years, decades, mean nothing to me.

We have a bond, a pact.

Come closer and I will tell you ...

Without realising it Kate had walked to the other end of the bridge and was on a cobbled sloping slipway that led to the water's edge. The flashes of sunlight were reflected in her pale grey eyes, now wide and open as if looking at something far distant. As the little eddies of water gently splashed over the toes of her trainers, she looked down at her full grey wool skirt and the high button boots whose pointed toes were just visible under the hem of her skirt. She pulled her shawl closer around her, feeling the chill icy wind as it whistled around her neck, tugging strands of her dark hair from under the bonnet where it had been scraped back from her forehead and secured with hairpins. Her hands in thin leather gloves clutched at the edge of her paisley patterned shawl and she felt the tightness around her body digging into her ribs and causing her to straighten her spine.

"Kate! Kate!" a shrill voice cut through to jar her ears and she could hear approaching footsteps, fast and running, getting louder and closer. At first she resented their intrusion and did not recognise the name being shouted. It was only as a hand shot out and grabbed her arm, causing her to be pulled off balance and back from the water's edge, that she was aware that the shouts were intended for her. 'But I am not Kate,' she thought, as she turned to look at her assailant. Opening her mouth to remonstrate with the stranger, she was struck by the bright colours and incongruous attire of a young girl, mousy hair flying out behind her.

"Kate! What are you doing? Come back! You'll be paddling next!" Kate heard a laugh and a giggle as she was pulled further up the path, the brightness of the water causing her screw up her eyes and feeling the dampness seeping through the toes of her trainers.

Her skirts had gone. Her shawl. Her gloves. Her shiny pointed button boots. Her name – but what was it ...? She could not recall it.

For a moment she resented the intrusion, and then the moment was gone and she allowed herself to be dragged back up the slipway and onto a bench seat at the top, where an old man sat dozing in the sun, completely unaware of the events of the last few minutes.

Sonja was still laughing and Kate hesitantly allowed herself a slight smile, then shook her head and joined in the laughter. By the time they had gone back to find Barney on his bench, Sonja was telling her about her phone call and everything seemed just as normal as it had always been.

"You'll never guess what Kate did!" squealed Sonja as she kicked Barney's foot to wake him.

But Kate knew that it was not Kate who had been standing there at the water's edge. And who – or what – else had been there also?

52

The year Henry turned eight, the autumn weather turned unseasonably wet and damp. William started to suffer from a hacking cough, that eventually had him in bed for the best part of a week as he came down with influenza. Between them Laura and Mary ferried warm drinks and heated ceramic pigs up to his room to keep him warm, while Laura tried to get him to eat some thin broth to keep up his strength. Once he had started to improve, he insisted that he wanted to come downstairs and wrapping a rug around him by the fire, Laura made sure that he was warm and comfortable. Over the next few weeks he began to regain some of his strength and appetite but he still would break into bouts of coughing when he came from the cool outside into the warmth of the house, or vice versa. At night, he would often waken Laura as he tried to tiptoe out of bed, and go downstairs, trying to avoid waking her with his fits of coughing, while gasping for breath.

It took many weeks until he felt well enough to enjoy walking with Henry to school, often detouring on his return to stand on the Ouse Bridge and look down the staith at the boats, arriving or departing, or being moored. The men he employed to sail his boats would bring any relevant paperwork to the house while he was laid up, but as he felt better and could walk down to the staith, he would often meet up with them there and drop into an inn on the way back for a pint of ale. The colour started to return to his cheeks and he began to fill out again, but his clothes still hung loosely about his previously stocky frame.

Never content to be idle, William still liked to have a purpose to his life. He was never a pipe-and-slippers type of man and it was something that Laura admired in him. Towards the end of December there were near-windless days of sunshine. In the mornings there was a crisp frost icing the grass and rooftops, which then dissipated by mid-morning. William wanted to go along with one of his crews taking a boat to Hull. He had some business to do there – meeting a prospective client, and he decided he would find the trip invigorating and healthful. Laura was not so keen on him travelling so far, but knew that her opinion held little sway with the thrawn Yorkshireman.

She bade him farewell on the door step early one morning, hugging him tightly and savouring the comforting smell of tobacco and woollen cloth that held the scents of oil, coal and sweat - his working clothes. He looked up and waved at the children, still in their night clothes waving from the upstairs window of their parents' bedroom, and giving her a final kiss upon her cheek, headed down the quiet street and turned the corner out of sight. The echo of his steps in his hobnailed boots rang out a familiar rhythm, the only other sound the approaching hooves of the milkman's cart in the distance as it turned in at the top of the street. Pulling her robe and shawl tightly around her, she shut the door and went into the kitchen where Mary already had the stove up to heat and the kettle was cheerfully boiling in preparation for a warming cup of tea. As Mary went into the living room to light the fire and bank it up with coal, Laura sat down and started making plans for Christmas. She hoped to buy a few small items for the children in town that day, while they were at school. And then together she and Mary were going to set-to making the Christmas pudding which would be left for a couple of weeks to soak in brandy and become infused with the warming flavours of the fruits and spices that they could savour on the day itself. A busy day ahead, she mused, and then standing went upstairs to dress and get the children off to school.

William savoured the fresh cold air that stung his cheeks, slapping his hands against his sides to keep the circulation going. That day they made good speed and moored up on the outskirts of a small town to spend the night. After finding a local inn where they got a hot meal and enjoyed a few pints of ale, they returned to bunk down in the cabin, something William had done many times. An eerie stillness fell upon the water overnight and they woke up to a thick and all enveloping freezing fog that hung thickly over the water and shrouded the banks and fields in the distance. They could hardly make out a boat's length in front of them so all that day progress was painfully slow, men taking turns to ring a bell or bang a pot or shout out 'halloos' to signal where they were, listening out for answering sounds to signal the approach of another vessel. The fog never lifted all that day, and the moist droplets lay on their clothes and hair, and noses dripped with the inhalation of the damp air. Every surface was wet and slippery and every task had to be done slowly and carefully. By that evening, William had retreated below, his cough returning and his chest aching with every spasm.

By the time they eventually berthed in Hull over a day and a half later, he was barely able to stand and needed help to step off the boat onto the quayside. His skipper walked with him from the dock and up Great Union

Street to a lodging he had arranged on Albert Street. Grateful to lay his head down and stretch out his weary bones, he lay upon the simple bed while the familiar landlady brought him some tea and a bowl of soup. All night he coughed and gasped for breath, hardly able to sleep for the constant interruptions cutting through his chest. His ribs ached and his legs were weak. He spent the next day barely aware of where he was, dreading the next bout of coughing. As evening approached his coughs seemed to ease and he drifted between waking and sleeping, grateful for the peace but his breathing was shallow.

53

L aura got news the next morning from a doctor who had looked in on William, having been summoned by the landlady who recognised that her lodger was far from well. Laura felt her heart sink and grasped the nearby chair to steady her as she read the short but disturbing message. Calling on Mary, she ordered her to pack some basic personal items for them while she collected together the few things she would need into a small leather case. Gathering the children to her, she explained as calmly as she could that their father was very unwell and that they were going down on the train to visit him. The children were quiet, recognising the seriousness of the situation which caused their mother to hasten them together and take the first train heading south. School was forgotten. They caught the train by lunchtime and were in Hull by mid-afternoon, the doctor having given her the address. It was familiar territory for her, and she quivered slightly as familiar streets and buildings came into view.

As they climbed the stair of the lodging house and were shown into the small but clean and well-kept room where William lay, Laura kept up a plea for his well-being running under her breath. The children hesitated in the doorway, unsure of whether to go in or stay back. Laura knelt down by the bedside and immediately was shocked by his grey pallor and sunken cheeks. His breath was fast and shallow and his hands above the covers were cold and clammy. Turning to the landlady who hovered in the doorway, she asked her to fetch the doctor who had been visiting him as she wished to speak to him herself. Then noticing the children, she beckoned them forward to stand by the bedside.

"Papa?" Henry implored, his voice thin and tremulous. Kate just stared, her eyes huge and her chin wobbling. At first he made no sign that he knew anyone was there but as Laura held his hand and gently stroked it, he roused himself enough to open his eyes and give a weak smile. He made to speak but then the effort of it threatened to have him start to cough again, albeit breathy and weak.

"Shush, my dear, just rest. We are all here. You will be fine," she whispered, with far more conviction than she felt.

Turning back to the landlady who had reappeared at the door, she asked if she would take the children downstairs, giving her a knowing look which the landlady immediately understood, shepherding the children ahead of her out of the room and into her own parlour on the ground floor.

Within the hour the doctor arrived. He was a tall ascetic man, with greying temples but a not-unfriendly smile as he introduced himself as Dr Willerby. He quickly explained that William was suffering from pneumonia and that he was very weak. The outcome was not good. Laura asked the inevitable question – how long? He shook his head and said that perhaps a day at the most. Laura explained that she had come down from York with her children, whom the landlady had taken downstairs for the present. But she didn't want the children witnessing their father's passing.

Nodding his head, he understood. Then he said quietly, "If you permit, I can take the children to my home where my wife can look after them for however long it takes. She is visiting someone not far from here, so I could take them with me now and we could take them back with us for the night. We live not far away." He paused, then added, "I will look in again in the morning, unless I am required sooner," fixing her with a look so that she understood the significance of the statement.

"Of course, I understand. That would be most kind of you. I did not think when I hastened to come that of course, the children should be spared this. I merely wanted him to know we were all here."

"Quite understandable," he replied as he pulled on his gloves and picked up his bag from the bedside where he had placed it earlier.

After hugging the children and assuring them that all would be well, Laura entrusted them to the doctor's care and returned to the room where her husband of seven years lay quiet and still. She spent a long night at William's side, hunched in a chair with a blanket over her, which the landlady had brought to the room with some hot tea and a simple supper for her. Laura was grateful of the drink but ate nothing, her stomach feeling like a stone sunken deep in her body. All night she listened to each breath, holding her own in the silent pause, then willing him to take the next. If she could give her breath to him, she thought, she dearly would. The candle by the bedside guttered and went out just as the first cold grey shades of dawn began to light the room. The frequency of William's breathing slowed so much that at times she was not sure if he was breathing at all, but then another slight lift of his chest and the merest whisper of air would pass through his dry parted lips. But then, eventually, the pause stretched out longer and longer, and no whisper of air seemed to follow. Then one deep inhalation, his chest fell as the breath escaped him, and he was still for ever more.

Laura sat numbed and unmoving. The minutes passed as she could not, would not, admit to herself that he breathed no more. But realisation came and she laid her head against his cooling cheek and sobbed silent tears.

After some time she went downstairs where the sounds from the kitchen were wakening the house. In the grey light, the landlady turned and saw her standing at the bottom of the stairs. Moving forward to wrap her arms around her, she understood fully. Sitting her down in the kitchen by the table, she pulled a small bottle from the cupboard and poured the clear liquid into a small glass which she put in Laura's shaking hands. She held them as she raised the glass to her lips and made her drink. Laura flinched as the sharp spirit hit her parched throat and coursed a hot path inside her. Gagging slightly, she put the half empty glass down and buried her face in her hands.

The landlady sent someone for the doctor and about an hour later he and his wife arrived with the children. Laura had returned to sit at William's side, unwilling to leave or cover him, wanting to etch the memory of his dear face into her mind forever. They had not met through love, but she realised she loved him dearly now, not in a passionate physical way but in the quiet comfortable way born of mutual respect and ease of being and growing together, matching each other in all they said and did. He had given her all she had craved – and now he was gone from her and she was alone again. Not quite alone, for she must plan for her children and make sure their futures were secure. Strange, she mused, neither of them was his …

The doctor came into the room and she stood as he gave her his condolences. He went over to the bedside and made the assessments he was bound to do, before covering William's face with the sheet and turning back to her.

"I am so very sorry Mrs Hoxton," he said in a respectful tone. "The children?" he added.

"I would not want them to see their father like this. Please let them stay downstairs. I will come down and tell them."

"My wife is downstairs with them at the moment. Would you excuse me? I have another patient I have to see?"

"Of course, and thank you so very much for what you have done," she responded quietly.

As he left, she took a few minutes to compose herself and try to think of the words she needed to tell the children. Closing the door behind her, she walked slowly down the stairs to the living room and pushed open the door. The children ran to her and buried the heads against her body. As she held them tightly she noticed the other figure in the room, standing by the window, partly silhouetted against the grey light that filtered through the lacy curtains that hung in front of it. She was a tall woman, well dressed with a modest hat and fur trimmed stole about her shoulders. Her face was less easy to distinguish under the shadow of her hat but there was a familiarity about the way she held her head that worried at the edges of Laura's memory.

The woman had now turned to fully face her, holding her small bag over her arm and folding her gloved hands together. She too seemed to freeze as she looked at her for long seconds that stretched out between them.

"Laura …?" she breathed.

And then recognition slammed into Laura, taking all her breath away from her.

"Martha …" she whispered. The older sister. The proud one that had nipped and pinched her, had made her feel the odd one out, the one who had stirred up the others to join in her bullying and nastiness. Her. Now.

There was no pretending that there could be any friendship or empathy between them, no more than a woman giving her condolences to a stranger. Little warmth was conveyed in the brief conversation that went between them. Laura thanked her for looking after the children. Martha offered to register the death on her behalf, saying that she would forward the certificate to her. Then Laura stiffly stood back and allowed her sister to leave the room. Outside Martha called to the landlady that she would see herself out and a moment later the door was pulled to and the latch clicked.

54

S ue returned to her To Do list, now sporting two ticks.

√ *Laura Emily – find her on 1871 census*

and

√ *find Laura's marriages*

Now to find out when Laura died, and where.

Returning to FreeBMD, Sue searched for the death of Laura Hoxton from the date of Laura's last marriage – 1876, and up to 1913 when she would have been aged seventy. A few results appeared but as there were now ages added to the records, none fitted the bill. She extended the search for another ten years, but still no suitable results. Adding another twenty years in sheer frustration still brought no results. She tried removing Yorkshire from the search criteria. Still no luck.

"Well, if she didn't die in England, where else?" she voiced aloud. Had she emigrated? Gone to Scotland? Or Ireland? America? The possibilities seemed endless and rather overwhelmed Sue when she thought of how she could track down Laura's death.

She tried again, this time taking out Laura's first name in case there had been an error in the record transcription. Screeds of names appeared with the surname Hoxton, male and female, and she sat back with a snort of annoyance. She added Yorkshire into the search again, which reduced the number of hits, but nothing suitable.

She slapped down the lid of her laptop in frustration and headed to the kitchen to make a strong cup of coffee.

Half an hour later, suitable refreshed and having calmed down a bit, she sat back at the table and looked at the To Do list again.

"OK, forget the death – for now. Newspapers? What did the tutor say?" she muttered under her breath. Shuffling her course notes, she found the scribbled words in the margin of the sheet – The British Newspaper Archive / Find My Past – has newspapers online.

But ten minutes later Sue discovered that both sites were subscription only (although she could have got three free pages as a starter on BNA). Unsure about subscribing to any other sites at the moment, she sat back and frowned, thinking about what to do next. Then she looked again at her notes and saw that she had drawn an arrow from the newspaper information in the margin to a double underlined phrase asterisked at the bottom of the page. Public Libraries usually have free access for members to family history sites.

"Great! Just need to find my library card then," she exclaimed and dived into her capacious bag dumped on the chair beside her.

The following morning just before 10am found Sue at the doors of the Public Library in Lincoln. As the librarian opened the door, Sue asked her about access to the computers, and after checking her card, the girl showed her to a terminal and explained how to log in and use the online resources. Explaining that she was a bit unsure of how to find what she was looking for, Sue told her that she was after newspaper articles relating to her ancestors and pointed to the file which was poking out of her large shopping bag.

The girl patiently went through how to log in and how to search the British Newspaper Archive and when Sue felt confident about using the search page, she left her to help another arrival at the next terminal, reminding her that she could print out any articles she wished for a fee per page.

Thanking her, Sue opened her file and started her search. She soon found that she had to zoom in to read the small print of the newspaper images and sometimes she found it hard to locate the actual article she was looking for. After an hour she had the beginnings of a headache and was about to give up for the day when she came across an article mentioning Laura Emily Shipton of Wheatley's Row, Lord Mayor's Walk in the City of York.

"Bingo!" Sue exclaimed out loud, drawing some looks from nearby library patrons. "Sorry," she whispered, and returned to peer at the screen.

She sent the image to the printer and soon returned with it in hand. Squinting at the small type she saw that it was a notice asking any people who had demands on the estate of George Shipton to contact Marr and Son, solicitors in York. She could see the date of death of Laura's second husband, who had died intestate and the legal details pertaining to the estate.

Thoroughly exhausted with the morning's efforts, she

packed up her file and notebook and shut down the computer. Paying her printing fee at the desk, she thanked the young girl who had helped her and headed out into the bright sunshine, realising that her stomach was grumbling and lunch and a large cake beckoned at her favourite café.

55

1882

T he skipper of the boat had organised everything. William would be brought back to York for burial, as he had wished, and as a mark of the respect he was held in by the watermen, a small flotilla would accompany his boat as they made their way north. Everything of the last twenty four hours had passed in a daze. Laura found herself swept along by the organisation of others, barely aware of what was being managed on her behalf. It was only as she stood at the dock side that reality hit. The coffin was being borne from the undertaker's cart onto William's boat, now empty apart from some boards laid across the gaping hull, void of cargo. She stood there under an umbrella held by one of the men, the rain pouring down in sheets and the winds gusting across the open expanse of the docks swept in from the Humber estuary. The muddy water frothed and swirled about, carrying any stray items that had been carelessly dropped or purposely tossed into the flood tide. Boats bobbed and rocked in the wind and Laura had to hold on firmly to her hat while the other kept her coat tightly grasped against her neck. The children huddled close against her skirts, their faces still pale and blotched from their tears as they watched the coffin being lashed to the boards of the boat and a tarpaulin laid over it and securely fastened.

Only as she was gently propelled forward to the edge of the dock by the waterman at her elbow did she fully comprehend that the journey they would all be making was by boat, upon the river, battling against the flow up to York. Her heart leapt into her mouth and she gasped, holding back and wildly looking about her, her hand going out to clutch at the children. But they were already being lifted across onto the rocking craft by strong arms and willing helpers. There was nothing for it but to join them ...

It was an unpleasant and perilous journey. Just battling their way out of the dock area and into the river that would take them north required all the skill of the crew. But as they nosed out of the city and made their slow progress homeward, the children became more excited by the experience and their earlier apprehensions were soon evaporating. They were all in the cabin at the stern of the boat, cosy and dry and not unfamiliar to Laura, reminding her of times long past. Memories came to her unbidden.

They made slow progress against the flow of the river, the water frothing up against the bows as the torrent forced its way downstream in the opposite direction. They were joined by three other boats that made up their little fleet, but as they were overtaken by faster boats or met others heading in the opposite direction, flying past on the sea-ward tide, they were hailed by toots and waves in salute, acknowledging awareness of the cargo they carried. Hats were removed and heads bowed as the river men acknowledged the passing of one of their own.

By nightfall they had made painfully slow progress and they had to pass the night bunked down together in the cabin, while the crew doubled up in the cabins of the other accompanying boats. The rain poured all night, lashing against the wooden sides of the boat and the wind howled through the bare trees on the bank and rocked them into a fitful sleep.

But by morning the worst had passed and the children were excited at the novelty of having their breakfast in the tiny cabin. For Henry this was a real treat. So often he had begged his mother to allow him to travel with William on the river and accompany him like other watermen's sons did, but she had always been adamant. Now here was his chance to explore and assume his rightful place, at least in his mind. As he left the cabin after their scanty breakfast, he stood up onto the edge that ran the length of the boat and made to walk along it as he had seen the bargemen do so often. Hearing his boots scraping on the wooden ledge, Laura flung open the locker door and shouted loudly at him, hauling him back inside and remonstrating with him, holding the arm of his jacket and shaking it furiously.

"Don't ever do that again! Do you hear?" she shouted.

He could see she was shaking and her face was white, her eyes wide and flecks of spit flying from her mouth. He had never seen her like this before and he was frankly terrified. Kate stood immobile at the back of the cabin, still chewing on her last bit of bread and butter. Her face was emotionless.

The little flotilla started up again and headed into the flow, another day ahead of battling the tide and cold weather. Whereas all sound had been blotted out by the previous day's wind and weather, now there seemed to be an eerie stillness broken only by the swishing of the water, the occasional conversation among the men or the bump as some item of flotsam was swept against the side of the boat. There were twigs and branches, some quite sizeable, that had been torn from the trees in the previous days' gales. The men were skilled at keeping away from the banks where there were tangled heaps of branches, pushed and twisted together into the places where curves and bends caused the waters to eddy and whirl, carrying anything in and on the water to be snarled into a jumbled stack.

The children soon became bored and she had to find things to entertain them. 'I Spy' and a pack of cards passed some time but inevitably they became restless. Laura's ears became more attuned to the sounds of the river and she fancied she heard things that weren't there. Or she thought they weren't ...

By mid-afternoon the day was already darkening and they were still well away from their destination. The men were signalling to each other when the lead boat spotted any hazards, large branches being swept along, turbulent water and so on and so they steered similar paths through the water, following each other like so many ducklings. Kate and Henry sat in the low area that led down into the cabin, sheltered from some of the coldest winds but nevertheless fingers and ears were getting numbed and blue. Henry's eyes never left the actions of the crew on board, nor their colleagues on the other boats, fascinated by the ease with which they traversed the boards and managed the steering, hopping nimbly ashore at the locks, grasping the mooring lines and securing the boat.

As the last of the natural light fell away, Laura could hear a rushing sound, unlike anything she had heard so far. As they neared the faint flickering lights of a small settlement ahead, the noise became more and more insistent. Her heart beat faster but she was unsure why. The children stood up in the cabin area and peered out over the edge of the boat. The men were signalling to each other and pulling the boat over to the starboard side, ready to enter a narrow lock set into one side of the river.

"'Tis Naburn Lock," announced one of the men, seeing them all peering ahead.

"So what is that noise?" asked Laura.

" 'Tis th' weir. Goes reet 'cross river blockin' our way. It be'int full flood wi' all that rain. But we go through t' lock around 't."

The man nimbly jumped up onto the towpath and soon had the boat secured fore and aft in the lock, quickly joined by another and together they rose as the lock filled and they reached the level of the river beyond the flow of the weir. Untying the boat, the man jumped aboard and soon they were nosing out into the stream to await their companions. Henry was fascinated and told his sister importantly how it worked and what was happening. She looked unimpressed but nevertheless was fascinated by the way they rose as the water torrented through the wooden lock gates, filling the lock.

By now it was totally dark and the only lights those of the lock keeper's house and an inn on the opposite bank some distance away, surrounded by a sprinkle of smaller lights marking the presence of cottages and a village. On the bow of the boat a lantern swung and inside the cabin the lamps had been lit.

As they were eventually joined by the other accompanying boats, their journey resumed and Laura went into the cabin to make some supper from what was available. She fervently hoped they would make York by that night and she would be sleeping in her own bed, the children tucked in and sleeping soundly in their rooms. But, she realised, she would be alone.

Clattering about in the cabin, she was unaware that Henry and Kate were still standing watching the passing of the village lights. Kate stood beside her brother, motionless, her head to one side as if listening to something that she couldn't quite discern. Henry was leaning round to look along the length of the boat at the crewman who was stowing the mooring lines previously used to secure the boat while passing through the lock. The boat was rocking in the turbulence of the water as it accelerated to rush towards the weir, some yards behind them further downstream. The man lost his grip on the coil of rope and some loops unwound and fell loose onto the tarpaulin covering the outlined shape of their father's coffin. Without hesitating, Henry stepped up onto the side ledge and leant forward to grab the loops of uncoiled rope to pass to the crewman. Kate leant forward behind him.

The only sound Laura heard was a louder than usual splash and a kind of sigh. Then a shout. Coldness gripped her, almost squeezing the air out of her as she flew to the open cabin door and stood up, looking downstream. All she could see was an arm and then it disappeared in a whirlpool of water. Without even hesitating, she put her foot upon the board and hoisted herself up and over the stern, her last sight the face of Kate looking at her with her clear transparent eyes.

As she hit the water, the shock of the icy coldness and the smothering blanket of water that covered her head caused her to gasp involuntarily. As she choked, it suffocated her and she tried to struggle but the weight of her heavy woollen skirt and flannel petticoats dragged her down. Losing all sense of direction, she could not fathom which way was up and could not think which way to strike out to reach the surface. The river had other ideas. It was holding her firmly, twisting her this way and that and utterly confusing her senses. Suddenly the coldness seemed to fade and the sound of the water in her ears became fainter. She fancied she could see a lightness ahead, a frothing whiteness that drew her forward. Reaching out blindly and trying to find that which she was struggling to grasp, she felt herself being swept about at the whim of that other power over which she had no sway. As her form was bounced and whirled, tossed and pitched about in the torrent, it was as if she was a partner in a mad dance, the tune of which she didn't know nor the steps, but her partner did and led her this way and that. As she tired and gave up trying to fight against the flow, she felt arms around her, strong and powerful, gently holding and caressing her as they folded around her and held her in their embrace. Fingers entwined and unravelled her hair, letting it fan out around and behind her, as everything slowed and motion became gentle and swaying. A feeling of peacefulness came over her and a sense of coming home. No fear now.

No loneliness.

A sense of belonging at last.

Those who are born of the river die by the river. Not always a gentle friend. Sometimes more sinister, grasping and avaricious. I knew friendship and fear. Something repellent, yet alluring at the same time. It was a constant battle inside me.

I kept away from you. Whenever I could. But you found

ways to seek me out. My life seems fated to be near you, or others of your ilk. You all conspired against me. You have a language of your own. Messages pass between you, unheard by us mortals. Mortals? What am I then? Half human, half – what? Whom did Mama meet, who lured her, caressed her, dripped sweet words into her ears, loved her, spilled their seed into her?

Who ... am ... I?

Who ... are ... you?

And in the end, she knew. It was ...

Always

the

River

56

T he University term was drawing to a close and Kate was already looking forward to time back with Gran and no studying, long lie-ins and lounging in the garden in the sunshine. The obligatory end of year parties and pub crawls were posted on the noticeboards around the campus and Jen was already planning her last few days in York before heading home. Kate was less keen to join the boisterous crowd that Jen hung out with, but she was looking forward to a night out with her whole tutor group at one of the local Chinese restaurants and the following day someone had organised a trip down to Naburn where they were planning to have a barbecue near the river in the evening if the weather held.

Kate lay back on her bed and answered the call coming in from Sue.

"Hi Gran, how are you? What have you been up to?"

The next few minutes were filled with small talk about Sue's classes and how the upcycled chair had turned out.

"And I've got a surprise for you," continued Sue. "I've found out quite a bit more about the mysterious Laura."

"Which one is she?" asked Kate, slightly confused with how many greats were involved.

Sue briefly outlined the generations then told her that she had been finding out information from the old newspaper archives, which immediately piqued Kate's interest. They chatted for a few more minutes during which Sue gave her a brief outline of how far she had got but said she'd let Kate see it all when she got back. There followed some clarification about which train Kate would be back on and when Sue could expect her that Friday.

"And what fun will you be getting up to for the end of term?" asked Sue.

"Well, I'm just going to a meal with the tutor group. I think the tutor said he'd come too. And the final evening we are going down the river to a place called Naburn, I think, and having a barbecue at the riverside. Barney's going to organise that. Lord, I hope there aren't too many midges!" Kate finished up laughing.

"Well, that's rather interesting – what a coincidence! But I'll tell you when you come home. Have fun! Bye love!" Sue finished up and Kate lay her phone down on the bedside table, her curiosity aroused.

A few days later the day dawned bright and sunny. The drizzle of the previous evening had disappeared, a pleasant breeze blowing it away and clearing the air. Kate woke and reached for her bottle of water at her bedside, her mouth dry and she felt she could still taste the Chinese meal from the previous evening. It had been a good get-together and their tutor had been quite a laugh – they certainly got to see another side to him, especially when he had put a large denomination note into the drinks kitty and made sure everyone was well lubricated with their drink of choice. Although Kate had had a couple of ciders, she ended up on water as she was aware of how awful she would feel in the morning if she overdid it, the voice of past experience echoing in the back of her mind.

She spent most of the day tidying up the flat and starting to pack the things she needed to take back home. Luckily they would have the flat again for their next year, thanks to Jen's parents, but in between it was going back on Airbnb for the intervening months – rental properties in York were always in demand over the summer tourist season. Any personal items they didn't want to take back home could be stowed in a lockable cupboard in Jen's room. And, noted Kate wryly, Jen was noticeable by her absence, her bedroom door closed tight shut. Kate had got back nearer midnight, but she was vaguely aware of the stumbling and bumping around the flat as Jen came home nearer three in the morning. Kate knew she wouldn't see much of her till early afternoon if things went as per normal. They were meeting up with the group going for the barbecue around six that evening, so Kate thought she'd let Jen sleep off most of her hangover and give her a knock after lunch.

Realising that there was only a drop of milk left in the fridge, she was glad to get out and have a walk down to the local Tesco and grab a small bottle to tide them over, as well as a packet of bagels which she was going to toast for lunch. As she walked along Lord Mayor's Walk and through Monk Bar, she realised how familiar York had become to her over the past few months. The places which were once new and unknown had become familiar. York had become a place where she felt a link that somehow bound her there. She recollected that Gran had mentioned that there were ancestors with connections to here so she wondered if she was picking up on those vibes. With her love of history, she liked the idea that there might be a thread that bound the present to the past, and perhaps linked the people to the place. She had been reading an article online the other day about a concept called Ancestral or Genetic Memory and she thought about this as she made her way back up Goodramgate, past the little alley that led to Holy Trinity Church and headed back to the flat. Perhaps she was walking in their footsteps.

Looking up at the walls as they came into view, she thought of all the generations of York citizens who had gone about their daily business, also looking up and did they, like her, wish the stones could talk? Shaking her head, she laughed to herself and thought that they probably had little time to have such fanciful thoughts and that the pressures of the daily grind were far more likely to be at the forefront of their minds.

The day continued bright and warm with a gentle breeze which she hoped would keep any midges away. They always seemed to find her a tasty treat. Barney had somehow managed to cadge a campervan from one of his cousins (of which there seemed to be quite a few) and they all piled in, squeezing the bags with items for the barbecue and various other requirements like rugs and cool boxes in the gaps between their legs. Jen had eventually taken two paracetamol and most of a bottle of water before she felt human again. However, she soon wolfed down the toasted bagels mid-afternoon and pronounced herself ready for the barbecue. Kate was amazed at her constitution!

The journey south to Naburn took about twenty minutes and Kate could see glimpses of the river through the hedges that lined the road. They pulled into a lane near a campsite and drove towards a grassy area by the water. There was rushing noise in the distance and at first Kate couldn't orientate where it was coming from. Seeing her trying to locate the sound, peering through the bushes and into the distance left and right, Barney informed her that the noise came from Naburn Lock. They could have a walk down later and see it. But first all hands were required to set out the rugs and get the portable barbecues going. The guys gathered round, taking on this task as their right, while the girls started sorting out the food and spreading items over rugs to stop them catching the breeze. Sonja from Kate's tutor group was there and a couple of others, as well as Jen and two of her sporty guys. They made a fun group and soon someone pulled a guitar out the van and one of the guys started playing.

As the evening drew in, they lit candles and a couple of lanterns. The sky went from blue to indigo, then became shot with peach and gold. The river glided along, so peaceful and calm. Occasionally the plants at the water's edge would tremble and a moorhen or duck would come swimming out into the open water, engrossed in its task. By now the trees were in full leaf, and the weight of foliage caused some of the branches to droop and almost touch the water. Barney came over to her, pushed his glasses up his nose and reached out his hand, pulling her up from the rug on which she was sitting cross-legged.

"Come on then. I'll show you the lock," he announced.

She had been feeling so relaxed and almost sleepy, that she was somewhat annoyed at having to move, but nevertheless she accepted his hand and hauled herself to her feet, wrapping her cardigan round her shoulders.

"Where are you two off to?" called Jen, with a giggle.

"The lock," announced Barney, which caused Jen to giggle even more.

"I'll bet," sniggered Jen, and Kate could not help but feel annoyed at her.

"Wanna come?" Barney looked over at Sonja, who would now be by herself.

"Yes, why not. Is it far?" Sonja replied, with a smile.

"No, just up the river a bit. Come on ladies!" and with that he set off along the path, well-trodden in the grass at the water's edge. Kate and Sonja followed, calling on him to slow down a bit and peering through the bushes at the river running past.

The sound of water gurgling and splashing got louder and soon they could see the concrete edges of a man-made inlet, off to the side of the main river. A small pleasure boat had just come through the lock and was heading out into the main stream to carrying it southwards. The river further out was marked by flashes of white water and the churned-up flow as it cascaded from an unseen barrier. They were able to cross the lock over a little walkway on top of the lock gate and from there they could see the source of the noise. To their right was a weir that stretched across the river, causing the water to be churned up and spat out in frothing white cascades to then re-join its calmer neighbour, which had been calmly channelled through the lock.

They could hardly hear each other speak over the noise of the water so Barney led them back over the lock gate to the pathway at the lock side. A slight bend in the path took them beyond the few buildings and then brought them out above the weir. The sound of the thrashing water faded and once more they could hear each other speak. They carried on walking for a few more yards and then stopped, looking at the string of small boats moored on the far side of the river and the lights of houses beyond.

They came across a bench set in a spot to admire the view through a gap in the trees. By now the evening was darkening and although they could still see to walk, the gloom caused by the surrounding trees added to the deepening shadows. It was so very peaceful that each of them became lost in their own thoughts, the only sound the faraway rush of water, a bird flapping in the trees or a far-off car engine receding into the distance.

Kate pulled her cardigan closer around her and buttoned it at her neck, a small shiver creeping along her arms and down her spine. Her eyes became attuned to the gloom, and she watched the swirl of the water as it caught on an overhanging branch or swept round the hull of a boat. It was all so very peaceful.

The flat-hulled boat was loaded high with cargo, a tarpaulin over it held down with ropes. The movement of men on deck caught her eye, wrapped up against the cold in scarves and with hats pulled low over their eyes. She watched as they threw the ropes across to each other. The darting motion drew her eye and a young boy in a tightly buttoned woollen jacket and cloth cap lunged forward to catch one of the ends of the rope which had slid off the edge of the deck. Behind him the white face of a little girl turned to look at the boy, and then she darted forward, her arms outstretched. The splash made Kate draw in a sharp breath as she watched the scene unfold.

A shout. The sudden movement of the men to the edge of the deck. The light suddenly bursting from the opening cabin door at the rear of the vessel. A woman's scream. Another larger splash. A few uncoordinated flails of her arms. Then silence.

Kate was mesmerised as she looked straight into the pale eyes of the little girl, seemingly unmoved, as she stood at the back of the boat and turned her gaze directly towards her.

And then Kate realised.

The little girl – was her...

57

A woman and her child were drowned near Naburn Lock last week. Every effort was made to recover the bodies but in vain until Thursday last due to the extreme flood conditions when the child was found and taken out of the river at Acaster Malbis. An inquest was held at Naburn yesterday when a waterman gave evidence that the alarm was given when the child fell overboard. On asking the little daughter how her brother had fallen in, she said he tipped over after standing on the side and then her mother had jumped in to save him. This is doubly heart-breaking for the child as the boat was returning the body of Mr Hoxton, a well-known and respected waterman and coal merchant and the husband of the family, for burial in York after his passing in Hull the previous week. Verdict : 'Accidentally drowned.' The body of the mother has not yet been found.

Yorkshire Gazette 15 Dec 1882

58

P roudly spreading out the family tree she had been working on for the last few nights, Sue smiled at Kate and sat back, watching Kate's face and looking for a sign of approval.

"Wow!" was all Kate could say. She took a few minutes to untangle the relationships, focus on the writing and trace the generations with her finger. "Gosh, you have been busy!" she finally exclaimed.

"Let me walk you through it all then," Sue replied, seeing the frown upon her granddaughter's brow. "And as we go, I'll tell you what I managed to find out about them all."

Pointing to the last name at the bottom of the sheet, she announced, "So - here you are," and then she began to relate the lineage.

"So, your mother was Debbie – Deborah Katherine Innes. And here I am Susan Martha Miles. I was born in Lincoln three months after my parents married."

"Oh!" exclaimed Kate, but she could see her Gran was non-plussed about that, certainly not ashamed.

"Now my mother was Maud Katherine Watkins and she was born over a year before her mother, Eliza Kate Davis," and here she pointed to the next box up, continuing, "was married to Henry Cecil Watkins in Lincoln. Sadly they later had a son who was drowned in a training exercise in the Second World War. But she had been born in 1901 in York. Her mother was Kate Eliza Hoxton, who married Herbert John Davis; again she was pregnant with Eliza when she married."

"I'm starting to see a pattern here ..." Kate interjected.

"Now, Kate Eliza Hoxton was also born in York," continued Sue. "She and Herbert had a son together but he died within a day or so of his birth. Kate Eliza's mother was Laura Emily Harrison. Now she is an interesting one. She would be your four times great grandmother. She was born in Hull in 1843. Her first marriage was to Samuel Cowper. He died the same year they married. Next, she married George Shipton in Leeds the following year and they had a son named Henry born very shortly after they married. George died just a month after the birth of his son. He was a waterman and he drowned near Wakefield. Laura married a third time to William Hoxton. He was a good bit older than her – almost thirty years older. But they had a daughter together – that was her, Kate Eliza, born a few months after they married. William died six years later in Hull." Sue paused to let all this sink in.

"So, every one of the women were either pregnant at their marriage or already had a child, all daughters by the look of it, illegitimately?" mused Kate aloud.

"Now – one more thing I just discovered the other day. I found it in the newspaper archive online at the library. I'm getting to be a regular there!" Sue laughed. "The son that Laura had by George Shipton, Henry, was drowned in a boat accident. And Laura jumped in to save him. They both drowned."

Kate went pale. "Where did this happen? Do you know?" she asked.

"Oh yes, it was at Naburn Lock. Near where you were the other day. They never found the poor woman's body. What a sad life she had. But I don't suppose we will ever know the full story, will we?"

Kate didn't answer ...

MESSAGE FROM THE AUTHOR

Thank you for reading '**Always the River**'. I hope you enjoyed it. If you could leave a review on Amazon that would be great - I love reading your thoughts and feedback.

If you enjoy books with a family history theme, you may also enjoy my previous novel, '**Prussian Blue**' - also available as an ebook and in paperback on Amazon. More details are at the end of this book. There are also more suggestions of books in this genre on the Facebook group page for the *Genealogical Crime Mystery Book Club* - follow this link:

https://www.facebook.com/groups/902684053599239

Please feel free to follow me by popping over to my author page:

https://www.amazon.co.uk/Leona-Thomas/e/B013QU3EW6/ref=ntt_dp_epwbk_0

ACKNOWLEDGEMENTS

My thanks go to the enumerable people who have researched, transcribed, digitised and added data to the many family history sites and archives over the years. Without them I would not have been able to research both of our families so thoroughly. It is from doing that, that I have come to know more about the social history of our ancestors, the places they inhabited, the lives they lived and their joys and sorrows - all through the archived documents, censuses, birth, marriage and death records, maps, and so on. The website at www.archiuk.com was invaluable with the Old Victorian Ordnance Survey Maps 6 inch to 1 mile.

I do also have to acknowledge the help I got from Jack Garrett who manages the *The Vikings of Bjornstad* website (www.vikings-ofbjornstad.com), who gave me some excellent suggestions for the name of the malevolent spirit and help with pronunciation. Also Wikibooks (en.wikibooks.org/wiki/Old_Norse/Grammar/Alphabet_and_Pronunciation). And of course, the Norse derivation pays homage to the past history of the East Riding of Yorkshire.

My thanks must also go to the author Nathan Dylan Goodwin whose encouragement and support have helped me get this and my previous project off the ground.

Thanks also go to my husband's late father and grandfather whose Yorkshire dialect echoed in our ears when we worked on the dialogue. For the purposes of ease of understanding, I made the decision not to use many of the stand-alone dialect words which might confuse non-British, even non-Yorkshire readers! I have tried to keep the dialogue as understandable as possible whilst acknowledging how working class people would have spoken in those times.

And finally thanks to my husband for allowing me to take such liberties with his family. Thankfully none of it is true - but the places and events I discovered while doing his family research gave me the background for this fanciful tale.

NOTE ON PRONUNCIATION *

I have used the 'name' *fljót vættr* for the spirit of the river and the pronunciation of this would be something lik this:

fljót vættr

fl-yoat vātt-ur

ó - *o* as in 'vote' (long)

æ - *a* as in 'cat' (long)

j - *y* as in 'year'

r - *r* as in 'roof' (trilled like in Scots)

* thanks to Jack Garrett and the 'Vikings of Bjornstad' website and Wiki-books Old Norse/Grammar/Alphabet and Pronunciation webpage

Prussian Blue

There are stories each generation can tell, but if the next generation isn't listening, they will be lost. Sometimes you realise you are the last link in that chain, and it is up to you to preserve them. So that is what I aimed to do. Taking the lives of three of my extraordinary ancestors – the apothecary, the surgeon and man-midwife and the sea captain, I have woven a narrative around the people, places and events that I have discovered travelling from 1809 in Prussia to the end of that century in N. Ireland.Discovering the innovative medical training which was being developed in Berlin in the 1840s and learning how that translated to the practice of a small-town medic in Pomerania, was both revealing and addictive, especially when I had access to my ancestor's handwritten archive material from that time. A distinguished surgeon and the first man-midwife in that area, he should have had an illustrious career, but that was tragically cut short. He left behind a young family and I followed his son who broke away and sailed the seas, eventually settling in N. Ireland. Discovering his notorious exploits were also a surprise.Handing over a box full of documents, files and folders left in my will to a distant cousin, who may or may not be interested in the family history, is not a guarantee of its perpetuity. Who is going to plod through all the research and notes I have made? So in order to ensure the information has a chance of being passed on and assimilated, I have constructed this story around the basic facts. I hope that readers, as well as my relatives, will enjoy finding out about my extraordinary ancestors as much as I did

Through Ice And Fire: A Russian Arctic Convoy

Diary 1942

On the Russian Arctic convoys in 1942, Leonard H. Thomas kept a secret notebook from which he later wrote his memoirs. These contained many well-observed details of life onboard his ship, HMS Ulster Queen. He detailed observations of the hardships that followed when they endured being at action stations and locked in the engine room, under fire from the skies above and the sea below, and only able to guess at what was happening from the cacophony of sounds they could hear. Thomas tells of how the crew suffered from an appalling lack of food, the intense cold, and the stark conditions endured for weeks on end berthed in Archangel in the cold of the approaching Russian winter. There are also insights about the morale of the men and lighter moments when their humour kept them going. These stories can now be told as his daughter has edited them into an account that illustrates the fortitude and bravery of the men who sailed through ice and fire to further the war effort so far from home.

Printed in Great Britain
by Amazon